The Zeros

nero lee

D1565539

The Zeros

Copyright © 2019 Nero Lee

For the ones who helped me face the storm

Chapter 1

Kaori

"Can I see that one?" I asked, staring into the glass case.

"Do you even know what that is?"

Darkened fingernails. Faint smell of hydrogen sulfide. **Burner**. *Cut off air supply to prevent gas exchange.*

I didn't know if the chubby, balding man was asking because I was a woman, or because I was seemingly so young. Either way, he should've been grateful to have anyone at all in his rat's nest. His place of business looked more like a looted thrift store than the antique shop he advertised. The shelves held more dust than merchandise, more junk than antiquities. I stood up from in front of the glass case and looked him in the eye.

"It's a stun gun."

"I'm impressed," he said with a look of uncertainty.

"Don't be. I've seen a lot of these in my lifetime."

"That weapon is over 200 years old and most people

haven't even heard of it, let alone seen one. How many could you have possibly seen?" he asked, defiantly sliding the stun gun across the counter.

"Does it work?"

I had piqued his curiosity a bit too much, and his uncertainty quickly turned to concern as I realized I had only made the situation worse.

"What would you need with a functioning weapon?" he asked as he slowly withdrew the stun gun.

"I might need to do some stunning..."

Being sardonic did nothing to allay his concerns. Attitude and patience, you used to tell me. Too much of one and not enough of the other.

"I'm gonna need to scan you."

I shrugged my shoulders in agreement as he pulled a handheld scanner from a holster on his belt. It bathed my face in a yellow light which turned green a second later. Satisfied, the proprietor returned the scanner to its holster.

"Yeah, it works," he finally answered, sliding the gun back towards me.

I picked up the stun gun and examined it. It was in surprisingly good condition for such an antique. I silently wondered how many drunks and meth heads it had subdued. I noticed something that looked like dried blood on the handle.

"What are you?" he asked.

"I'm Japanese," I responded without looking up.

I was still engrossed in Exhibit A: Blunt Object.

"Why would I care about your race? What's your Class?"

"Oh, I'm a Class 1 Shocker..."

"No wonder you need a weapon," he laughed.

I feigned a smile and prepared to make a snarky response, but the crescendo of young boy breaking merchandise distracted me.

"I'm so sorry, Sir!"

The boy couldn't have been more than sixteen. He was frail and timid like most humans, and bore a zero branded on the back

3

of his left hand.

"You buggered Zero!"

"One twenty-fourth of an ounce," I interjected my distraction.

The proprietor turned his attention to me and away from the hapless boy.

"I'll take one twelfth. I can easily get a quarter," he countered.

"For a 200 year old weapon that no one has ever heard of? Or needs?"

He furrowed his brow and folded his arms. As I smugly placed the gold on the counter, my eyes found those of the cowering boy, and my pride melted into shame. I had delayed his pain by only minutes, so I had no more reason to smile than he. I placed another twelfth on the counter, much to the surprise of the proprietor.

"That's the only stun gun I have."

"It's for whatever your Zero broke. Can't be worth that

much," I snidely replied, looking around at his wares.

He cocked his head to one side, now more suspicious than ever.

"You a Zero sympathizer?"

"I'm a lady who just got a great deal, so I'm in a good mood."

I smiled at the boy but saw more confusion than gratitude. One day's reprieve hardly made up for a lifetime of pain. I made my way to the door as the proprietor's eyes followed.

"Is that a Tomahawk!?" he asked.

He had caught sight of my motorcycle through the window.

"Yeah. 2003."

"Wow! Where did you find a 212 year old mobile cycle? Do you know a Class 100 Skipper or something?" he asked jokingly.

My eyes began to water as I forced myself to answer the innocuous question.

"You could say that…"

It's crazy how something so simple could trigger old feelings so easily, but I guess nothing was simple anymore.

"How much do you want for..?"

I left the store before he could finish. I saw the young man through the window as he gingerly gathered up everything he had broken. If only I could've done the same. I placed the stun gun in my satchel, climbed onto my bike and drove away.

Driving back roads and living in the shadows often made me forget what life was like for humans, existing only as slaves or prisoners. But I guess I was a prisoner as well, a prisoner of time. Unable to face a painful past, unwilling to look ahead towards a hopeless future. So, all I ever had was that second, that current moment in time wrapped around me like a cocoon, hoping it could preserve my sanity.

My wandering mind almost proved deadly as I rounded a corner and found traffic at a dead stop.

"Dammit!"

I swerved to avoid the car ahead of me, nearly dumping my

1,500 pound behemoth of a bike. The driver in the car ahead looked back nervously. I tried to show my contrition with an apologetic smile, but I don't think it was well received.

I looked ahead to see what was causing the hold up and saw four Enforcers, also known as local law enforcement. Enforcers were real hard asses, more concerned with keeping people in their place than keeping the peace. But I guess that was one and the same to them. As I moved up the line, I checked my palm for the faint green light.

It was finally my turn, and one of the Enforcers approached me.

Shaky hands. Accelerated breathing. Narrow eyes. **Speeder**. *Use magnetic pulse to purge kinetic energy stored in cells.*

I remember thinking their all-black uniforms made them look more like sous chefs than cops. The one before me was young, mid twenties, a little younger than myself, or a lot younger, depending on your perception of time. His sheepish grin made it clear he had taken a shine to me.

"That's a nice mobile cycle, Miss."

He wouldn't have been so nice if he had known at the time what I was. I got off my bike and stood in front of the baby-faced officer. His badge said Simmons.

"It's called a motorcycle, and thanks."

"The side mirrors are missing," he observantly noted.

"I use a rear cam instead."

"Oh. I've only seen these in holographs," he mused as he knelt down to pore over my bike. "Didn't these run on petroleum? Where do you find the fuel?"

"It's been adapted to run off of batteries," I replied.

"Incredible. Well, I just need to scan you."

"Be my guest."

Simmons raised his scanner to my face. Yellow light, then green, followed by a reassuring beep.

"You're all clear, Miss."

I smiled a silent lie.

"So what's your name?" he asked.

"Noneya," I replied

"That's a pretty name."

It was fun to mess with people in the future. It was like I had my own language at times.

"Where do you live?" he pressed.

"I don't."

"You don't live..?" he asked, clearly confused.

"Hey!" called a fellow officer from a couple cars away. "Court citizens on your own time! I don't wanna be out here all day!"

Spiky hair. Nystagmus. **Shocker.** *Stun gun to disrupt the parietal lobe.*

As I climbed back on my bike, I noticed a couple being scanned a few cars ahead. Even from that distance, I could see their worry. The man rubbed his brow and nervously smiled. The woman clutched her chest as if she was trying to keep her heart from bursting out.

9

"Have a good day, Miss," Simmons said to me.

My would-be suitor's manhood seemed somewhat bruised as he shamefully shuffled away.

"You didn't have to embarrass me like that!" he told his partner.

"You never had a chance anyway!" the ineffectual wing man retorted.

He was right. Simmons never had a chance, but neither did anyone else. Not since... you. The paradox of love is that sometimes the emptiness in your heart becomes so great that it starts taking up space, leaving very little room for anything else.

My attention had turned back to the couple when I saw another figure emerging from their car. I guessed that she was around seven or eight. A towheaded little girl in a blue dress holding a doll like it was her own precious baby. The father was sweating. The mother was shaking. At that point, it was clear what their daughter was, and they had every reason to worry.

The Enforcer scanned the little girl, but there was no green light, only red and then a banshee-like siren. I hated that sound. I had come to associate it with pain and death. But I was lucky, because most Zeros only hear it once.

"We got one!" an Enforcer cried out.

My admirer and his partner rushed to assist while the other travelers watched in surprise as the officer grabbed the child by her arm and looked at her hand, knocking her doll to the ground.

"Aaaahhhh!!!" the poor girl screamed.

"There's been a mistake!" the father cried as he reached for the officer's arm.

The father's protective instincts were quickly rebuffed by a blast from a neutralizer, causing him to fall helplessly to his knees.

"Daddy!!"

Please," the mother begged. "Don't hurt them!"

"She's not even branded!" the officer yelled. "Put these three in the vehicle!"

The family was mercilessly shoved into a van on the side of the road. Simmons tried to ease the crowd, which was more

11

disturbed by the little girl's presence than by the officers' callous behavior.

"Everything is okay, everyone. The situation has been handled."

"You can't save everyone," I told myself as the van drove away.

But I hadn't saved anyone. All this time I had been trying to save the world and hadn't really managed to save a single soul. Then along comes this innocent little girl who didn't ask for this life, and I was trying to look the other way. I tried to put it out of my mind, but I caught sight of her abandoned doll lying in the road.

I wasn't sure at the time what made me get off my bike and walk over there. I just focused on my palm, turning the green light to red, walked up behind Simmons and grabbed the doll that lay near his feet. He turned around, startled by my presence.

"Miss, you need to return to your vehicle...," he said, pointing with his scanner.

But as he did, the scanner passed my face and his finger hit the trigger. Much to his surprise, there was a glow of red this time, and the wailing siren once again startled the crowd.

"But, but you were clean…"

"She's a Zero! I thought you scanned her!" his partner lectured as he approached me.

"I did! She was green! I don't know what happened!"

"What happened is you weren't doing your job!"

The Shocker struck me in the head with the grip of his neutralizer, and I fell to the ground. As I slipped away, I realized what I had done. My life was never going to be same.

"They're coming!" I yell as I rush into the lab with Protos right behind me.

"We're out of time!" Cordell replies.

He runs over to a safe and quickly opens it. Inside it is a canister.

'Take this!" Cordell exclaims, handing the canister to me.

"We gotta go!" Protos yells just as gunshots echo down

the hall.

I woke up seated in an interrogation room surrounded by gray walls and a concrete floor. My head was pounding like a bill collector at the front door.

"What kind of man hits a woman like that?" I thought.

Chivalry was clearly dead, and that Shocker was going to join it soon.

I pulled up my sleeve and looked at my wrist. My bio-clock under my skin lit up and read 15:00, 05-10-2218. I had only been out for an hour. I noticed my chair didn't have restraints. That's how little they thought of us. Enforcers didn't even have weapons for Zeros. They used neutralizers on other Classes to deal with criminals and Sympathizers, but Zeros were considered no threat to them at all. And that was their biggest mistake.

"Hello, Zero. I am Detective Aiden Price. And you are?"

Thin. Atrophied. Bulging eyes. **Mover.** *Blind to disorient.*

The Enforcer looked to be in his late 50's, but Movers aged prematurely due to atrophy and poor diet. They had the biggest

God complex of all Classes. This guy was suspiciously feminine, but most people didn't care about such things anymore. Mankind had found new ways to label and discriminate. His predecessors had fought hard for the right to wear that ring on his bony finger, but since then, their sacrifice had become meaningless. The detective was bald with eyes so black they seemed to tug at my very soul. His lips were pursed, and he held his head unnecessarily high. As smug of a man as I had ever seen. He had my satchel with him which he placed on the table in front of me. He seemed annoyed when I didn't answer his question.

"How is your head?" he asked.

His insincerity didn't warrant a response.

"The arresting officer claims he scanned you, and you were clean, then minutes later, you approached him, and you were flagged by a second scan. Can you explain that?"

"Faulty scanner?"

"Faulty scanner… Why did you approach him when you were free to pass?"

15

"I had to get the little girl's doll."

The Mover looked at the wall to his right. I figured that was where the family had to be, in the adjoining interrogation room. The detective reached into my satchel.

"You mean this doll?" he asked, lifting it up. "Do you know this family?"

"I'm afraid not."

"You are not afraid of what?"

I never knew which expressions had survived until someone looked at me like Jodie Foster in Nell.

"I do not know the family," I replied.

"You are telling me that you sacrificed your freedom, perhaps even your life, for a doll belonging to some child you do not even know?"

"It's a collector's item."

"A collector's item," he chuckled. "Well, you do have quite a collection," he said as he dumped the contents of my satchel on the table in front of me.

Price picked up some of the items as he spoke.

"Some kind of electrical device, an electromagnet, an antiquated communication device, a watering gun filled with a cleaning solution, some odd type of eyewear, a bottle of nitrocodone, a handwritten book in some foreign language and a fellow officer tells me this is an acupuncture needle? What need do you have for such things?"

"I deal in antiques."

"Worthless antiques?" he asked.

"One man's trash…"

"What man's trash? Whose belongings are these?"

"No," I replied shaking my head, "one man's trash is another man's treasure."

The detective tilted his head to one side, confused by my vernacular.

"And what about this?"

He pulled the bottle of nitro from my bag.

"What about it?"

17

"5,000 milligrams of nitrocodone?"

"So what?" I responded. "It's a pain reliever."

"You must be in a lot of pain."

"You have no idea."

Next, he picked up my journal.

"What language is this?"

"It's cursive," I smirked.

"I have never heard of such a language."

"It's like Latin. It's a dead language."

"Dead. Yes, that sounds about right. You are not marked. Can I assume you are not sterilized either?"

I didn't respond.

"I suppose that is a yes. How did you make it into adulthood without ever being caught?"

"Lucky, I guess."

"Are there other lucky ones like yourself?"

There was no one like myself. And if there were, they certainly would not be considered lucky. I had lost everything I had ever loved. I had lost everything I had ever known, including myself.

As Price handled the journal, our photograph fell out.

"Oh what a pretty photo capture," he said mockingly.

I reached for it, but he pulled it away.

"It looks like you and a gentleman caller at some kind of costume party?"

He was thrown off by our clothing. I guess not all fashion comes back around. Agent Price turned the photograph around and showed it to me. It was from our last Christmas party at work. I was a little buzzed, and told you I loved you for the first time. The edges of the photo were tattered and the image was faded from water stains on some parts. It was the only photo I had of you, and time was eating it away.

"If you cooperate, I can make this easier for you. I can arrange for you to be sold to an elderly man with only a few needs, but if you do not cooperate, it could be a brothel where the needs are endless."

I sat there for a moment, looking at my belongings scattered on the table, but my interrogator's patience had worn thin.

"Answer me, you filthy piece of…!"

"It used to be you," I said, breaking my silence.

"What?"

"Your kind, you used to be the ones oppressed. You were the ones treated as subhuman and despised."

"Ha! You stupid woman, Classes were never treated as such!"

"Not Classes," I replied. "People with your… desires," I said, pointing to his ring finger.

Price looked down at his wedding ring then defensively covered it with his other hand.

"What are you saying?"

"They called you queers and nearly every culture on Earth saw you as an abomination."

Although I saw doubt in his coal-like eyes, my words made

him increasingly unnerved.

"You were oppressed, harassed, beaten, ridiculed. You were blamed for everything from disease to natural disasters."

"That is not true..."

"Along comes the Event mutating 40% of the world's population and suddenly you become exactly like the very thing you fought against. I guess deep down your kind is just as bigoted and hateful as everyone else."

His doubt was joined by anger as his brow furrowed and his eyes squinted.

"You are a filthy, lying Zero! Your kind knows nothing of history!"

"Check the Archive. There you'll find the truth."

"How do you know of the Archive? And what does a Zero know of truth?"

"I know plenty... Mover."

I had caught him by surprise.

"How do you know...?"

"You're a typical Mover," I said. "Smug, frail and weak."

With that, Price leaped to his feet, raised his hand and used his psychokinetic powers to lift me into the air by my throat. Clearly, I had used a poor choice of words.

"How is that for frail and weak!?" he taunted.

I was worth far more alive than dead, so I knew he wouldn't kill me, but self-preservation forced me to struggle for breath as I dangled in midair, futilely fighting against the invisible hand around my throat.

"Your errant tale has earned you a most undesirable fate," he said, releasing me from his grip.

I fell onto the table with a thud and took a raspy breath of air. I noticed the water gun near my hand.

"Now tell me, Zero, who is the weak one?"

"You are!"

I grabbed the ammonia filled water gun and shot him in the face.

"Aaaahhhh!!!" he screamed in agony while clutching his

eyes.

I reached for the acupuncture needle and leaped over the table towards my tormentor. Most Movers depended far too much on sight for their powers and became disoriented when they couldn't see, so Price was no exception. I slammed him against the wall and plunged the needle into his neck.

"No, stop! Stop! What are you doing?! Help me!!" he cried.

Suddenly, two Enforcers burst through the door.

"Let him go!" they ordered.

I grabbed the Mover's arm, aimed it at the other Enforcers, then wiggled the needle in his neck. A concussive force erupted from his hand, sending the Enforcers through the wall.

I turned his arm in the direction where I suspected the family to be.

"What are you doing!" he cried.

"Making your predecessors proud."

I moved the needle again and forced him to rip a hole in the other wall. My suspicions proved correct. There stood the family of three along with two interrogators, all of which stared back in shock.

I used my puppet's powers to fell the two officers with ease. More Enforcers came barreling through the first hole I had made.

"Get her!" one of them ordered.

Thinking me a Class, one of them hit me with a neutralizer. It did nothing to me, but it effectively zapped Price's psychokinesis. I kicked him towards the other officers, and followed behind, rushing the Enforcers while they were off balance. Much to my enjoyment, the nearest officer was the Shocker whom I owed a favor.

"I should've killed you in the street!" he said.

He balled his fists, building a charge as I reached for the stun gun. I slid across the table towards him and shoved the gun under his chin.

"I could've told you that."

The first jolt dazed him. I spun him around towards his

fellow officers and delivered a second, stronger jolt to the base of his skull. To his dismay, a burst of electricity shot from his eyes and mouth, frying his friends… and his brain.

He still had a charge in him, and I used it to hit a light fixture. The surge plunged the whole building into darkness. I reached around for my night vision goggles and threw the rest of my belongings back into my bag.

I quickly made my way into the room where the family stood huddled in the corner while the Enforcers ran about like blind mice in the darkness. I reached for the father who was startled by my touch.

"Who's there?" he asked in fear.

"I'm someone like your daughter. Take my hand, and I'll get you and your family out of here."

I scooped the girl up in my arms.

"Mommy?" she cried.

"It's okay, baby. Mommy is right here."

The father grabbed my hand and the mother grabbed his.

We raced down the hall towards a back door.

We made it outside near the impound lot, and I removed my goggles.

"Does your car have a biometric starter?" I asked the father.

"Yes it does," he replied.

"Good, no need for keys. Let's go!"

"Stop!!"

An Enforcer had followed us outside. It was Simmons from the checkpoint. He was kinda cute for an oppressive neo-Nazi, so I almost felt bad for what came next.

"You can't escape! Surrender and you will be treated fairly!"

"As fairly as I was treated by your partner?"

Simmons scowled and launched himself towards me. As you know, a Speeder's speed comes from his ability to store kinetic energy in his cells. In order to stop smoothly, a Speeder must purge all kinetic energy in a controlled manner. Well, I figured out that an electromagnetic pulse disrupts the cells, causing them to purge suddenly, bringing the Speeder to a dead stop. The average Speeder can move eighty-eight feet per second. At that speed, Simmons could reach me in 1.14 seconds, but I could draw on a man in .15. I hesitated briefly before pulling out the electromagnet and dropped him at point blank range. Simmons stopped a mere three feet in front of me, as if he was suddenly frozen in time. I put him down with a blow to the head before he could recover.

"There are more coming!" the mother exclaimed.

I looked up and saw a dozen or so Enforcers charging out the back door. I heard one of them through Simmons' com.

"She's a Zero! Your neutralizers won't work! Use your Classes!"

I looked at the mother and then the father.

Partial heterochromia. Muscle spasm in eyelids.

"You're a Trickster?" I asked the father.

"Ye- yes," he replied nervously. "How did you know?"

"Make us all invisible!" I said.

He shook his head in fear.

"I cannot guise so many people. I mean, I never…"

I grabbed him by the collar.

"Try!!"

The father closed his eyes and clenched his fists. A second later we were out of sight.

"I thought they said she was a Zero!" one Enforcer said.

"It's not her! The Trickster is the fa.. aaarrgh!"

Cloaked with invisibility, I began taking them out one by one.

"Where is she?"

Their blind attempts at hitting me resulted in friendly fire on their own men. I was halfway through them when I began to flicker back into view. The father couldn't hold it together any longer.

"Stop the Sympathizers from helping her!"

An Enforcer rushed the family, but the father used what

strength he had left to only cloak me that time. I caught up to the Enforcer and slide tackled him from behind, a throwback to my varsity soccer days. I reached the family just as I became visible again. The other Enforcers were closing in.

"We have to find your car!" I said

I grabbed the little girl by the hand, and we all ran through the impound lot, ducking around the cars. We managed to lose the Enforcers in the maze of larger vehicles.

"Split up, form a perimeter around the back half then close in on them!" an Enforcer ordered.

I peered through a car window and saw more Enforcers joining the fight.

"What are we going to do?" the mother asked.

I looked around and noticed an old natural gas meter. Some of them were still used as recently as fifty years ago. I smelled hydrogen sulfide. I quickly turned back to the mother and my satchel rubbed against her arm. A welt appeared immediately.

Skin writing. Premature graying.

"You're a Skipper?"

"Yes," she replied.

The Enforcers were getting closer, so I had to act fast.

"Take your family and skip thirty seconds ahead."

"Why?" she asked.

"Just do it! Thirty seconds. Now!"

Time travel was like diving into cold water. You instinctively close your eyes and hold your breath. There was this sense of sinking deeper and deeper until you bottom out, then you began to rise. What seemed like forever took no time at all, and the illusion ended when you surfaced and gasped for air.

The family returned to time and found me holding a Burner in a chokehold in the middle of what looked like the aftermath of Hiroshima. The father stepped cautiously towards me.

"You're not harmed?"

"Burners have a protective perimeter around them. Stand close enough and the flames won't hurt you either."

Having outlived his usefulness, I threw the Burner to the

ground.

"We have to go."

"But you destroyed everything," the mother replied.

"Not everything." I pointed to a corner of the lot that was untouched. There was my bike and the family's car. Some lot attendant was sitting on my bike, and his earbuds made him oblivious to the situation. When we reached him, I tapped him on the shoulder. He turned around to see ground zero and decided it would be a good idea if he gave me my bike back.

The family jumped into their car, and I hopped on my bike. I tore through the fence onto the road with the family close behind.

We drove for about an hour down several back roads. When I was certain we were safe, I pulled over to the side of the road. The father did the same, and I walked over to them as they exited their car.

"Where are we?" the father asked.

"Middle of nowhere. You're safe for now."

They looked around, and the father turned back to me.

"So, should we go home?"

"You can't go home... ever again."

His face turned pale and sullen, and my heart broke for him, for I knew that feeling all too well.

"Well, wherever you're going, may we come with you?" the father asked.

I was taken aback by his request.

"No, that's not possible."

"Please, miss," the father pleaded. "We'll die on our own."

"Were it not for me, you would already be dead. Besides, I'm on the Enforcers' radar now, so they're going to come for me, and after what I did, they won't stop. When that happens, I won't be able to protect your whole family."

"If they can find you, then what chance do we have?" the father asked.

"I'm sorry. I've done all I can."

The father's eyes dropped to the ground, and the mother looked down at their little girl by her side.

32

"Then just take our Gracie," she said, nudging the confused girl in my direction.

"Caroline! No! We can't leave our daughter with a stranger!" said the father.

"John, that stranger just saved all of our lives, and we can't protect Gracie, but she can."

"Mommy, I want to stay with you!"

"My life is no place for a little girl," I said.

But Caroline replied, "This world is no place for a little girl, especially when she's a Zero."

Her words brought back my shame and weighed heavy on my heart. John looked at his daughter and softened his protest.

"They will find us, and they will take her. And you know what they will do to her," the mother continued.

She was right. Even a girl young as Gracie was not immune to their depravity. I guess when you decide someone isn't human, it's easy to commit unspeakable acts against them.

"Please, miss," Caroline begged again.

"I can't. I'm sorry."

Again I was walking away, but I had done all I could. At least that's what I told myself. In reality, I had done no more for them than I did for the boy back at the shop. I had simply bought them a little more time. As I attached my satchel to my bike, I remembered why I had done this to begin with. I reached into my bag for the doll.

The family looked at me curiously as I walked over and squatted down in front of Gracie.

"I believe this is yours," I said, handing her the doll.

And there it was. The brightest, most beautiful smile I had ever seen, like the light from Polaris beckoning me home.

"Annie!" Gracie exclaimed.

The look on that little girl's face awakened something in me that I thought had long since died. For the first time, in such a very long time, I felt joy. I felt hope.

I stood up and looked at her father, then her mother, and I nodded my head. Caroline swallowed hard then hugged me

34

tightly.

"Keep my baby safe," she whispered in my ear.

I felt the warmth of her tears against my cheek. I nodded again, choking back tears of my own.

When I turned to John, I could still see the reluctance on his face. He slowly held out his hand, but I pulled him close instead.

"They won't get her," I assured him.

I could see the fear coming over Gracie's face.

"Mommy..?"

Caroline picked up her daughter and buried her face in her golden locks.

"My sweet baby, I love you so much."

"I love you too, mommy. X O"

"X O, baby."

John kissed Gracie on the top of her head and the three of them held each other tightly. Their bodies trembled, and the impending separation triggered my anxiety, so I had to look away.

I pulled the pill bottle from my pocket and shook it slowly it like a rattle.

"Daddy and I have to go away for a while. This nice lady is going to take care of you while we are gone."

"No, Mommy," said Gracie, gasping for breath between her sobs.

"It's okay, sweetie. She can keep you safe from those bad people. Mommy and I will be back for you as soon as we can."

"No! Please, do not leave me!" Gracie begged.

She was about to lose everything she loved, and I was the one who was going to take it all from her. The father broke the embrace and turned to me.

"We do not know your name."

"It's best if you don't know, in case..."

"I understand," he replied.

"You need to leave first," I told them. "Go in that direction for an hour or so. It should lead you to familiar territory. John nodded and Caroline gave Gracie one last kiss.

"Don't leave me... please, Mommy!!"

"It'll be okay, baby. I promise."

"Daddy!!!"

I squatted down and pulled Gracie close to me as she fought to reach her parents as they headed for their car.

"Please, don't leave me!! Please!! Mommy!! Daddy!!"

I opened my mouth to tell her it was going to be alright, but all that came out was a gasp. Her parents got into their car and started driving away, and Gracie's cries got louder, piercing my ears... and my heart.

"MOMMY!!!!! MOMMY!!! Come back!! Please come back!! Daddy!!!"

She cried well after the car was out of sight. I don't know how long we stayed out there with Gracie sobbing in my arms and me on my knees with my head on her shoulder, but eventually, the sun began to set, and her cries were reduced to shallow breaths. She reached up and touched the side of my face, so I released her, and she turned around.

"What is your name?" Gracie asked me with short gasping breaths.

"My name is Kaori."

Chapter 2
Josiah

I am Josiah Griffin, Special Agent with the Gendarmerie, and this is my account of the events surrounding the fugitive, Kaori Maru.

I arrived at the Enforcer station at eighteen o'clock, approximately three hours after the attack. I was immediately shocked by the amount of damage she had caused. Bodies lay everywhere, the power was out, every server and backup had been destroyed, and the impound lot looked like a meteor had crashed there. The officers I initially interviewed provided me with minimal information, as they had paid her little mind when she arrived. To them, she was just another Zero, until she brought the place to the ground.

"Josiah, what in Gehenna has happened here!?"

The Governor of North America, Mathias Ross, usually didn't get involved in local matters, but a Zero taking out an entire

Enforcer department warranted his attention.

"Hello, Governor. So far, it appears a husband and wife were arrested at a roadside checkpoint for having an unregistered Zero child. An unrelated adult Zero was arrested separately at the scene, and she broke them all out of the facility while doing considerable damage in the process."

"You're telling me this is not just the result of one person, but of *one Zero*?" the Governor asked with incredulity.

It was hard to believe any Zero could take out a Class, much less a few dozen of us, but there we were, standing in the middle of the aftermath. We had never given Zeros much credit for strength or creativity, and it appeared she had used that arrogance and lax attitude against us.

"One Zero, sir. That is what I have been told thus far."

"How? She was in custody. Did she get ahold of a neutralizer?"

"No, Governor. She controlled their powers with primitive tools they found on her."

"There is no way one of those animals could destroy a whole station with just a bunch of party favors!"

"Look around, Governor. There isn't a single weapon in here that would harm Zeros..."

"Why would we need weapons for Zeros? We are the weapons!"

"That's exactly the problem. By not considering them a threat and becoming too dependent on our Classes, someone was finally able to exploit our dependency and use it to her advantage."

The Governor was a man of pride. He didn't like hearing that our undoing was due to our own crippling hubris.

"Just find her, Josiah, and bring her to me. Alive."

I watched the Governor storm off and wondered how long it would be before he interfered with my case.

"Excuse me, I'm looking for Detective Aiden Price," I asked a passing officer.

"His office is the last one on the right," she said as she pointed down the hall.

I made my way down the hallway and knocked on his office door.

"Detective Aiden Price? I am Special Agent Josiah Griffin with the Gendarmerie."

There was no response, so I opened the door and walked inside. There sat Aiden Price at his desk with reddened eyes and a blood stained neck, holding an ice pack to his head.

Aiden removed the ice pack from his head but didn't look up.

"Well, that took longer than I expected," he said.

I took a seat across from the wounded officer, and looked around the room. I could tell he was organized to the point of being anal. Everything on his desk was evenly spaced, no dust in sight. Even his trash can was clean.

"I had a lot of people to interview. I was told that you spent the most time with her," I said as I placed my holo on the desk to record the interview.

"Yes, I did the interrogation," Aiden replied.

"I tried to recover the video, but it was destroyed when the server room burned down. You'll need to tell me everything you remember, Detective."

Aiden took a stuttering breath before he recounted the massacre. His voice continued to tremble throughout the story, more so out of anger than fear. He was so embarrassed that he had been beaten so badly, but he had probably never faced a real adversary. After the war, the Gendarmerie took the fight out of the Zeros, so they spent most of their time hiding in the shadows. Since then, the most action Enforcers saw were rowdy, drunken teenage Classes. If anything really serious happened, the Gendarmerie was called in. As I watched Aiden tell his story, I saw the shame in his eyes.

"What can you tell me about her?" I asked.

"She talked differently. Unlike anyone I have ever met."

"Like an accent?" I inquired.

"Not really. Mainly strange phrases. And she talked like she knew a lot about the past."

"The past? What do you mean?"

"History. Things that happened before the Event..."

I sat up straight and looked Aiden squarely in the eye.

"That's impossible. The Event happened over 200 years ago, I was told she was thirty at the most, so she would've needed to travel through time to get here, and no one can skip that far."

"But she spoke of things I had never heard. She said that *we* used to be the Zeros."

"We..?"

"People like myself.... and my husband..."

I looked at Aiden's hand as he rubbed his ring.

"She said we were the ones that were hated."

"That's absurd." I responded. "Why would anyone care about who your mate is? She was just distorting your mind. She knows nothing of the past."

"She knows about the Archive," he replied.

Aiden really had my attention then.

"What did she say about the Archive?" I asked.

"She just told me to check it, to verify the things she said."

Most law enforcement didn't even know the Archive existed, so her awareness of it was very concerning. I sat silently for several seconds.

"Come down to Gendarmerie headquarters tomorrow morning. I want a Reader to scan you."

Chapter 3
Kaori

As I tore down the road on my bike, it felt like the wind would whip away at my soul, eroding me to nothing. I increased my speed, making it harder to breathe, but I barely noticed, or maybe I just didn't care. I was almost at 150 when I felt her tiny nails digging into my skin and her rapid heartbeat pounding against my back. *Shit*. I wasn't used to having a rider, and I realized how scary it was for Gracie at that speed. I eased up on the throttle and downshifted then looked over my shoulder and barely saw the top of her golden curls pressed tightly against my back. Slowing down did nothing to loosen her death grip, so I pulled over on the side of the road.

I shut off my bike and turned to the side. Gracie looked up at me with tear stained eyes. She had released my flesh but still had a good grip on the sides of my jacket.

"I'm sorry I was going so fast. Are you okay?"

Gracie simply nodded but her fearful blue eyes told me otherwise.

"We're almost there. I'll go slower."

Gracie nodded again and regained her death grip, closing her eyes and burying her face in my jacket. I kept it under fifty all the way *home*.

We pulled up behind an abandoned automobile factory, and I triggered the motorized gate. With all the rust and weeds, no one would have ever suspected that it was a hideout.

We entered one of the buildings through a garage door. When I went to help Gracie off the bike, I got another look at her face. I grabbed a handkerchief from my jacket pocket and wiped her face clean.

"Where are we?" she asked looking around.

"When I was a kid, this was a factory where they built cars," I replied as we walked down the hall.

"They don't anymore?"

"Not for a couple hundred years."

Gracie wrinkled her brow.

"How old are you..?"

I laughed at the thought of what must have been going through her little mind.

"I guess I have a lot to explain," I said as we entered the cafeteria.

"I guess you do," said Godspeed.

Gracie quickly cowered behind me and clutched my leg while keeping a watchful eye on the four new strangers before her. I ran my fingers through her hair.

It's okay, sweetheart. These are my friends."

I went around the room introducing the group to Gracie. The young black guy was Gadget, a genius with technology. He was a cross between MacGyver and the Professor from Gilligan's Island. I told him that once, and he just stared at me blankly. The fair-skinned ginger was Medic. She secretly received medical training from her master's wife and became an incredible physician. She had saved all of our lives more than once. The old

48

white dude was Deadeye, the deadliest shot I'd ever known. And Godspeed... he was... he was just a really good driver.

"And what is your name little lady?" Medic asked, squatting down to eye level.

"Gracie, " she replied cautiously.

"That's a beautiful name, Gracie."

"Where are her parents, Kaori?" asked Godspeed.

Gracie dropped her head and leaned against me.

"They went another way," I replied.

The four of them looked at each other trying to make sense of my words.

"Gracie is human; her parents are not. I saw them being arrested at a checkpoint, so I broke them out of an Enforcer station."

"Tell me you aren't serious..," said Godspeed.

Medic saw the whole thing going sideways and decided take Gracie away.

"Hey, little one. I bet you're hungry. How about we go find

you something to eat?"

Gracie looked at me, so I nodded and gave her a wink. She took Medic's hand and disappeared into the kitchen. Godspeed waited until they were gone before continuing his lecture.

"Do you have any idea what you've done?"

"I saved a little girl's life."

"At what cost?" he asked.

I didn't reply. I just looked away instead. Godspeed took his plate and left the room.

"Well, I like kids," said Gadget, leaving as well.

I gave a smile of gratitude.

We had been living in the shadows unseen for so long, and no one even knew we existed. All of that was about to change, and it was all my fault. How could we complete the mission if we were constantly on the run? And how could we live life on the run with Gracie? I looked over at Deadeye, and he gave me a look that you'd get from your grandpa after your parents scolded you.

"So, they got picked up at a checkpoint, eh?" Deadeye

inquired.

"Yes," I replied. "I saw them being carted off, and I had to do something."

"I would think taking on three or four Enforcers at a checkpoint would be easier than taking on the whole station."

"I didn't decide to act until they were gone."

"I guess it's too bad you don't have a bike capable of reaching 300 miles per hour. You could've caught them before they made it back to the station."

Deadeye never said much, except when he did. Then it was way too much.

"You missed supper," he added before walking away.

I joined Medic and Gracie in the kitchen and found them eating some grapes. The two had warmed up to each other quickly, but that was no surprise. Medic was a nurturer. I had known many physicians that treated the body, but she treated the person. I always told her that she was a nurse trapped in a doctor's body. She always took it as a compliment.

51

"Looks like you two are becoming fast friends."

Gracie's eyes widened.

"Are we becoming Speeders?"

Medic smiled and gave Gracie a hug.

"No, sweetheart. I think she means that you and I are quickly becoming friends."

"Oh..."

Gracie looked disappointed with the news that there would be no mutations, but quickly turned her attention back to her treat.

"Look, Kori. Medic gave me grapes!"

"I'm sorry you two missed supper," said Medic. "Deadeye made the most wonderful pigeon chili."

When you spend your life in hiding, you make do with what you have. Adjusting to the delicacies in the afterworld was pretty hard. Things my mom used to kill with a shoe became main courses. It wasn't so bad once I got used to it, but it took a *really* long time to get used to it.

"I have never had pigeon chili," Gracie replied. "Have you,

Kori?"

"Yes, I have. And Deadeye is a great cook."

Medic smiled.

"I'm going to ready myself for bed. I can prepare bedding for Gracie if you like, Kaori."

"Thanks, Medic."

Medic left, and I sat down next to Gracie. She offered me a grape.

"Thank you.".

"Kori, why do all of your friends have funny names?"

"They're humans."

"Everyone is human," she replied.

"I mean they're Zeros, Gracie. Do you know what a Zero is?"

Gracie lowered her head.

"It is someone who is not very special," she said.

I lifted Gracie's chin so she could see my eyes.

"Gracie, a Zero is the last truly special thing in this world."

Her face lit up again, and I knew bringing Gracie back with me was the right decision, no matter what happened.

"You and I are Zeros. Why do we not have weird names?"

"Well, parents give children their names out of love, but most Zeros don't know their parents. "

"That is sad."

"That is sad. You and I knew our parents, my friends did not. Usually Zeros wind up being named something awful by the bad guys, or they name themselves. When that happens, they tend to choose a name that reflects what they do."

"Were your parents nice to you?"

"Very much so. In fact, my dad used to work here in this very factory."

"Really?"

"Yup."

I told her about how they built cars, and she thought it was the most amazing thing, which was funny because her parents could do magic and travel through time. My dad would bring me the factory, and I'd have to wear ear and eye protection which was so neat to me at the time. Sometimes, when no one was looking, my dad would let me tighten a bolt or two. I remember hoping I'd never wind up owning one of the cars that I worked on. He'd take me into the cafeteria, and the cook would bring out special dishes that he made just for me. Seeing Gracie sitting there reminded me of those times. I never told you any of that before.

"Where are your parents now?" Gracie asked.

"They're dead."

"How did they die?"

"I don't know."

"Then how do you know that they are dead?"

"Because no one lives to be 260 years old."

"Kori, I do not understand."

"You know how your mommy skips time? Well, I used to have a co-worker, and he could skip a lot time, years in fact..."

I proceeded to tell her about the *mysterious* Event that mutated human genes and how some people developed superhuman abilities: flight, psychokinesis, magic, speed, strength, electricity, fire, telepathy and time travel. Unfortunately, it wasn't at all like what we read in the comic books. Hubris spread throughout the superhuman community like the plague as people fancied themselves gods. They began to abandon religion and looked to superhumans for salvation. But benevolence quickly became tyranny as the Classes sought to rule the Zeros.

When I arrived in the future, it was clear you hadn't fixed things yourself. I learned there had been a civil war between the Classes and the Zeros. The End War spread to Canada and Mexico and the death toll reached into the hundreds of thousands. The Zeros had heart, but they were hopelessly outgunned and they were defeated a year after the conflict began.

When the war ended, North America became one country, and the Zeros faced oppression like never before. Many of them fled to Cuba, the Dominican Republic and parts of South America. Back in the states, there was a growing fear that the Zeros' inferior genes would taint the gene pool, so laws were passed requiring registration and selective sterilization for them. Wary of civil unrest of their own, other countries adopted similar laws. The Zeros numbers dwindled to 30% of the general population. They became victims of horrible cruelty. Before all that, everyone had something to blame for the demise of America: immigrants, religion, minorities, gays, but in the end, it was arrogance and a lack of compassion that did us in.

"What made people change into Classes?" Gracie asked.

My eyes found the ground before my lips could find the answer.

"No one knows. Some thought it was a radiation leak, or an electrical storm, but no one ever found out what caused it."

"No, Kori. What made them change into bad people?"

For a moment, I was at a loss for words.

"I don't know, Gracie. I guess no matter how great or powerful we become, there's still this emptiness inside of us, and you can either fill it with love or hide it with hate."

"I think my parents filled it with love."

"You filled them with love, sweetie."

Gracie grabbed my hand and nestled her head into my side.

"Why did you travel here?" Gracie asked.

"It was a mistake…"

Chapter 4
Aiden

History will not be kind to me. It will tell a tale of cowardice and weak moral fortitude, so I am writing this so that you might know the truth. So that you will understand that I did this for us. For all of us.

I finally returned home several hours after the ordeal, but it was still very fresh in my mind. My thoughts alternated between the intense pain and vengeance. I walked into our building and took the lift to our floor. By day's end, I usually levitated my way back home, but the effects of the neutralizer hadn't completely worn off, and getting around without any psychokinetic assistance at all took some getting used to.

I wearily reached our front door, but before I could touch the biometric scanner, the door swung wide open.

"Aiden! Honey, are you okay!!?"

You rushed to greet me at the door because you were

worried. The news of the incident had spread throughout the country, but the officials were calling it a gas explosion. There would have been mass panic if the public knew a Zero took down so many Enforcers.

You immediately threw your arms around me.

"I kept trying to reach you but the department said you were unavailable! They said you were fine but look at you!"

I walked inside and sat down on the couch while you followed closely behind.

"It is ok, Carson. I am not as bad as I seem."

"Well, I hope not, because you look horrible!"

You tried to dote on me, but I wasn't in the mood. I had not been in the mood for a long time... I had allowed my dissatisfaction with my work to affect us and that incident had only made it worse. I wanted revenge, and all you wanted was love.

"Carson, please..."

"I am sorry, but I was worried, okay? I saw the reports about the gas explosion, and officers were killed, and I was just going crazy when they wouldn't let me speak with you."

"I am sorry. I should not have barked at you, but this has been a trying day."

"It's okay darling. I'm just glad you are home."

You snuggled up to me, but I was less than affectionate. For the first time in my life, I found myself more obsessed with a woman than a man.

"I might be going away for awhile," I said.

"Why?"

"I owe a young woman a favor, and it is important that I pay her back."

Chapter 5
Kaori

I stood in the shower letting the hot water wash over my body. I remembered being baptized as a child and the preacher telling me the water was the blood of Christ and it would wash away all of my sins. I imagined the shower was doing the same, washing every bad thing I had ever done down the drain. Instead, I saw my sins spiraling around and around but never going away.

I heard him coming. I could have turned him away. I should have, but I knew his touch would mitigate the burden of my yoke. Nothing would change, but for the moment I could pretend to know love again.

His hands met my waist just above my hips as his lips barely touched my neck. He kissed his way up to my ear and a warmth flowed throughout my body. He pressed his thumbs into the small of my back then slid his hands easily across my wet skin. When he reached my stomach, he pulled my body against his, then wrapped his strong arms fully around me. I wanted to feel his love, but I didn't know how to give any in return, and I couldn't keep hurting people, including myself.

"Godspeed, stop..."

When he didn't, I looked down and saw my hands held tightly to his arms. My body had betrayed me, telling a truth that words tried to keep hidden. I pushed his arms away from me and faced him.

"Last night was a mistake," I said.

"And the night before?"

"The same."

I hoped I had only hurt his pride, for I couldn't bear to hurt his heart again.

"Why do you do this, Kaori? I know you feel something when we're together, because I feel it too."

I did feel something. I felt desperation, loneliness, and sadness and Godspeed's love was a drug I used to numb the pain. It was a powerful drug when inside me, but the effects quickly wore off and coming down from that high left me even more empty than before.

"Things are different now," I replied.

"Does this have anything to do with that girl?"

"Her name is Gracie."

"We've seen a thousand little girls over the years, Kaori, and not once did you rescue any of them. What makes this one so special? What does she mean to you?"

"She means I'm still alive."

"And what do I mean?"

"I'm sorry, Godspeed."

"Sorry that I mean less to you than a stranger's child?" he asked.

"I'm sorry that I cannot give you what you want, and I'm sorry that you do not have what I need."

There was no doubt that I had hurt his heart that time. It showed on his face and poured over his body.

"Do you know what's worse than loving someone who

doesn't love you in return?" he asked.

"I didn't know there was anything worse," I replied.

"Not being able to tell that person you love them. Whoever hurt you, I am not him."

"I know..."

As Godspeed walked away, the hot water turned cold.

The walk back to my room felt longer than normal, and the nighttime chill of the factory was made worse by my damp hair. I was more than ready for that day to end.

My room *(which was really just someone's old office)* was so toasty when I returned. I was thankful to Medic for lighting the heater. She was sitting with Gracie on my bed *(which was an old couch)* and telling a story.

"So, the Providence will save us from the Classes?" Gracie asked.

"Yes," Medic replied. "The peril that we face now is only but for a while. His coming will see to that."

Medic looked up and saw the displeasure on my face. She

nervously smiled.

"Look who's done with her shower, Gracie..."

"Now you look more like a girl!" Gracie mused.

"Is that so?" I asked smiling.

I hadn't thought much about it before, but I guess I was putting out somewhat of a butch vibe with my cropped leather jacket and biker boots. There wasn't time or much of a reason for primping in the afterworld anyway.

"Are you surprised to see a girl under all that dirt and soot?" I asked.

"I knew you would be pretty if you were not so dirty like a nasty boy."

I sat on the other side of Gracie.

"Boys are nasty, aren't they?" I asked while giving her tummy a tickle.

"Ha ha haaa! They are the worst!"

It had been so long since I had heard the laughter of a child. I had forgotten how much joy that warbling song could bring. I

66

picked up a book that lay near the couch and handed it to Gracie.

"Wanna read this for a bit? I need to speak with Medic."

"Okay," Gracie shrugged and began reading softly to herself.

Medic slowly followed me over to the other side of the room. She knew what was coming.

"I appreciate you looking after Gracie, but I would prefer you not present fairy tales as truth," I said firmly.

Medic didn't like confrontation, and I kinda felt bad for giving her the business.

"I'm sorry. I was just sharing the story of the Providence. I thought it would help if she had something to believe in."

Apparently, while I was sidestepping a couple of centuries, someone came up with the idea that an individual called the Providence would come to their rescue. I wasn't sure if he was supposed to be a god or what, but the story spoke of a powerful being who would stop the Classes and liberate the Zeros.

"How does believing in lies help her?" I asked.

"It has been prophesied…"

"Medic, I was there before any of this came to be. There was never any talk about a Providence. Throughout history, anyone who ever claimed to predict anything was proven to be a fraud. Even after the Event, predicting the future was impossible. Besides, you're a scientist."

"That doesn't mean I can't have faith," she replied unapologetically.

"In what? Some stranger's words? The only future we can predict is the one that we create ourselves."

"Okay, Kaori, but what does it hurt if she has something to believe in?"

"As long as she thinks someone is coming to save her, she will never save herself. Again, I appreciate your help, but I will give her something to believe in."

"You mean like this?"

Medic showed me the bottle in her hand and my heart leaped into my throat.

"It fell out of your jacket," Medic said cautiously.

I released the arrested air from my lungs and stood there shaking my head. "They're for pain."

"You hate pills, Kaori, but you've been carrying this bottle for over six months with just the right number to kill a woman of your weight and tolerance."

"What are you saying, Medic..?"

"I thought you were better," she said.

"I just got better at pretending..."

An all too familiar hurt washed over Medic's face.

"No one wants you to pretend, Kaori. We love you."

"I know that. But compassion and sympathy are not in infinite supply. My life has just become a really bad movie. Everyone hopes it will get better, but if it doesn't, they'll eventually walk out."

Medic stepped closer and placed her hand on my face.

"I'm not walking out."

She put the medicine bottle on a table next to me, which

69

was totally unexpected.

"We all find comfort by putting our faith in something. I cannot take your faith from you and not replace it."

Medic leaned forward and kissed my forehead then held me close.

"Stay," she said.

She then turned to Gracie to tell her goodnight.

"Good night, Medic!" said Gracie.

Medic left, and I reached for my comb on a side table and worked my way through my raven locks. Gracie watched with great interest.

"You have really pretty hair, Kori."

"Not as pretty as yours."

Looking around, she curiously asked, "Why do you not have any mirrors? How do you get ready in the morning?"

"I know what I look like."

My words had more bite than I intended, and Gracie's fragile feelings were clearly bruised. I handed her the comb and smiled to provide levity.

"There's no one here I need to look good for anyway," I said.

Gracie took the comb and ran it through my hair.

"You do not have a boyfriend?"

"I do not."

"Do you have kids?"

"No."

"How old are you?"

"I'm almost thirty, or 230. Depending on the day."

"That is old!"

Smiling I replied, "Yes, it is. It's getting late, and we should get some sleep. Tomorrow will be a long day."

Medic had made a pallet for me on the floor next to the couch, so I got down there and tried to get comfortable.

"Kori, you did not tuck me in..."

"I'm sorry."

I knelt beside the couch and pulled the blanket over Gracie, just up to her chin.

"Better?"

She nodded.

I'm pretty sure I had already started dreaming when she spoke again.

"Why is tomorrow going to be a long day?"

"Because we have a lot to decide."

"About me?"

"About all of us, Gracie."

"Kori?"

"Yes, Gracie?"

"I miss my mommy and daddy."

"I know, sweetheart."

Gracie dropped her arm over the side of the couch and spread her fingers. I reached up and her little hand wrapped around two of my fingers.

"X O, Kori."

"X O, Gracie."

Chapter 6
Aiden

"Hello, I am Detective Aiden Price. I am here to see Special Agent Josiah Griffin. He is expecting my arrival."

I arrived at Gendarmerie headquarters early in the morning as requested. I was rather apprehensive, partially because I was still reeling from my beating, but also because I was about to have my brain prodded by a Reader. The average Reader could only get inside your mind if you let him, but an upper Class could use brute force and shred your mind into pieces. I had seen more than one person lobotomized by a determined Reader.

"Welcome, Mr. Price. Have a seat, and I will see if Special Agent Griffin is available."

The receptionist at the front desk might as well have been a robot for the amount of emotion he showed, and that did not help relieve my anxiety at all. I took a seat and attempted to relax

Although I had been in law enforcement practically my

entire life, I had never been to Gendarmerie headquarters. The Gendarmerie rarely interacted with any branch of government below the federal level, and I think that created a shroud of mystery around them which discouraged anyone from getting on their bad side, including Enforcers.

Everything in the building was white, including the walls, floors and the furniture. There were accents of green and brushed nickel here and there, but everything else was like a hospital. It made me uptight, nervous and afraid to touch anything.

I tried to send out psychokinetic waves to get a feel for the place and its occupants, but it was in vain, as I knew it would be. The Gendarmerie buildings were oversized neutralizers that suppressed powers of anyone not on staff. The Gendarmes themselves had implants that made them immune to the neutralizers. I, however, was rendered powerless on their home turf, which was all the more reason to be anxious.

"Aiden, come with me."

I looked up to see Josiah at the front desk, welcoming me

with a stoic expression.

"Hello, Special Agent Griffin," I replied.

"Josiah is fine, takes less time to say. The Reader is waiting."

I followed Josiah into the lift which carried us to the 13th floor.

"I had heard that people used to think the number thirteen was unlucky, so some buildings did not have a thirteenth floor," I said, making conversation.

"I heard that people used to be really stupid."

"I believe I heard that too," I replied.

With that, I remained silent for the remainder of the ride.

Josiah led me past the main office area down a long hallway towards a row of rooms with large glass windows. We stopped at a room occupied by a rather unprofessional looking woman. She was in stark contrast to the other Gendarmes with her form fitting black and red shorts and a matching tank top. She wore red boots that reached her mid-calf and was covered in tattoos, including some on her face. The tattoos on her face were inverted hearts that ran down the right side of her face like tears. She had jet black hair with the exception of a chunk of red in the back. Her feet were propped up on the table in front of her as she leaned back in her chair. Although I had never met her, I knew she could only be Riser Kilroy, one of the world's most powerful Readers, and leader of a group of mercenaries known as the Reapers. Josiah waved at her through the window, and she gave barely a nod in response. Josiah placed his palm on a biometric scanner to open the door.

"Detective Aiden Price, this is..."

"I know who this maniac is, and she is not getting anywhere near my brain!"

Riser sat there, clearly amused by my objections.

"Aww, you done hurt my feelings..."

"There's nothing to worry about," Josiah interjected. "Riser is very professional."

"A professional killer!"

"Don't be afraid. Ah won't hurt ya, 'less you like it that way."

I frowned and looked over at Josiah. Reapers were nasty creatures, drugged up on nitrocodone, or Nitro, as it was called on the street. Very few Classes could handle a Nitro overdose, but those who did saw their powers increase tenfold. Those with such a tolerance were usually identified in their youth. They were called Outliers.

"Ooh, but ah'm knockin' on the wrong door, aren't I, pussycat?"

Riser made me increasingly uncomfortable. I felt vulnerable without my powers, and I hated her manner of speaking which was a result of lifelong drug use. I greatly regretted my decision to let a Reader scan me, but I did not really have a choice.

"Riser, settle down. I just need you to pull a woman's image from his memory," said Josiah.

"Repressed memory? Amnesia?"

"No, nothing like that."

"Then what you got me outta bed for, Griffin? Any level one Reader can pull a image from a willing mind."

"I need it to be as accurate as possible, and I need any details about her that he may have forgotten or overlooked."

Riser looked over at me, then back at Josiah. She stood up and leaned over the table.

"This about the lady that brought hell fire to the Enforcer station all by her lonesome?"

"Scan him, Riser, and give me everything I need."

"Fine."

Riser responded with a decided lack of enthusiasm and walked over to me . She reached out, but Josiah quickly grabbed her hand.

"Whatever you learn here, stays in this room. Do you understand?"

Riser cut her eyes sharply at Josiah.

"Yes, ah do. Now, do you understand that if you grab my person like that again, ah'ma scramble your brains so bad, the cafe will be servin' em with bacon 'n French toast?"

Josiah had no fear of Riser, but he needed her, so fighting was out of the question. He released her hand.

"Do you care if he lives?" Riser asked.

"I most certainly care if I live!" I quickly interjected.

"Leave his mind intact, Riser."

"As you wish. Sit down. This might hurt a lil'."

I pulled a chair out from under the table and nervously sat. Riser climbed onto my lap, straddled me then wrapped her arms around my neck.

"Hey wait..,"

"Settle, pussycat. This is no pleasure for me either."

She leaned forward and placed her mouth on mine, which I found disgusting. Out of the corner of my eye, I saw Josiah pull a holoprojector from his belt and place it on the table. An image pulled by a Reader was only as accurate as the subject's memory, but, in the absence of video, it was the next best thing.

Riser's veins glowed like fire wire throughout her body and

80

my eyes rolled back into my head. In my mind, I saw the Zero sitting in the interrogation room across from me. Most of our altercation was replayed but the images vanished at the part where she blinded me. The cacophony of sounds remained, but the replay became fruitless after the Zero left the room. Riser released me and stood.

"You was bested by a Zero?"

"She bested us all," I defended while holding my head. My brain felt like it had been sliced by razor blades then dropped in acid. Riser turned to a dissatisfied Josiah.

"Looks like that pussy has claws. Bring me the other survivors. I wanna see everything that happened," said Riser.

"I know what happened," Josiah replied. "She took over a Shocker and then a Burner and practically destroyed everything."

"Took over??"

"She used the tools you saw on the desk. She is just very clever at using Classes' powers against them."

Riser glared doubtfully at Josiah. He impatiently snatched

81

the holo off the table. I learned later that he hated working with Reapers.

"You can go now, Riser."

"When you gonna admit you over your head and call in the Reapers?"

"I have no further use for you or your drug addicted, hooligan friends," Josiah replied.

Riser's eyes flashed red and Josiah instinctively reached for his neutralizer.

"Go 'head, Burner. Pull out your gun," Riser taunted.

Josiah stood there for a moment then removed his hand from his weapon.

"You know neutralizers don't hurt Reapers none. You do better to throw it at me. Ha ha haaa!"

Riser raised her hand and pointed her index finger at Josiah with her thumb extended and her middle finger pointing downwards. It was a common gesture amongst a lesser class of people and not very nice.

"Ah be expecting your call, tomcat."

Riser walked slowly towards the door, waving over her shoulder.

"Don't forget. You are not to speak of this," Josiah ordered.

Riser gestured again as she walked out of the room.

"I want to help," I said forcefully.

"You just did. I'll call you if I need anything else."

"I want to be there when you catch her," I demanded.

Josiah shook his head, "Detective, what the Gendarmerie do is not quite the same as..."

"I know what you do, and I want to be there when it is done. I am a ten year Chief Detective and a Class 6 Mover. I can help you catch her. I will not be bested again."

Chapter 7
Kaori

"Why is she here?"

Godspeed was none too pleased that I strolled into the situation room with Gracie by my side. She was having trouble sleeping the past week, so she spent a lot of time with me. She cried a lot, but that was to be expected after losing the only life she'd ever known. I made some clothes for her out of old tarps and rags. She looked so cute standing there in her outfit from the ghetto Von Trap collection while leaning over the table looking at a map of the city.

"She shouldn't be hearing the things we have to say," Godspeed insisted.

"What are you worried about?" I sighed. "Think she's gonna tell someone?"

"Maybe. If she's caught…"

Godspeed looked around at Gracie, Gadget, Medic and

Deadeye and realized he was saying too much. He had become jealous of the time I spent with Gracie, because he thought she was the reason I was pushing him away. He acted petty, but it wasn't all his fault. I hadn't been very kind to him.

"Perhaps this should be discussed at another time," said Deadeye.

I quickly pulled Godspeed aside.

"So, you're more worried about our plans getting out than her getting captured?"

"You know that's not what I meant. But yes, that's a valid concern," Godspeed replied.

"Understand that if Gracie is taken, it will only be because all of us are already dead. And then our plans won't matter at all."

I returned to the table where everyone was sitting.

"What is all of this, Kori?" Gracie asked, peering over the map.

She was referring to all the red X's that covered the map. We had combed every inch of every building you had ever lived or worked in or bought underwear from. At least the ones that I knew of. Most places from our time were long gone, and the few we found produced nothing. I just didn't understand. At some point you knew we skipped too far, so why didn't you leave a note or a clue or a treasure map? Why didn't you use the cure yourself? We even checked out all of my old stomping grounds. I thought for sure we'd find it at the Arboretum where we shared our first kiss. The Arboretum remained, but there was no sign of the cure. Maybe you didn't even survive that day.

"So now what?" Gadget asked.

"We move. Now, tonight," Godspeed demanded.

"We're not leaving tonight," I replied. "We have time."

"Truly?"

At the time I thought Godspeed just wanted to fight. I realized later that fighting was the only time he had my undivided attention.

"How many 200 year old motorcycles have you seen around here?" he continued. "How many of them were driven by

Asian women?"

"Come on, Godspeed," said Deadeye.

"No, Deadeye, how many have you seen? Five? Six?"

I shook my head.

"You're giving me a migraine…"

"We've probably all seen the same number that everyone else in this town has, one. And when the sightings narrow the search down to this city, the authorities will throw a noose around it and pull until it strangles us all. We've already stayed here too long."

He was right. They would narrow it down quickly and my impulsiveness would prove to be my folly. But I couldn't give him that.

"They only know about Gracie and myself. The rest of you are safe."

"You can't be serious, Kaori," said Medic. "We won't leave you behind, no matter what happens."

"Typical Kaori," said Godspeed. "Completely unaware of

how her actions affect others."

He was right again, and that only angered me more.

"Everything I have done with my life for the past three years was for others! Do you have any idea of the sacrifices I've made? I've lost my parents, my family, my home, career... love. I've lost everything!!"

My words silenced everyone, except for Godspeed who didn't miss a beat.

"I'm sorry that you've lost so much. But you've lost things that we've never had. You've had to live like this for three years, but for us, it's been our entire lives."

And there it was. A solid argument against my petition for martyrdom. I was no saint, just another sinner seeking atonement.

Gadget spoke just before the silence smothered us.

"So, what now?"

"The Archive," I replied without looking him in the eye. "I need to know what happened the day I left. The Archive should be able to tell us that."

One hundred years or so ago, the powers that be decided that information was power and gathered up all physical and digital historical documentation and archived it on five giant servers, two of which were in North America. All of the servers were offline, so they could only be accessed directly. After a while, mankind had forgotten all of the evil things it had ever done, and predictably repeated all of the mistakes of the past. But I was not given the luxury of having my past archived, so I was forced to live with it everyday. Anyone who tells you they have no regrets is a liar, heartless or has a very short memory.

"How do you plan to get to the Archive?" asked Deadeye.

"D'Arco," I replied.

"D'Arco..?" Gadget asked.

"You cannot be serious," said Godspeed.

D'Arco was... another mistake. What he and I had wasn't love. It was obsession. It was volatile. We took everything we hated about ourselves out on each other and tried to say it was passion, but really, it was nothing more than assisted suicide.

89

D'Arco was one of the first people I met when I arrived in the future. He wasn't traditionally handsome, but he had these eyes. They were a deep brown, and I knew instantly that they would either warm my heart or burn my soul, and I was willing to accept either. Of course, I often wound up with the latter. Towards the end of our relationship, I met Godspeed. He was kind to me, and between D'Arco and the mission, I had grown so battle weary. Godspeed allowed me to breathe, and I desperately needed that. I wrapped myself in his affection let myself be. Of course, things got ugly between the D'Arco and Godspeed, but that was my fault. My indecisiveness and selfish deceit made things far worse than they needed to be. D'Arco hated Godspeed and me after that, so we went our separate ways.

I soon learned that you can't steal happiness. You have to earn it, and I had earned nothing. I was Goldilocks, moving from bed to bed when the last one did not suit me. Unfortunately, the problem was inside of me. Godspeed became another casualty of my careless heart, but I couldn't run this time, so I was forced to see his pain everyday. Soon our love became cyclical like the ocean tides, and that day, it was ebbing.

"Do you believe D'Arco wants anything to do with you? Or any of us for that matter?" Godspeed continued.

"D'Arco cared about the mission," I replied.

"Kaori, D'Arco cared about you," said Medic.

"He's our best shot at the Archive," I insisted.

"We could try negotiating. D'Arco is a businessman. We'll give him something he wants," said Deadeye.

"What if he wants Godspeed's head?" Gadget snickered.

I figured that was a very real possibility.

Chapter 8
Aiden

I was sitting in my home office, no more than twenty feet from where you were in the next room, but I might as well have been a thousand miles away. Had I looked, I would have seen you down the hall in our living space, slowly drifting away. I realize now that I stopped looking at you. I looked around you and through you, but never at you. I suppose if I had, I would have seen the pain that filled your eyes, eyes that I had forgotten were such a pale shade of blue. I put my needs so far ahead of your own that it was as if you had none at all.

As I sit here writing these words, I imagine that if I told a different tale, our story would end another way. Alas, my pen cannot turn back time, as my regret would not turn back your heart.

As usual, all of my attention was on my work. I was unshaven and disheveled from working for several days straight, but I had no intentions of letting fatigue slow me down. It had been a long time since I had a real case, and even longer since I had been bested. I sat in front of my holo looking at a map of the city. I had already marked several areas indicating sightings of the fugitive. I made a circle around one marker in particular, highlighting it in yellow. It was an antiquities shop whose proprietor had sold our fugitive a weapon. I thought that would make a great place to start.

As I pored over the data, you suddenly appeared in the doorway. Even after being startled, I still did not look directly at you. In fact, I did not even acknowledge your presence. You finally spoke with a breath of exasperation.

"You have a guest."

"I am busy," I replied without looking.

"Too busy for me?" a familiar voice spoke.

I looked past you and saw Josiah, so I quickly stood up.

"Special Agent Griffin... What brings..."

"Let's not play coy, detective. I'm sure you're well aware that I was advised to take you on as my partner during this investigation. Apparently, you're well connected."

Josiah's displeasure was obvious from his tone. He had no patience for politics or special favors when it came to doing his job, and he had no problem making that known.

"I agreed to this, but understand that I'm not going to babysit you. If you fall behind, you will be left. If I have to choose between saving your life and capturing the fugitive, you will die. Getting this Zero is my priority, not playing your elitist games. Do you understand?"

"Understood. Now, if you are ready to begin, I have our first lead."

Josiah looked over at the holo, noticing all of the markers. He was secretly impressed as my leads matched nearly all of his own. Josiah pointed to the yellow highlight.

"The antique shop?" he asked.

"Yes," I responded. "The proprietor says he sold her a stun gun..."

"The weapon she used to control then kill one of the

arresting officers," replied Josiah. "Let's be on our way then."

I eagerly followed Josiah to the door, stopping briefly to speak to you.

"I will return late," I said in a tone that seemed more like an afterthought than any type of consideration, and I was gone.

We drove to the dusty edifice mostly in silence. Josiah wasn't very talkative, but that was common for Gendarmes. They were never interested in polite conversation. Every word and action was a deliberate means to an end. That was well with me because idle chatter was not a priority at the time.

The proprietor looked out of his storefront window when we arrived. I was certain he immediately regretted calling the authorities. He had placed a call to our department but had no idea Gendarmerie would arrive. No one liked dealing with them. They had a lot of leeway with regards to the law and were free to dispense justice in any way they saw fit. That often meant trouble for anyone receiving a visit.

"Rick Harris?"

"Yes, sir," the proprietor nervously replied as he greeted Josiah and me at the door.

"I'm Special Agent Griffin, and this is Detective Price. We're here to speak with you about this woman," said Josiah as he displayed her holograph.

"Yes, of course. But I was expecting the Enforcers. I wasn't aware that this was a Gendarmerie matter."

"There's nothing to worry about," Josiah assured. "Just tell us everything you remember about her."

Rick wiped his brow and swallowed hard.

"Well, she asked about a stun gun I had for sale. I was surprised she even knew what it was, being a couple centuries old. Then she asked if it worked, which I found odd because..."

"Because what does a Class need with a functioning weapon," I added.

"Exactly!" said Rick.

"Did you scan her?" Josiah asked.

"Yes. And she cleared."

Josiah and I looked at each other.

"You know, so then I wondered if she was a Sympathizer, especially after she paid for some things my Zero broke."

The proprietor went on to describe how she looked, how long she spent in the store, a lot of irrelevant details that I had no patience for. Josiah was more tolerant of the nervous blabbering. He was used to people spilling every minutiae of their lives in the presence of a Gendarme. I, on the other side, had all I needed and was eager to leave.

"Anything else, Mr. Harris?" asked Josiah.

"She talked weird," he replied.

Our return ride was slightly more wordy as we discussed the case.

"She received two clear scans by two different scanners then failed the third," said Josiah.

"Electronic implant," I replied.

"Why electronic and not biological?"

"She obviously could turn it on and off. That would be a

much harder feat if she had some type of biological masking. Besides, technically, that ability would make her a Class."

Josiah smirked at the possible irony.

"She is planning something," I said.

"What makes you think that?"

"She can mask who she is, which means she could live a nice quiet life among us. Instead, she collects weapons to use against us, as if she anticipates a fight, and then she goes looking for one. And she is not alone."

"You believe there are others like her?"

"Maybe not like her," I replied, "but someone is helping her."

"Why?"

"The ancient mobile cycle, tricking the scanners, implants, unconventional methods of defeating Classes. These things require the skills of a mechanic, an engineer, a surgeon, a tactical strategist and probably several other disciplines. It is possible she has acquired a vast number of skills, but it is more likely she has a network."

As Josiah pondered my theory, Dispatch messaged him through the car's com.

"Special Agent Griffin?"

"This is Griffin."

"Sir, the child's parents have been located."

"Where are they now?"

"They were spotted in Zero Alley and are currently under surveillance."

"Tell the officers to stay on them but don't make a move. We're on our way."

You knew of Zero Alley, but I doubt you had any real concept of what it was like. After the war, it became a den of drugs and prostitution. It was one of the few places in the country where Zeros were allowed to roam freely, as free as poverty stricken, drug addicts could be anyway. Everything seemed gray, even when the sun was shining brightly. The buildings, the streets, even the trees and the people were all gray. Zero Alley was so bleak it almost did not seem real. Trash and debris was so prevalent, one might think they were design elements, purposely laid out to convey desolation. Structures were missing so many bricks and mortar, it seemed impossible that they could stand. The buildings looked as if they had been afflicted with some disease. The walls shed their skin in large flakes and the metal succumbed to cancerous rust. Water stains appeared to be dried tears as if the edifices themselves were crying out in pain.

The Zeros were less like people and more like permanent fixtures in the monochromatic landscape. You rarely saw their eyes as their heads always hung low. I did not know if it was so no one would notice them or so they would not notice anyone else. We blamed them for their living conditions because they took no pride in themselves or their surroundings, but, in all honesty, we were the ones who took their pride. Not only that, we took their families, their homes, their freedom. We even took their names. Tell a man he has no value long enough, and sooner or later he will believe it. Then he will grow to hate himself... and you. I see that now.

Every now and then, Enforcers would venture down to Zero Alley to shake things up, but for the most part, we let them be. Occasionally the denizens made good informants, but if the average citizen was unfortunate enough to find himself in Zero Alley, it was unlikely that he would ever find his way out.

We pulled into an alleyway behind an afflicted apartment complex, and an undercover officer disguised as a vagabond approached our vehicle.

"They're up there, room 324," the officer motioned with his head towards one of the more dilapidated buildings.

"Thanks..." Josiah replied as I jumped out of the car.

Josiah quickly exited the vehicle and cut me off.

"Slow down. I'll take the lead on this."

"I am perfectly capable of doing an interrogation," I angrily retorted and began to levitate.

"Yes, we saw how well your last one went," Josiah quipped as he grabbed my leg.

My eyes narrowed as I stared down at Josiah.

"The stairs, Aiden."

I lowered myself to the ground and grudgingly followed Josiah into the back door of the building.

Josiah walked up the two flights of stairs with me behind him growing increasingly more impatient. The building reeked of urine and calcium nitroxide, the latter of which was a byproduct of making Nitro. Josiah stepped over a rag covered fellow sleeping in the hallway while I gave him a psycho-kinetic shove, using far more force than necessary. Josiah gave me a disapproving glare, but I did not care. My heart beat harder with every step we took. My pent up anger was coming to a boil.

"324," Josiah said, pointing to the faded numbers on the door.

He knocked three times before announcing our presence.

"Gendarmerie! Open the door!"

Immediately, we heard the occupants scurrying about inside the apartment.

"What are you doing?" I asked.

"I'm knocking..."

I shook my head then placed my hand against the door, shredding it with a concussive force. Dirty and disheveled squatters scattered like leaves in a strong wind but it was to no avail. I pinned the eight or so people against the walls nearest them.

"Where are Caroline and John Whitacre!!?" I demanded.

"Aiden, relax..."

I levitated my holo and displayed Caroline and John's images then quickly looked over the room and spotted them. I dropped the other vagrants immediately and jerked the couple towards me, dropping them at my feet.

"I said relax!" repeated Josiah.

He walked over to the couple and squatted beside them. He pulled out his holo and showed them the fugitive.

"Where is this woman?"

John looked at the image and then at his wife.

"I-I do not know," John stammered.

"Do not lie to us!!" I shouted.

"Aiden, I need you to calm down. John, where is your daughter?"

John looked at his wife, she shook her head slowly as tears streamed down her face.

"Caroline, where is Gracie?" Josiah asked.

Caroline continued to shake her head as she sobbed loudly.

"Aiden, scan the apartment."

I bathed the room in psychokinetic energy, *feeling* every inch of the apartment, then the entire building.

"There are no children anywhere in this building," I declared. "Their child must be with the Zero. Tell us where she is!"

I started squeezing the life from John as his wife cried out.

"Please stop! We do not know where she is or even who she is! We do not even know her name!"

"Where did you go when you left the station!" I asked.

"Aiden..."

Josiah was losing his patience with me. I continued my

assault on John, but he refused to give up his daughter or the Zero.

"If you do not value your own life, perhaps you value that of your wife!"

I released John and levitated Caroline by her throat.

"Now, tell me where they are!"

"Put her down, Aiden!" Josiah yelled.

"No, no..." John whimpered.

He could not bear to see his wife tortured, so he closed his eyes, but I would not have that.

"No, you will watch what happens to your beloved!"

I mentally pried John's eyes open, forcing him to witness his wife's torment.

"Tell me where they are!!"

Josiah reached for his neutralizer.

"Aiden, that is enough! Let her go!"

But I couldn't. I was too consumed by hatred and rage. I levitated the gun from Josiah's hand and smashed it against a wall. Josiah ran over to me and stood in front of my face, speaking forcefully but calmly.

"Do you really think he'll betray his own child?"

The raw anger in me ebbed with Josiah's words. I looked at the mother and father and briefly imagined if the child was someone I loved. I was still angry, but I understood. I released the couple from my hold.

"We'll get a Reader and pull their thoughts," said Josiah.

I nodded in agreement as I held my head low, trying to regain my composure.

"But..," Josiah continued.

His body turned bright orange, instantly raising the temperature by 400 degrees. I could not react in time and dropped to the floor. The heat was affecting my brain making it impossible for me to concentrate.

"...if you ever use your powers on me again, I will kill you. Is that understood?"

I used what little strength I had left to nod a "Yes."

Chapter 9
Kaori

We put on our flack vests while Gadget loaded up the van with weapons, real weapons: guns, knives, grenades. D'Arco lived in the bad part of the slums and probably wanted us dead, so we weren't taking any chances. Deadeye and Godspeed volunteered to come along. I advised Godspeed that his presence might hurt negotiations, but he insisted. I wondered if he was more concerned about what would happen between D'Arco and myself than he was about my safety. We were all set to go when Gracie appeared, tugging at my jacket.

"I want to come too, Kori."

I turned and saw Gracie rubbing her eyes. My plan had been to slip away while she napped, but clearly that wasn't going to happen.

"Go back to bed, sweetheart," I said as I brushed the hair from her face. "Everything is okay."

As I tried to reassure her, Medic came running up.

"I'm sorry, Kaori. She slipped away while I was in the lavatory. I thought she was still napping."

"It's okay, Medic. I was just about to tell Gracie that we have to leave for a bit."

"But what if you do not return?" she asked with fear welling in her eyes.

"Gracie, we're just going to visit an old friend."

"Then why are you taking so many guns?"

Looking at our arsenal, it was pretty clear that we weren't headed to a playdate. Gracie was young, but she wasn't stupid. She had a target on her back almost as big as mine, so playing make believe would be doing her a disservice. I foolishly thought I could give her a normal childhood, but that wasn't going to happen. Instead of protecting her with lies, I had to arm her with the truth.

"Gracie, we're going to a very bad town to meet with a guy who probably wants us dead, so I need you to stay here with Gadget and Medic. They will keep you safe."

"No, Kori! What if the bad men come for me?!"

I wanted to tell her not to worry, but she had every right to. I couldn't risk her being abandoned again.

"Gadget, bring the smallest flack vest you can find."

Gracie's eyes lit up like Christmas lights, but Godspeed was not quite as ecstatic.

"Are you insane, Kaori? Allowing a child to come with us is the second worst idea you've had!"

"I think allowing you to come with us is at the top of that list. Yet here you are," I replied flippantly.

"I'm being serious," said Godspeed.

"So am I. And she's right. What if they do come here? You said it yourself, we don't know how much time we have. No matter what, trouble will come calling, and I'd rather be at her side when it does."

Gadget returned with a vest and helmet.

"This the best I could find, but I'm sure I can make it work. Come here, little one."

Godspeed shook his head as Gadget strapped the makeshift vest to Gracie. I could tell the others weren't keen on the idea either, but they knew how stubborn I could get.

"I do not want to wear the hat! It makes me look like a boy!" argued Gracie.

"No one could ever mistake that pretty face for a nasty boy," I assured her.

She smiled in a way that sent waves of joy through me.

"I hope you know what you're doing," Godspeed said.

"If I can break her out of an Enforcer station, I can certainly keep her safe in Zero Alley."

We had all piled into the van when Gadget grabbed the sliding door and leaned inside.

"I want you guys to be aware that your protective gear is pretty strong, but D'Arco has access to some pretty serious weapons, some of which can tear right through your gear."

"If you're telling us to not get shot, that was kinda the plan all along," I said smiling as I shut the door.

It was a long, quiet drive, which was good because I didn't have much to say. Godspeed drove while Deadeye rode shotgun. Gracie and I were in the second row bench seat. All the other seats had been removed for our arsenal.

Occasionally, I would catch Godspeed watching me in the rear view mirror. I wanted to tell him to watch the road, but I just looked away instead. He wanted to engage me, but I wasn't in the mood for another fight. Gracie lay her head on my shoulder, so I put my arm around her, and she sighed deeply.

"Are you okay, sweetheart?"

She just shrugged her shoulders and buried her face in my side. I knew it was crazy to bring her to what could very well be a gunfight at the OK Corral, but I thought, even in a shootout, she'd be safest with me. Or maybe I was the one who needed to feel safe. I couldn't bear the thought of something happening to her, or the thought of her dying alone. That was a fate reserved for someone less deserving. Someone like me.

It took us a couple of hours to reach Zero Alley, a place so

111

dark and depressing that even the animals kill themselves. It was a monochromatic landscape so dark and gray that the sun seemed to shine less brightly there. It was a place for burned out Zeros to disappear. Even some wayward Classes made their way down there. It was the epitome of lost hope. Everyone there was pretty much dead already. They were just waiting around for it to be official.

Every now and then, law enforcement would go in and shake things up, just to remind them of their place, but for the most part, they left the Alley alone. No one there was a cause for concern. Well, except for D'Arco. But as far as the law was concerned, he was just a mid-level drug dealer doing the world a favor by thinning the Zero heard. The truth was, D'Arco was connected to any and everything. He could get you pretty much whatever you needed, but it came with a price. And sometimes that price was pretty steep.

"Stop here," I said to Godspeed.

He stopped the van in front of a hole in the wall bar, and I hopped out.

"I'll be right back."

I walked inside, and it felt like the wind was knocked out of my soul. I saw faces with eyes so hollow I could almost hear the echo of hopelessness. I'd say they were full of broken dreams, but these people never had dreams. Most of them were born into something they had no idea how to escape. They probably couldn't even conceive of anything else. When faced with seemingly insurmountable obstacles, you can be overwhelmed and give up, or be encouraged and press harder. I had no idea how I felt, so I decided to keep moving until I did.

I walked up to the bar and took a seat. The bartender had his back to me when I placed my order.

"One River Juice on the rocks."

The bartender paused and took a deep breath before turning around.

"Welcome back, Kaori. What do you want?"

"I'm hurt, Whisper. Why can't this be a social visit?"

"Because I know you too well, Darling."

Whisper jumped over the bar, wrapped his arms around me and lifted me off my stool. He was a middle aged, slender man with blonde hair and matching stubble. He had pale skin that provided sharp contrast for his many tattoos. Zeros were not allowed to own businesses, but the rules in Zero Alley were rather lax. Years ago, Whisper was my go to guy whenever I needed info, and, at one time, he was my best friend. He looked around then took me off to the side of the bar away from everyone.

"Are you the one the feds are looking for?" he asked.

"Probably," I said.

"Well, watch yourself. They've been sneaking around lately, and I heard they might be coming to the Alley today."

"Great... Any idea why they're coming?"

"An arrest maybe. I'm not really sure, so you make sure you watch your ass."

"Oh, Whisper, that's what I got you for!"

We occasionally flirted, but in reality, he was just a really good friend. No matter how much time would go by, we could always pick up right where we left off.

"Okay, I know you didn't come back just to see my pretty face. What do you need?" Whisper asked.

"I need to know where D'Arco hangs his hat these days."

Whisper was taken aback, then he looked at me as if waiting for a punchline. He soon realized there wasn't one.

"I believe you're the last person D'Arco wants to see," said Whisper.

"I'm aware, but I desperately need his help."

Whisper gave me this crooked smile then shook his head.

"You always did have a bit of a death wish, Darling."

"No one lives forever."

"Go to the Dead Mall on Ludlow. Look for the office spaces."

"Thanks, Whisper. I owe you one."

"You owe me fifty-one."

I hugged Whisper tightly and kissed him on the cheek.

"See you soon, Whisper."

"Be careful, Kaori."

We drove for another few minutes then stopped in front of a building that seemed the least likely to support adult humans. We knew D'Arco had high tech surveillance cameras everywhere, and since we wanted an audience with him, we didn't bother sneaking in. Gracie had dozed off, so I gently woke her from her slumber.

"Gracie, we're here."

She groggily opened her eyes and looked around before furrowing her brow. She was clearly appalled by the conditions before us.

"Where are we?" Gracie asked

"We're in Zero Alley," said Godspeed, "the last place on earth you ever want to be."

Gracie turned to me, "Your friend lives here? Is he homeless?"

We all exited the car and grabbed our gear.

"No, he's far from homeless. He just likes to stay hidden."

I bent down to secure Gracie's vest.

"I need you to stay close to me, okay?"

Gracie nodded, and we proceeded to enter the belly of the beast.

"Let's get this over with," Godspeed insisted.

He always gave the best pep talks.

Surprisingly, the front door of the building was unlocked. We entered and found crumbling walls and debris covered floors. It used to be full of offices and shops, but that day it looked like the aftermath of a military training camp.

"Hello?" I called out. "D'Arco? Bully?"

Bully was D'Arco's muscle. He never cared for me, especially after I broke D'Arco's heart. Nevertheless, I was hoping he could help me out with D'Arco. Suddenly shots rang out all around us.

"Get down!" Deadeye ordered as we darted behind a wall.

The shots were coming from a balcony, and they had us pinned down.

117

Godspeed turned to Deadeye, "Cover me! I'm gonna run for the stairs!"

"No!" I yelled. "No one fires back!"

"Are you insane?!" Godspeed asked. "They're trying to kill us!"

"If they wanted to kill us that, first shot would have been in one of our heads instead of the floor!"

Deadeye lowered his gun.

"She's right. Those are just warning shots."

The shots ceased.

"Bully?! Is that you?!" I asked while still hunkered down behind the wall.

Poor lil Gracie was holding onto me for dear life.

"What you doing here, Kaori!" Bully asked.

"So, you do remember me?" I asked gleefully.

"Why you think I shot!"

So much for the welcome wagon.

"We're here to see D'Arco!"

That was obvious but more talking meant less shooting, and less shooting is always good.

"What you want with D'Arco?" Bully asked.

"I need a favor."

Dead silence. You would've thought I just told my fiance that I was a man.

"Bully..?"

"You hit your head since I see you last, Kaori?"

"Please, Bully. Just let me speak with him."

Silence again. I had started to think the plan was a very bad idea.

"Throw out your weapons!" Bully ordered.

"No way!" I replied.

Instead of silence, this time I got laughter.

"Same ol' Kaori," Bully mused. "You come into our house; you ask favors. You want to take everything and willing to give nothing!"

I sighed heavily then placed Gracie in Deadeye's arms. I

threw my weapons out into the open.

"What are you doing!" Godspeed cried.

"I'm coming out!"

As I stood, Godspeed grabbed my arm.

"Don't be foolish!"

"Do not go, Kori!" Gracie begged.

"Bully is right. I have to give them something. I'm coming out!"

I walked into the open with my hands raised. Bully was on the second floor, same bald head, dark skin, ghastly nose ring and every bit of 400 pounds. I had hoped his yellowed smile was an indication that he was happy to see me.

"I going to enjoy this!" he said.

His henchmen came out of hiding, all twenty of them. Guess I was wrong again.

"Kaori, you can't go in there alone!" Godspeed said, almost pleading.

"I'll be fine, just stay here."

"No way!"

Godspeed threw out his weapons, raised his hands then walked over by my side.

"I can't let you do this by yourself!"

"What are you really worried about, Godspeed?"

My cynicism was too much and hurt washed over Godspeed's face. He looked away without responding, and I instantly knew I shouldn't have asked that.

"Kori, do not go with those bad people!" Gracie pleaded as Bully and his cronies approached.

"I'll be fine. I promise. We aren't going far."

"Do not leave me here!"

"Don't worry. They're crazy, but they wouldn't hurt children, especially Zero children. Besides, Deadeye is the best marksman ever. He won't let anyone hurt you."

"But you are hurting me..," her voice trailed off as tears streamed down her face.

Before I could respond, Bully was upon us.

"Aaaw, boyfriend stands by your side. Bring them!"

I tried to look back but I was forced to keep moving ahead. I caught a glimpse of Gracie turning away from me.

They took us upstairs and down a long hallway. The spiders didn't bother me at all, but the rats, *shudder*. I did a great job of pretending not to care when one ran across my foot. Godspeed smirked and shook his head. He knew better.

We finally entered a dark room that was in the middle of the building, so it had no windows. They walked us over to a large wooden desk. D'Arco stood at the far end of the room with his back to us, arranging some bric a brac on a shelf. Even if I had happened upon him by accident, I still would have recognized him, the way he stood, the shape of his head.

"Let me do the talking," I whispered to Godspeed.

D'Arco spoke without turning.

"I was shocked when I heard you were back in the Alley. I thought my sources were mistaken. Then you drove up to our headquarters and parked right outside. When you walked inside, I thought, you must be lost. Maybe this was some sort of coincidence, because there is no way Kaori would just sashay into my house uninvited after all of these years and bring him…"

"D'Arco," I breathed.

He suddenly spun around

"And now you are asking for favors, Bella?"

D'Arco walked over to the desk and stood behind it.

"You walk into my house with this puta…"

Godspeed moved forward, but I grabbed his arm.

"…and you have the gall to ask me for favors?" D'Arco continued.

I wanted to speak, but I couldn't think of anything that wouldn't make it worse. Godspeed's eyes were red with fury and his jaw was clenched like a bear trap. D'Arco smiled.

"Don't worry, puta. I will get to you shortly. Then we can finish what we started."

D'Arco tilted his head and looked quizzically at the both of us.

"Ohhh, but I don't have to. She's already caused you more pain than I ever could."

D'Arco was a level 3 Reader, and with Godspeed's emotions on his sleeve, he was an easy read.

"Who did you move onto, Bella? Gadget? Deadeye? Not Medica?"

D'Arco laughed which only angered Godspeed more, so I tried to stay on topic.

"D'Arco, I'm desperate..."

"I owe you NOTHING!!!"

His words echoed throughout the room with such a boom, I could feel the reverberation in my chest.

"You took everything I had until I could give no more and still you seek to take!"

I knew I had hurt him, but I thought most of the pain would have subsided by then. He had aged slightly around the eyes and temples, but his heart remained stuck in the past, much like mine. I released Godspeed's arm and stepped forward with my arms extended out from my sides.

"Whatever it is you need to heal, take it from me. Be it my dignity, my body, or my life, take it. It is yours to do what you will, but help us first. Then take your pound of flesh from me, but only me."

D'Arco sat down in his chair and leaned backwards. He looked over at Bully who only shrugged.

"You must be desperate, Bella. What do you want from me?"

"The Archive," I replied.

D'Arco chuckled, "I don't have the Archive."

"But you can tell us how to get to it and give us access."

"That's asking for a lot."

"I'm offering everything I have."

"Keep your flesh, Bella. I learned a long time ago that a pound of flesh is the most expensive cut of meat you will ever buy."

"Then what do you want?" I asked.

"A Backtracker named Shift."

"There's no such thing as a Backtracker. It's just a myth."

"I've seen him, and he owes me a substantial amount of money. Sixteen ounces to be exact."

"Why would I be able to find someone that the resourceful D'Arco cannot?"

"Because he is hiding from me, but he is looking for you," he replied.

I was perplexed. I knew for a fact, there was no such thing as a Backtracker. We proved beyond a doubt that no one can travel backwards in time. Nevertheless, I wondered why that charlatan would be looking for me. How would he even know my name?

"What does he want with me?" I asked.

"I don't know, but he has been searching for you for over a year now."

"If you knew he was looking for me, why didn't you just track me down and wait for him?" I asked.

"I did," D'Arco replied.

"You've been watching me all this time just to catch him?"

D'Arco looked away.

"Yes, Bella. Just to catch him..."

It was probably only five seconds, but the silence seemed to last forever.

"We weren't there everyday. We just kept tabs occasionally, but I suppose he was not a very good hunter because he never showed. I would've put the word out where you were to help him, but I didn't know who else might be looking for you."

"I've attracted a wee bit of attention lately," I admitted.

"Ask around about a Backtracker. Eventually he will find you. Bring him to me, and I'll get you access to the Archive."

Suddenly, I felt body warmth and smelled sandalwood and grapefruit.

"Hello, Jinx."

The child-like Trickster popped into view, squatting on the table in front of us.

"How you know I was here, KK?"

Jinx was a twenty year old, Level 9 Trickster born to Nitro addicted Classes. She had an intellectual disability, so she never matured past eleven, but being a Level 9 meant she didn't just perform illusions. Jinx could actually alter reality. D'Arco took her in as a teen, and they were peas in a pod ever since.

"I smelled your perfume, Jinx," I replied.

"Ooh, sneaky, KK. What you want the Archive for?"

"I think Kaori is looking for the truth about something," D'Arco answered.

"But KK knows all the truth. The only one that does," replied Jinx.

My heart skipped a beat when Godspeed gave me a funny look.

"I remember you!" Jinx exclaimed pointing at Godspeed and thankfully drawing his attention away from me. "You the driver!"

"Hey, Jinx," said Godspeed.

"Are you staying this time, KK?"

"No, I'm afraid I won't be staying."

Just then some of D'Arco's men entered with Deadeye and Gracie then Jinx disappeared. She liked to surprise people.

"Kori!" Gracie exclaimed and rushed to my side.

I looked at Deadeye.

"She wouldn't stop crying, and I didn't know what else to do."

"I told you I'd be okay, lil one."

"The bad men scared me."

"Well these guys aren't so bad," I assured her as I looked at D'Arco.

Jinx suddenly appeared right in front of Gracie.

"Boo!" Jinx exclaimed.

Gracie was startled but thrilled.

"Ha ha! You are funny," Gracie mused. "You are just like my daddy."

"Your papi is a Class?" D'Arco asked.

"And my mommy," Gracie replied. "I look like her."

D'Arco seemed a bit confused. Just then one of his guys burst into the room.

"D'Arco! The Gendarmerie is here!" the kid exclaimed.

D'Arco leaped to his feet.

"Where are they?" he demanded.

"They are a few blocks over arresting a Class couple. A husband and wife."

"Sympathizers?" D'Arco asked.

"No," the boy replied. "I think it has something to do with the accident at that Enforcer station a few weeks back."

Deadeye, Godspeed and I all stood there with mouths agape, but Gracie was too distracted by Jinx. I pulled the boy to the side.

"What are their names?" I demanded.

"I don't know."

He turned to D'Arco.

"It's a Trickster and Skipper, I believe. They're also asking about a young girl."

I jerked him back by his arm.

"Shut your mouth…"

But Gracie had heard him that time.

"My mommy and daddy…?"

D'Arco stood up and leaned towards Gracie while looking at me.

"Were you and your parents at the Enforcer station during that accident?" he asked.

Gracie looked at me uncertain if she should answer.

"Let her be, D'Arco." I said.

"What have you brought into my house, Bella?"

"The accident at the Enforcer station was actually me. I broke Gracie and her parents out, and now the Gendarmerie are looking for us, but I had no idea her parents were hiding here."

"But you still came knowing the two of you are wanted," D'Arco replied.

"D'Arco, I'm sorry. We'll leave."

"Kori, if my parents are here, you have to save them!"

131

Gracie remembered what happened the last time they were arrested, and it was not a fond memory.

"Gracie…"

As I looked into her pleading eyes, my words failed me.

"We have to go now!"said Godspeed.

""No," I replied. "They're only looking for Gracie and myself."

"You think you're leaving by yourself?" asked Godspeed.

"No, Gracie comes with me," I replied. "If they find me, and I'm alone, they'll tear this place apart to find her."

"Then just stay hidden here," D'Arco insisted, softening his stance.

"They don't know if we're with her parents or not. There's a good chance they'll do a sweep to find us just in case."

"You're not going out there without us!" said Godspeed.

"We can't let them know there are more of us. It's the best advantage we have."

Godspeed knew I was right. Everyone did, but no one liked

it. Gracie especially.

"Kori, I want to see my parents!"

"We can't, sweetheart. Not right now."

Her eyes welled with tears speaking even louder than her words.

"But they are being arrested. You have to save them, like you did last time."

"Last time I took on local Enforcers by surprise. This time we're dealing with Gendarmerie, and they're well prepared. It would be safer to run."

Gracie's face made it clear she couldn't accept that, and I couldn't blame her. Her parents were possibly a few blocks from us, and I was asking her to run away.

"We'll come back…"

My words crumbled to dust as they left my mouth.

Don't protect her with lies. Arm her with the truth.

"I can't save them this time, Gracie. They're going to die…"

"Noooo!!!"

Gracie let out a cry that tore through my heart as she fell to her knees.

"Do not let them die, Kori! Please! Do not let them die!"

I knelt down in front of Gracie and placed my hands on her face.

"I promised your parents I would keep you safe, and they were more than willing to give their lives to help me keep that promise. If I try to take on the Gendarmerie now, we'll all die right along with your parents. That's not what they want for you, Gracie. Do you understand?"

She turned away from me and nodded her head, and I knew the only thing she really understood is that I was letting her parents die. I figured she was going to hate me for a while. I had no idea how long.

"We're leaving. I have my com on. Godspeed, Deadeye, stay here until I let you know I'm safe," I instructed.

"Be careful, Kaori," Deadeye advised.

Godspeed just gave a look of disappointment and pain.

I turned to D'Arco, who was hesitant to look me in the eye.

"I'll return with your *Backtracker* as soon as I can. Godspeed, Deadeye, I'll see you back at home."

"Wait!" D'Arco warned. "There are Gendarmerie patrolling out front."

His holo showed several of them outside right beside our van.

"We need another way out of here," I said, knowing D'Arco always had contingency plans for such occasions.

"Jinx, take them out through the basement and get them out of the city," D'Arco ordered.

Jinx's eyes grew big along with her smile.

"I got it for ya, D! Les go, KK! Follow me!"

Jinx knew how to protect herself, but her naivete made her oblivious to serious danger sometimes. Everything was a game to her.

We followed her back down the stairs to the first floor, then we ran towards the back of the building and down another flight of stairs into the basement and wound up at a dead end.

"Did we make a wrong turn?" I asked.

"There is secret door!" Jinx insisted.

She waved her hand over what looked like an old concrete wall, but there was indeed a door hidden there. She ushered us in then closed the entrance just as she had opened it. We ran down a long, dark corridor guided only by the light from Jinx's hands.

"Look out for the mices!" Jinx instructed.

But they were hardly mice. They were full on rats, and you know I how I felt about rats, but I couldn't have a freak out moment in front of Gracie, so I kicked the ones that got too close and continued down the corridor.

After several twists and turns, we came to the end of the path where a ladder awaited. Jinx climbed the ladder and beckoned us to follow. We surfaced at a loading dock between two buildings. There was only one way out so we headed that way.

"Wait," said Jinx. "I can make you see through."

Jinx waved her hand and Gracie and I vanished, but we quickly came back into view.

"Sorry," Jinx said as she tried again, but we just kept flickering back.

"Jinx, what's going on?" I asked.

"Sometimes Gendarmerie bring dampers. I can beat them now and then. Want me to try real hard?" Jinx asked.

"No," I replied. "Flickering suspects will draw far more attention than we need right now."

A damper was a short range neutralizer that was sometimes used when arresting large numbers of rogue Classes or Sympathizers. It didn't fully knockout powers, but it could handicap a Class quite a bit. Gendarmerie had internal devices to protect them from dampers and anyone assisting them were given protective bracelets to wear on their wrists.

"Okay, follow me," Jinx instructed.

We cautiously stepped out onto the sidewalk and crossed to the other side of the street. Save for a few addicts and some prostitutes, the streets were pretty clear. Nevertheless, we kept our heads low. I removed Gracie's helmet and pulled her hood over her head to hide her hair and face. I had hoped our escape would be an easy one, but that hope was shattered when we saw three Gendarmes round the corner half a block away. Jinx shoved us into a narrow alleyway between two buildings before they could see us. We hastily made our way to the other side, but I kept looking back, and that was a big mistake. I was so worried about what was behind me, I failed to see what was in front. We stepped out of the alleyway onto the sidewalk and saw them. John and Caroline were being escorted out of an apartment building by Detective Price and three Gendarmes. We all froze, staring at one another. No one moved or said a word for several seconds. The only movements were the tears of a mother, then the silence was broken by the cries of a little girl.

"Mommy! Daddy!"

Price raised his hand, so I grabbed Gracie and yelled.

"Run!!"

Jinx lead us back down the alleyway as a concussive blast smashed the walls behind us. We returned from where we entered and ran right into the three Gendarmes from earlier. Jinx fell on top of one and another grabbed me by my arms. I shoved my pistol under his chin, but he was a Glider, and he carried me five stories into the air before I could even blink. I looked down and saw the last Gendarme chasing Gracie. My gun was still under the Glider's chin, and he looked at me smugly.

"You wouldn't dare," he smiled.

The hammer said otherwise.

As I fell, I took aim at Gracie's pursuer and nailed him in the back. I reached for a nearby fire escape, but I was falling too fast and nearly ripped my arm from its socket. My grip slipped, and I continued falling. I didn't think I would die when I hit bottom, but I didn't imagine I'd be walking any time soon either. Luckily, Jinx made quick work of her Gendarme and teleported up to the fire escape. She grabbed my arms as I passed her, further tearing at my shoulder. My ear piercing cry belied the gratitude I

139

felt for my rescue.

We rushed down to the street and over to Gracie as sirens whined, and an emergency call came over the coms. I grabbed Gracie with my good arm and we ran into a nearby abandoned office building. We saw stairs on the other side of the room, but someone opened the door behind us, so we darted behind a reception desk.

"I'll check the north end. You take east, you take the south," said one of the Gendarmes.

"That sounds like three," I whispered.

"One for each of us?" Jinx asked.

"I don't think Gracie is capable of fighting grown men."

"Oh."

"Gracie will stay here, and you and I will dispatch them ourselves."

"No," Jinx responded. "You're hurt. I deal with them."

I heard footsteps getting closer.

"You can't beat three Gendarmes alone with a damper

draining your powers."

"Don't need to beat them, KK. Just need to hold them off 'til you to escape."

I wanted to argue, but her idea was our best bet of surviving. I nodded, and Jinx leaped over the desk and laid into the Gendarmes. Cut off from the front door, Gracie and I ran for the stairs.

We reached the second floor and found a large conference room. I was hoping to find a window we could safely jump from, but my arm was hurting too badly. As we entered, we could still hear the barrage from the floor below.

"Gracie, I gotta fix my arm before I pass out."

"Okay," she replied.

I grabbed a dry erase eraser and bit down on it. Then I tied my hand to the door handle and reached for the underside of the conference table. I thought I would vomit as I slowly pulled my arm back into place. I dropped to the floor and spat out the eraser.

The pain was excruciating, so I reluctantly reached into my

pocket. The rattling was almost enough to settle my pain, but I opened the bottle anyway. Gracie looked at me curiously, perhaps pondering my hesitation. I hated pills. I had known too many addicts in my life, including you. I couldn't do it. I stubbornly decided to fight through the pain. Just then the noise of battle stopped. Gracie and I looked at each other, listening closely. We heard footsteps coming from down the hall, and Gracie ducked behind the conference table. I pulled a knife from my pocket to cut myself free from the door, but the footsteps stopped, and I smelled hydrogen sulfide. I stepped closer to the wall as the door handle turned. It was halfway opened when I jerked it towards me then slammed it back as hard as I could against the Gendarme. He let out a pain filled moan, and I cut myself free just as he kicked the door back at me. The door clipped my injured shoulder, knocking me to the floor and making me drop my pills. The Gendarme raised an impact gun, and I hurled my knife at him. It penetrated his side and caused him to miss his target. The blast didn't do any damage upon impact, so it was apparent he was only trying to incapacitate me. Even still, I needed to get inside his protective zone. He wouldn't burn me to death, but he could easily subdue me with a burst of heat. As he removed the knife, I rushed him and knocked his gun away. I held him close as we exchanged blows. He wasn't going to kill me, but he clearly had no problems hitting me like a man. I found it odd that even when he managed to put some air between us, he made no attempt to flame up. Nevertheless, I continued to engage him up close. I grabbed his collar and kneed him in the groin, side, and face. I guess that was all he could stand because he shoved me across the room and tried to flame. I grabbed a ceramic mug and threw it at his throat. The brief tracheal collapse snuffed the flames he was producing. I grabbed a stapler from the table, extended it, ran over and slammed staples into his neck and face. He knocked the stapler from my hand, so I shoved him against a wall with my forearm against his neck. I pummelled his midsection as he struggled to breathe. He managed to loosen the pressure against his neck and raised his other hand as he looked over my shoulder.

143

"You're the only one I need alive," he said in a raspy voice.

I turned my head and saw he was aiming a ball of fire at Gracie. I couldn't risk it, so I released him. He grabbed his neck and let out several dry coughs before introducing himself.

"I'm Special Agent Josiah Griffin and you are under…"

A sudden blast from behind and Griffin was down. I looked up and saw a disheveled Jinx holding an impact gun. She was battered and bruised but still managed to offer a smile. I was so relieved to see her face. When the sounds of fighting stopped, I had feared the worst. Seeing her alive brought tears to my eyes as I went to hug her.

"You don't look so good," I said smiling through my tears.

"You not belle of the ball either, KK," she replied.

"Belle of the ball," I laughed. "You've spent way too much time with me."

I looked at Gracie and beckoned her over to me.

"Come on, sweetheart. It's okay."

She stepped cautiously towards me, but hesitated when she

neared Agent Griffin.

"No worries, Gracie," Jinx assured. "Is not dead, but is not getting up anytime soon."

Gracie stepped over him and ran into my arms.

"I am scared, Kori."

Just then we heard a commotion downstairs. More feds had entered the building and were headed for the stairs.

"We need to get to the roof, Jinx."

"Will do, KK."

I grabbed my bottle of Nitro, and Jinx lead us into the hallway, towards the stairs.

"But they are in there, Kori!" worried Gracie.

"Jinx knows what's doing, sweetheart."

We entered the stairwell and saw a group of Gendarmes and Enforcers rushing up the stairs. Jinx quickly produced a cloud of smoke to hide our escape, and we ran towards the roof. Gracie stumbled as I pulled her behind me.

"Kori, slow down!"

"You gotta keep up, baby."

Her little legs weren't cut out for that. I felt so badly for pushing her so hard, but that was what her life had become. Gracie nodded through her tears and pushed on.

We reached the roof, then Jinx and I pushed some old AC unit in front of the door. I figured our best bet would be finding a way down on the side of the building or jumping to the next roof if it was close enough. That was no longer an option when we saw Price levitate to the roof.

"Glider?" Jinx asked.

"No, Mover," I replied. "And this one has an axe to grind."

Price lowered himself to the rooftop and looked Jinx and I up and down. Gracie was obscured by the AC unit, so he was unaware of her presence. He walked towards us, staring with his coal black eyes and taunting us with his smug grin.

"I have been burning for a rematch ever since our first encounter," Price said, "and I began to doubt if I would ever have one. But then I walked out of those apartments and could not believe my fortune. It was like you had been delivered to me from someone above."

All I had left was my knife and two grenades, neither of which were much good against a Mover at that distance. Luckily, I had Jinx with me, and we knew each other well.

"Let us see how you fare when I am not caught off guard, Zero."

Price raised his hand, and Jinx teleported behind him while I took off running towards them. Jinx covered Price's eyes with her hands and washed them in a blinding light.

"Aaaaaahhhh!!" he screamed.

He expelled her off his back, sending her sailing off into God knows where. I had no time to contemplate Jinx's fate as I only had a narrow window to act. Price couldn't see, but he had learned his lesson from the last time. He sent a concussive wave in my direction, but I knew it would branch out like a shotgun blast, widening the further out it went. I just needed to get under it before it reached me. Relying on my trusty soccer moves again, I slid just

147

in time and took Price's feet out from under him. He landed on top of me and I tried to stab him the chest with my knife. Unfortunately, he was wearing an impact vest, and I barely pierced his body. Still blind and in a panic, he sent me sailing over the side of the building. It was enough force to slam me into the side of the next building across the alleyway, but I managed grab onto a window ledge as I fell. I carefully dropped down to two more ledges before I reached the ground. The pain in my shoulder was becoming unbearable.

I looked up at the building from where I was hurled and saw Price leaning over. His eyesight had not returned and he was trying to *feel* me with his powers, so I hid next to a dumpster. Suddenly, he stopped and left the ledge. He leaned back over and yelled down.

"It seems you have left something behind!"

Gracie! He had sensed her, and I immediately began to panic. There was no way I could scale the building, and she would be caught long before I could run back inside and up to the roof.

My heart was pounding its way out of my chest. My breathing was labored. I thought I knew fear before. I thought I knew loss, but nothing compared to what I was feeling at that moment.

"Gracie!!" I screamed. "Gracie, I need you to jump!"

Silence.

"Gracie can you hear me?! Gracie?!"

Silence.

"Please, baby! I need you to jump!"

My heart tumbled into my stomach, and they both sank to my feet. My world was ending again, and I couldn't do anything to stop it. But then I saw this little person fly over the edge of the building swinging her arms and legs like an Olympic long jumper. Tears of joy filled my eyes. I didn't know if I could safely catch her or not, but I was prepared to die trying. Then, like a guardian angel, Jinx teleported into Gracie's path, caught her, and they both landed safely on the ground.

I grabbed Gracie and squeezed her as tight as I could. I turned to Jinx to thank her, and I noticed she was clearly exhausted.

"Are you okay?" I asked.

I was worried that resisting the damper had proven to be too much.

"Fret not," Jinx unconvincingly replied. "Is a little left in me."

"We need to go now," I insisted.

We started to leave, but three Gendarmes stood blocking our path.

"Don't move!" one of them ordered as they approached us.

A second later, Price flew down from the roof and landed with such force the ground shook. He had regained his sight and his anger.

"Leave them to me!" he demanded.

He pinned the three of us against a wall, and we hung there like living graffiti unable to move a muscle, not even our mouths.

"You worthless Zero. Agent Josiah wants you alive for now, but the traitor..," said Price while looking at Jinx, "that treacherous dog that aids you does not hold the same value."

He used his powers to force my head in her direction.

"Watch her, Zero, and see what will soon be your fate."

Jinx's eyes grew large with fear as her body began to tremble. I heard her bones snapping as her body contorted. Blood dripped from her eyes and ears. Price was crushing the life out of her, and she couldn't even cry out in pain. Finally, he ended her torture and snapped her neck. Her lifeless body fell from the wall and into a muddy puddle that slowly turned dark red. Price stood there smiling, as smug of a man as I had ever seen. He was quite pleased with himself. That was until the six of us began to flicker. Price realized that Jinx had tricked him into pinning the three Gendarmes against the wall instead of us, but by then I was right beside him and stabbed my knife all the way through his bracelet and his wrist. He cried out in pain and tried hurl me away, but without the bracelet blocking the damper, his powers felt more like a light breeze. I punched him in the face then Gracie, Jinx and I ran off.

We exited the alleyway and ran down the street looking for a vehicle. We were no longer in any position to fight, especially Jinx. Fighting the feds with a damper sapping her powers had taken a serious toll on her, and she could barely even run.

We rounded a corner and saw a man getting into an old pickup truck. As we made haste towards him, a Gendarme drove into our path, blocking our escape. The fed opened his door and pulled out his gun, so without missing a beat, I did a flying kick to the door, slamming his legs against the car frame. He screamed in agony as the door crushed his legs. I grabbed the gun from him and continued towards the truck. I would've hijacked his car, but a fed's car was impossible to steal without the right tools, or Godspeed.

Just as we reached the truck, several more feds came speeding around a corner.

"Hurry!" I yelled.

There was no way that pickup was outrunning a federal vehicle, but I had a plan. To the driver's surprise, we all jumped on the open gate and into the bed of the truck. I pointed the gun at him through the open back window and gave him an order.

"Drive!"

The man sped off as a half dozen or so Gendarmerie vehicles gained on us. When I figured they were close enough, I hurled one of my grenades in their direction and fired off a shot. My timing was perfect as every one of those cars was reduced to scrap metal. Only a huge cloud of smoke remained. Then my com started buzzing in my ear.

"What's up, Godspeed?" I asked.

"I've been trying to reach you since you left!"

"Sorry, I didn't hear you. I've been a little preoccupied," I replied.

"Are you okay?" Godspeed asked.

"Well, that depends. By okay do you mean are we alive? Or by okay do you mean are we okay? Because we are alive but definitely not okay."

"Kaori, turn on your tracker! I'm coming for you!"

"No, way Godspeed. We're in the back of a pickup heading out of town. We'll be…"

"Kaori, I cannot hear you! Kaori! Speak to me!"

I was distracted by a shadowy figure emerging from the smoke. It was a Speeder, and he was closing in fast.

"It's a Speeder, Godspeed."

"Is he fast?" he asked.

"He's faster than this rusty bucket we're in right now!"

"Tell me where you are!"

"No! I'll take him out!"

I let off several rounds, but this guy was way too fast. I was going to run out of ammo before I ever hit him, and he was getting closer.

"Did you get him?!" Godspeed asked.

"No, he's too fast!"

"Turn on your tracker, Kaori!"

I should have, but I was just too stubborn. Gracie was terrified, holding on for dear life, and Jinx was slumped in the corner, exhausted, barely hanging onto the side of the truck. I stuck my gun back through the window at the driver.

"Drive as fast as you can! When I tell you, slam on the brakes!"

The terrified driver nodded as he put on his seatbelt. I turned back around to Gracie and Jinx.

"Hold on tight."

The Speeder got within a foot of us when I yelled.

"Now!"

The sudden deceleration caused the truck to nosedive and the bed to rise. Just before the back of my head smashed into the window, I saw the Speeder decapitate himself on the gate. I looked down and saw the Speeder's head by my foot. I quickly kicked it away before Gracie could see it.

"Kaori, what happened?! Talk to me!" cried Godspeed.

I groggily looked around and saw Jinx lying on the ground. She looked like she had been hurt badly, but I could see she was still moving. The driver was dazed but okay nonetheless.

"Gracie, are you okay?" I asked.

"My arm hurts…"

Gracie raised her arm and I was horrified to see it bleeding so badly.

"Don't worry, baby," I said with more confidence than I had. "Just hold still."

Still dazed, I tore part of my shirt and made a quick tourniquet for Gracie's arm. Then I gave her half of a nitrocodone pill for the pain.

"Kaori!" Godspeed cried through my com.

"I got rid of the Speeder, Godspeed… but we had a little accident," I replied.

I stumbled out of the truck and made my way to Jinx. I asked where she was hurt but she only shook her head. She was out of it.

"Tell me where you are!" screamed Godspeed.

"I'm gonna head… towards the Miller bridge. Once we cross… I'll blow it, and we'll be safe."

"Kaori, you don't sound well. What's wrong?"

"Godspeed, don't wor..."

I looked into the distance, and there was another car.

"They're still coming..."

"Kaori!"

I turned on my tracker alerting Godspeed to our location.

"Hurry..."

I wearily dragged Jinx to the truck and managed to lift her into the cab, then I pulled the driver out.

"Thanks for the ride."

I grabbed Gracie from the back and put her up front with Jinx, then I climbed into the driver's seat and sped off, but the fed was hot on our tail.

I drove as fast as the rusty bucket of bolts would go, which wasn't nearly fast enough. The bridge up ahead was four cars wide, long, rickety and wooden, and to make matters worse, it was a hell of a drop if we fell. I just needed to get to the other side before the feds caught up, but that didn't seem likely as the driver got close enough for me to see his face. It wasn't a fed. It was Price. That guy would not give up.

He pulled right up behind me and then attempted to go around. I managed to block him a few times using moves I saw on Talladega Nights. Unfortunately, that truck was no race car, and Price quickly got around me. I wondered why he didn't just pass and block my path, but that soon became clear when he slammed his car into us. He was no longer interested in keeping me alive. He was trying to run us off the bridge.

We were halfway over the bridge, but we couldn't last much longer. Price was slamming into us hard and each time we were closer to flipping over. He lowered his passenger window and held out his hand. We were out of range of the damper, and his powers were returning. All I had left was the grenade, but that would have killed us all. We needed a miracle, and it came in the form of the best driver I had ever known. In my rearview, I saw Godspeed racing up behind us in what I assumed was one of D'Arco's sports cars. Price was unphased, or he didn't notice. All of his attention was on us as he released a concussive blast that sent the truck careening on its side. We were going over, but Godspeed raced up to the passenger side just in time and caught us with the side of his car. He then swerved to the left and set us back upright. Next, he sped off then cut in front of Price then slammed on his brakes. It looked like Price tried to blast him out of the way, but he didn't react in time and crashed into the back of Godspeed. The cars spun around dangerously close to the side of the bridge as I flew past them. We reached the other side, and Price climbed out of the window and fell to the ground. I could see blood on his forehead. I wasn't in much better shape as I got out of the truck and slumped to the ground as well. Godspeed climbed through the roof of his car and ran towards us. Price raised his hand but couldn't focus and dropped it back down. Godspeed reached me, and I saw the worry he had in his eyes. It looked a lot like how I felt when I thought I had lost Gracie. I smiled and handed him my last grenade. He pulled the pin and hurled it towards the bridge. I blacked out before it exploded.

Chapter 10
Aiden

I woke up in a hospital bed attached to machines with two blurry figures at my side.

"Aiden? Can you hear me, love?"

I do not know why I was disappointed or who I was hoping would be there, but I should not have been surprised to see you.

"Carson?"

"Yes!" you replied with a voice filled with equal parts of joy and fear.

I suppose I should have known then how much you really loved me. As my vision returned, I could see Josiah on the other side of me, standing stoically with his arms folded.

"Did we capture her?" I asked.

"Capture her?" Josiah replied. "I thought you were trying to kill her."

"No. I was somewhat aggressive, but I know we need her

alive…"

I did not recall everything I had done at the time, but I did know that I was lying. I wanted her dead.

"She got away along with the Trickster, the Zero child and an unknown male," Josiah informed me.

I could tell by his tone that he was not convinced of my innocence. I tried to adjust my position and suddenly realized how badly injured I was.

"Ugh!" I grimaced. "Every cell in my body hurts."

"You had a nasty accident, love. Don't try to move."

"You were in an explosion, and then you fell 200 feet to the ground below," said Josiah. "You must have managed to create a protective barrier around yourself before you landed."

"Apparently, it did not protect enough. I feel like a building was dropped on top of me."

"Well, it's good you had a few days to rest," you said.

"A few days?"

I tried to sit up, but that proved futile.

"Aiden, please don't try to move!" you pleaded.

"How long have I been here?"

"Four days," Josiah replied. "There probably isn't a lot you can tell us now. I'll return in a couple days and get your report. Rest well. Goodbye, Carson."

You smiled and waved as Josiah left the room.

"Sit me up," I told you.

You carefully leaned me forward and rearranged my pillows for support.

"Is that better?"

"Yes," I replied.

Moving increased my agony, so I reached for the PCA system to administer a dose of pain medication. You saw my struggle and pressed the button for me then reached for my hand.

"Thank you."

I thought I had friends or at least caring coworkers, but none of them were there. Only you.

"Do you wish to talk about what happened?" you asked.

"I could not even if I wanted to. My head is just, it is just cloudy right now."

"Well, what do you want to talk about?"

"I do not care," I replied. "Tell me about your day…"

My words came as much of a shock to me as they did you. I could not remember the last time I had asked you about your day, and I did not know if you were more pleased or surprised.

"Well, there's this old woman at the home and she is 200 years old!"

"No one is that old," I replied.

"Okay, I'm exaggerating, but just a bit. She's around 180."

"180 years old? How is that possible?" I asked.

"Her Class slowed down her metabolism, cell division or something. Basically, it made her age really slowly. Too bad it did not slow down her attitude."

I smirked.

"Another testy old woman?"

"You can not conceive! She was so hate filled and nasty!

Combative, throwing her food, screaming obscenities."

"Sounds like you had your hands full," I mused as I started drifting back to sleep.

"I had eight hands full! And she kept calling me queer."

Queer. I wondered why that word sounded so familiar. *Why did it cause me such anxiety?* Suddenly, I was fully awake.

"Queer?" I asked.

"Yes. Queer. I think she meant it as an insult..?"

"I am certain of it…"

You stayed until the nurses made you leave so I could sleep, but I could not. Your words kept ringing in my ears,

"She kept calling me names like queer."

How could the fugitive have known about that? Had she also encountered someone with metabolic retardation? But that did not explain the mobile cycle or the ancient weapons she carried. I needed to find out the truth, and I had a plan.

I reached over to the com beside my bed and called the nurse.

"Yes, Detective Aiden?"

"I am in a lot of pain," I replied.

"Is your PCA empty?" she asked.

"No, I just need something stronger."

"Okay, Detective Aiden. I'll be right there."

Chapter 11
Kaori

"Take this somewhere safe!" Cordell insists.

"Where?" I ask.

"Anywhere!" he replies. "Travel through time if you have to!"

I look over at Protos, and he glances cautiously at Cordell.

"How far?" he asks.

"A few days, a week. A year if necessary! Just don't lose it! I have reserves, but if that's destroyed, this will be all that's left!"

I woke up in a strange bed surrounded by blurry figures. My head felt like it was filled with Doozers jackhammering my skull. Everything was fuzzy for a bit, and I couldn't remember where I was or why my head was hurting so badly. Slowly pieces were coming back to me. I remembered Zero Alley, D'Arco, fighting and...

"Gracie!!"

I sat up in a panic.

"Relax, Kaori," said a blurry Godspeed. "She's fine."

"Take me to her! I want to see her!"

"You hit your head really hard. You don't need to be up walking around," said Deadeye.

Seeing that Deadeye had returned safely made me feel better, but I was still concerned about my little girl.

"I don't care, Deadeye. Take me to her now!"

"Okay, okay."

He and Godspeed helped me out of bed, and as we walked down the hallway, my vision slowly returned. I could see that Gadget was the third figure.

"Gadget," I smiled and reached for his hand.

"Glad to have you back."

We continued down a second hallway past numbered rooms.

"Where are we?" I asked as I ambled along.

"Well," Deadeye began, "we didn't want to be on the run

with the three of you injured, so we packed up and moved a few cities away to this office building."

"Three of us..? Jinx!"

I had forgotten that the fight had taken everything out of her and how she flew out of the truck.

"Is she okay?"

"Am fine, KK. A bit bruised is all."

Jinx limped out of a nearby room with her arm in a sling, but she was still her usual chipper self. I reached out and hugged her tightly.

"Did good, KK?"

"You did great, Jinx."

We continued a little further down the hall and about ran into Medic exiting another room.

"What is she doing up?"

Medic was normally passive, but if you disobeyed doctor's orders, Mama Bear would come out.

"She wanted to see Gracie," Gadget explained.

"She has a hairline fracture in her skull, so it doesn't matter what she wants!"

"Then you can be the one to tell her to go back to bed," said Deadeye.

Medic looked at me and saw the determination on my face. Even beaten and half conscious, I was stubborn as a mule.

"Fine. But only for a few minutes," Medic obliged. "I'm sure you're in terrible pain."

"It's not so bad," I winced.

"It would be a lot better if you'd let me give you stronger pain meds like Nitro."

"You know how I feel about that…".

We all followed Medic back into the room, and there was little Gracie lying on a bed facing the far wall. Her doll was behind her hanging off the other side of the bed. I let out a heavy sigh with such force I thought my body would float away. Gracie barely turned her head in my direction.

"Kori," said Gracie with far less enthusiasm than I had

hoped for.

It was more like she was acknowledging my presence than greeting me. Nevertheless, I pulled away from Deadeye and Godspeed and made my way to Gracie on my own. I leaned down wrapped my arms around her. She hugged me back, but barely.

"You've been asleep for days," she said.

I looked back at the others.

"Days?"

"You've been in and out of consciousness for a while," said Medic.

"I guess I hit my head harder than I thought."

"Okay, Kaori needs to go back to bed," Medic insisted.

"Okay," said Gracie.

She looked at me and handed me a casual smile then squeezed me a little tighter, and I grimaced. She quickly released me.

"I'm sorry, Kori."

"It's okay, Gracie. But maybe I should lie back down."

I leaned back over and kissed her on the forehead.

"I'll see you in a few hours."

"I'm glad you're okay, Kori."

"Thank you, sweetheart."

Medic escorted me back to the door while Gracie waved goodbye. Just outside of the room stood Gadget next what was left of a wheelchair.

"What's that?" I asked.

"It's a wheelchair," Gadget replied.

"Seriously? You once built a bomb using a can of hairspray, a nine volt battery and an egg timer, and this is the best wheelchair you could come up with?"

"Hey, it has a seat and wheels!"

Laughing, I sat down in the chair.

"Any progress on the Shifty guy while I was out?" I asked.

"We put out feelers," said Godspeed, "but nothing so far. However, there is a great buzz about a Zero laying waste to the Gendarmerie."

"I'm not sure if that's good or bad, but the skirmish might have gotten Shift's attention. If it did, then Whisper would know. We need to reach out to him," I replied.

"Well, I don't know how available he will be," Deadeye began. "The Gendarmerie came down hard on Zero Alley after your exhibition."

"D'Arco..?"

"D'Arco and his crew escaped unharmed," Deadeye replied.

"No word on Whisper?" I anxiously asked.

"Not so far, but we'll keep checking."

"We have eyes down there. As soon as we hear something, we'll decide what to do," said Godspeed.

"For now, you need rest, Kaori," said Medic.

She offered to take me back to my room and told the others they could visit with me later. It was clear she wanted to speak to me alone.

"There seems to be a lot of medical equipment around here.

What kind of office building is this?" I asked.

"Doctors' offices were in here. We chose this place so the three of you could recover."

We returned to my room and Medic helped me back into bed. Once I was situated, Medic sat at the foot of my bed.

"Let me guess, you have good news and bad news?"

"I only have news," Medic replied. "Gracie lost a lot of blood and needed a transfusion. She has a rare blood type, AB negative and since you're O negative, yours was the only blood I could use."

I looked down at a bandaged area on my arm where she had drawn blood.

"Okay..?"

"Well," Medic continued, "when I was testing your blood, I noticed you had a virus."

"What kind of virus?"

"I have no idea. I had to continue with the transfusion or Gracie would've died. Later, I looked closer at the virus, and it appeared to be dormant."

"And now Gracie has it..?"

"Yes, but as near as I can tell, it's harmless."

"And what if it becomes active..?"

Medic sighed and looked at the floor.

"I don't know."

"My blood might kill her..."

"Don't say that, Kaori. I was the one who gave her the blood."

"But it was my blood!"

"It had to be done to save her life."

"Her life wouldn't have needed saving if I hadn't taken her out there to begin with."

Medic tried to calm me, but it was in vain. She made sure I was comfortable, then hesitated before leaving. She pulled my pill bottle out of her pocket and set it on the nightstand beside my bed.

"I replaced the missing pills," she said as I choked back tears.

Medic understood, and she trusted me.

"I know you're doing your best," she said.

As she left, I reached for the bottle and slowly began shaking it as I cried myself to sleep.

"This way!" cries Protos as we race down a hallway and into a stairwell.

I look back at the laboratory door and a feeling of dread overcomes me.

"Come on, Kaori!"

I follow Protos down the stairs and into the parking garage. We hear the noise of rioters, so we duck behind a car. They pass, and Protos beckons me on. We reach Cordell's Tomahawk.

"I'll drive!" says Protos.

"Why you?"

"Because I have the keys!"

I look up and see that we have been spotted, so there's no time to argue. Protos hops on the motorcycle, and I climb on back.

I start to place the canister in my pocket and I realize I am not wearing my jacket. I hold the canister tightly against me instead. The mob gets closer, and I urge Protos.

"We should probably leave now!"

"Don't let her get away!" yells one of our pursuers.

We take off with such force I nearly fall. We whip around cars and unsuspecting people as we make our way to the exit. Protos takes the ramp and we spiral our way towards the street. Unfortunately, another vehicle heads up towards us, Protos takes a detour to another level. As we race across the lot, two other vehicles come at us.

"This doesn't look good!" cries Protos.

"Try to lose them!"

"That's not so easy in an enclosed space! We're gonna have to skip!"

"No!"

"You heard Cordell! We have to keep it safe!"

Protos cuts hard between two parked cars, and as he does,

177

the canister flies out of my hand.

"Protos, I lost it! Don't skip!"

But it's too late. I look back and see a dark skinned man picking up the canister.

I had that dream intermittently over the past three years, but it had become more frequent in the weeks since my accident. I tried to ignore it, but I couldn't. Reality was frequently an unwelcome travelling companion on my life's journey, but she had the map, so it behooved me to listen.

I awoke in the middle of the night, and only the ambient light of the moon illuminated the hallway outside of my room. I made my way to the door and down the hall. I had no idea where anyone was in the new facility, but I knew how to find him. Every night he would fall asleep reading Of Mice and Men, so I just needed to find the room with the light.

It wasn't long before I found the door with a sliver of light beckoning from underneath. I followed the flickering flame of the candle inside and went over to his bed. He lay there in a shallow, restless sleep with a furrowed brow as if he was struggling to solve a riddle which had no answer. I reached for the book which lay open on his chest and curiously looked to see where he had left off. Lennie and George were gonna *"live off the fatta the land."* I placed the book on a nearby table, making sure to save his spot, then placed my hand gently on his chest. His heart was beating too quickly for someone asleep, like one of his car engines idling too high. Bad timing I suppose. Godspeed opened his eyes, looked at me and placed his hand on top of mine. His heartbeat slowed until we were in sync. He brought my hand to his lips and kissed it softly before resting it on the side of his face. He closed his eyes and smiled ever so slightly, seemingly awash in contentment for having found the answer to his riddle. I caught my flickering shadow dancing on the far wall, and I followed her lead. I took his hand to my mouth and kissed the back of it, then ran it down my neck, to my breast, then my belly. He closed his hand around a section of my thin gown and pulled it downward. I watched as it slid easily over my shoulders and arms and fell at my feet. He sat

179

up and reached for my waist, then pressed his mouth against me just below my navel. His hands slid around to my back then moved upward, pulling me closer. He inhaled me deeply, breathing me in and my scent filled him like an opiate. He exhaled and tasted my scent on his tongue. I watched our silhouettes as his powerful arms lifted my body on top of his. I straddled his legs and our eyes met in the dimly lit room. He reached for my hips and pulled me further up his body as he lay back down. I leaned forward and placed my hands on the wall behind the bed while his face disappeared between my thighs. I raised my head and arched my back as the movement of his tongue reverberated throughout my body. His hands grasped my thighs, pulling my *lips* closer to his. My hips began to rock, desperately searching for his mouth every time it left my body. My breaths became gasps as I quivered with euphoria. Then silence. My body was motionless until my raptured spirit returned, and I exhaled suddenly as I had forgotten to breathe. Beneath me, he continued traversing my body which proved to be too much in my sensitive state. I pushed myself down his body leaving my nectar from his chin to his waist. I looked at him and saw everything I ever wanted in his eyes. He sat up, and I wrapped my legs around his waist then gasped as his body merged with mine. Our lips embraced and my body rose and fell to match the rhythm of his. I locked my legs around his waist and pulled him deep inside so he could feel what he was doing to me. With my hand on his head and my lips on his ear, I whispered.

"I love you…"

And he said the same.

Hours later, I was fully awake lying with my back to Godspeed when he began to stir. The candle had long since burned out and without the dance of shadows, I was left with nothing but darkness. Several minutes passed before anyone spoke.

"I know you'll leave me," he said.

"Then why do you stay?"

"Because no matter who leaves, the pain is the same. If I stay, at least I get to know the pleasure of your heart for as long as I can."

Godspeed's love was foolish and unrepentant, but it was also true. Lying there I wondered when I had last been the object of such affection, if ever at all.

"Do you think there's something wrong with me for loving you the way I do?" he asked.

"Yes," I replied.

"Why?"

"Because I know there's something wrong with me."

Chapter 12
Josiah

My first experience with the rogue Zero was eye opening. It was clear that our meeting in Zero Alley was a chance encounter as all parties were equally surprised to see each other. We immediately went after Kaori, the child and an unnamed female Trickster, but Detective Aiden was a bit too zealous with his initial strike. When I caught up to Kaori, I attempted to subdue her using traditional means, but I was soon forced to use my Class. Unfortunately, she knew my weaknesses as a Burner and exploited them well. I was only able to gain the upper hand when I cowardly threatened the life of the child. My heart bleeds not for Zero children, but there is no honor in winning a fight by targeting the weak. I was shot from behind as I was arresting the outlaw, and I can only assume it was the Trickster. I had thought she had been dispatched by Agents Hull and Perkins, but I learned later that she had dispatched them instead. The Recovery team gathered as much

183

of them as they could find. I was amazed how much power the Trickster retained in the presence of a damper. I could only imagine what she was capable of at full strength. I intended to clean the matter up quickly and quietly, but Governor Mathias had other plans.

I entered my office to find him sitting at my desk. He had my framed photo capture of my family in his hand.

"May I help you, Governor?"

He graciously offered me a seat in my own office. He stayed seated behind my desk. I expected a lecture about the incident in Zero Alley and my failure to capture the fugitive, but the Governor could be unpredictable at times.

"How do you feel about Zeros, Josiah?"

I leaned forward and took the photo from the Governor. I expected outrage, but he simply grinned.

"I understand that we failed to capture the fugitive and now everyone knows Zeros are behind the attacks, but I will get this under control."

"Do you remember the last election?"

"Yes, of course."

"It was close, Josiah. People are getting along. When people are united in love, they hold hands and sing songs. But when you divide them with fear and hate, they sacrifice their freedoms for security."

"I don't understand…"

"Getting Classes to fear the scourge of Zeros was a hard sell, and now Sympathizers are on the rise, but these latest attacks will stymie their bleeding hearts. Josiah, this Zero will get me re-elected in a landslide. Find her quickly. But not too quickly. We need to shake the Classes without emboldening the rest of the Zeros. Or don't find her. I could finally justify releasing the hounds."

"Sir, those *Hounds* will bring destruction!"

"Like the Zero?"

The Governor left me to dwell on his words. By law, Reapers were considered a branch of the military and were very limited when it came to domestic operations. If the Governor could get Congress to bring back martial law, the Reapers would have free reign, and that would mean danger for us all.

With the Governor gone, I was able to sit behind my own desk, so I dropped into my chair with a frustrated sigh. I actually had the fugitive in my hands, and she slipped away. I had to know this woman's secret. I pulled the odd weapon that she used to assault me out of my drawer. It was not exactly lethal, but it was certainly painful. Based on its appearance, I assumed it was rather old. As I pondered its origins, I received a call from the front desk.

"Special Agent Griffin, Detective Aiden Price is here to see you."

"Aiden? He's supposed to be in the hospital. And our appointment isn't for another few weeks."

"Would you like me to send him away, sir?"

I figured he must have some very important information if he was dragging himself out of his hospital bed, so I was quite curious to hear what he had to say.

"No, send him up."

Aiden took longer to reach my office than before because he was struggling with his wheelchair. He was still badly bruised and the restorer had not finished healing all of his broken bones. I greeted him at my door.

"Hello, Aiden. I would offer you a seat, but…"

"Amusing," he replied dryly.

It was a cheap shot, but he had it coming for his behavior in the Alley.

"So, Aiden, I'm quite eager to hear what brought you off your near-death bed so soon."

"I believe she is really from the past."

The man I met a few weeks before was not the man sitting before me then. Of course he had been this ever evolving character the entire time. He started broken and confused, became hate-filled and vengeful, and now he was... scared..? I didn't understand why he seemed so unnerved. He was fine when I left him at the hospital, so it wasn't the fight that changed him.

"So we're back to that theory now? What has happened since I last saw you?"

"There is this woman whose powers have slowed her aging process. She is 180 years old…"

"Yes," I interjected, "she probably has metabolic retardation on the third genome, and she probably looks quite old. The Zero in question is young and has no mutations."

"True, but they knew the same things. And this Zero, she is not like any I have ever known. She is strong and confident, and she fights back. She had that ancient vehicle, all of those artifacts she used as clandestine weapons. She knows our weaknesses. She destroyed an Enforcer station killing over a dozen officers. She killed nine Gendarmes."

"Let's say that she is from the past. What does that mean?" I asked.

"It means she knows how we began. Which could mean she knows how we end."

Aiden had a point. If she was from the past, that would

explain a Zero having intimate knowledge our powers, but travelling that far was impossible. There had never been any record of a Skipper being able to move more than a week at a time. Even using increments, no one could come close to skipping 200 years in a lifetime.

"What do you propose we do, Detective Aiden?"

"We go to the Archive and find out who she is and why she is here!"

I walked over to my door, closed it, then turned to Aiden.

"I realize you have certain connections, but knowledge of the Archive isn't supposed to exist below a federal level, so it's not in your best interests to broadcast your awareness."

"But you are allowed access. You could get us inside."

"Having access does not give me carte blanche to go digging around in classified information without justification."

"I would think a rogue Zero on the loose killing law enforcement officials would be justification. Please, Josiah."

Begging. Why was he begging?

189

I had no doubt that his interest in the Archive was connected to the woman, but there was something else he was seeking. There was something he wasn't telling me, but it mattered not.

"I can't help you, Detective."

He was quite disappointed, but he didn't seem too surprised,

"Oh, well, thank you anyway, Josiah."

He leaned forward and held out his hand. I shook it but felt a sharp pain and quickly retrieved my hand.

"Aah! What was that?"

"I am sorry! My powers have been a bit unpredictable lately."

"How would your powers be active in here..?"

"Uh, the restorer. I was told as it heals, it can cause power spikes. It is only temporary though."

It was true that a patient on a restorer device could see a spike in their powers, but I doubted they would spike enough to cancel out a localized Gendarmerie neutralizer. Something didn't seem quite right. Aiden's eyes were wild and sunken, and he was awfully jittery. Granted he had almost died just days before and was undoubtedly taking lots of pain medication, but there was something else going on.

"You have a good day, Agent Griffin."

I watched him leave my office then turned my attention back to the weapon. I needed an expert on antiques, and I just happened to know one. I gave Rick Harris a call and pulled him up on my holo.

"Mr. Harris."

I took control of his holo and force it answer my call. He was startled by my image suddenly appearing on his holo, and he dropped the boxes he was carrying.

"Special Agent Griffin!? Uh, what can I do for you, sir?"

"You collect old things. Can you tell me what kind of weapon this is?"

I placed the weapon on my holo and scanned it. When Rick

received the image, he cautiously smiled, presumably at my ignorance.

"Uh, sir, that's no weapon. It's an office tool called a stapler. It was used to bind pieces of paper together back when paper was used more. Where did you find it?"

"The woman I spoke to you about grabbed it off of a table and used it to attack me. She shot little pins into my neck and face."

I focused the holo back on myself so that he could see my face.

"I see. Well clearly she has a passion for all things old."

"Why do you say that?"

"Well, that's old. Really old. If she had simply grabbed it and used it as a blunt object, I would've thought nothing of it. But grabbing it in the heat of battle and using it that way indicates she already knew how it functions. She not only knew that it ejected sharp objects, but she knew how to open it so she could staple your, um, face."

"Perhaps she had seen one recently and figured it all out then?" I said offering another theory.

"Unlikely," Rick replied. "These are extremely rare. She's either a historian, or really, really old."

"Thank you, Mr. Harris."

Rick gave me a nervous smile, and I disconnected the session. Minutes later, I was stepping off the elevator on the first floor and looking around. I thought for sure Aiden would've been gone by then, but he was clearly a lot slower in his hobbled state.

"Aiden!" I called across the lobby.

Aiden turned his wheelchair around with a look of confusion on his face as I raced over to him.

"I've changed my mind."

He didn't ask why. He simply nodded his head and said, "Okay."

Aiden followed me back into the elevator, and he watched closely as I placed my hand on the biometric hand scanner. I realized then that his attention to detail was quite purposeful. After

I scanned my hand, the elevator came to a complete stop, which startled Aiden causing him to tightly grab the sides of his wheelchair. The display panel showed options for a set of hidden floors, and I chose A. A hidden door behind us opened, and I motioned for Aiden to follow. We traveled down a long hallway past numerous doors. Aiden wasn't seated quite high enough to view through the windows but I noticed he still tried in vain to stretch his neck as we passed each one.

We reached the end of the hall where I was required to scan my hand again. The door ahead of us opened to a long, narrow hallway.

"Do you need help with your chair?"

"I will manage."

Aiden rolled behind me down the hallway to one final door that lead to the Archive Room. It was a circular room located in the middle of the floor. The walls were one continuous piece of impact proof glass with a single door. I scanned my hand again, and we reached our destination.

I had only been in the room once before, and that was years ago, but I remembered being as shocked as Aiden was when I saw it for the first time.

"Where is the Archive?" he asked.

"Right there," I replied.

Aiden sat there in amazement for several seconds before speaking.

"How does this work?"

"The user asks questions or thinks them. The Archive can read minds."

I pulled my holo from my belt and produced an image of the Zero.

"Can you identify this woman?" I asked.

The Archive projected images of all matches that were found.

"My facial recognition records go back over five centuries resulting in over three million possible matches."

"That is a lot," said Aiden.

"I'm aware. Check over the past 200 years."

"Over 1,000,000 possible matches."

"Can I pose queries?" asked Aiden.

"Pleased do."

"Limit your search to North America," said Aiden.

"Over 700 possible matches."

I began to doubt the effectiveness of the idea.

"How many owned a Tomahawk?" asked Aiden.

"A tomahawk is a North America axe that resembles a hatchet. It was used by colonial Europeans and Native Americans as a general purpose tool and sometimes a weapon. Records for tomahawk ownership were not kept."

"No," said Aiden. "A Tomahawk mobile cycle."

"Did you mean motorcycle?" asked the Archive.

"Yes," he replied.

"The Dodge Tomahawk was a concept vehicle introduced in 2003 at the North American Auto Show. The vehicle was never put into mass production and only nine were known to be sold.

None of the women from your query were owners."

"Show us the owners," I demanded, growing impatient.

Archive projected nine men in front of us. None of them seemed assuming. I wasn't sure where to go from there. Thankfully, I had a seasoned detective with me.

"How many lived within a hundred mile radius of here?" Aiden asked.

"One. Cordell O'Riordan."

"Who are his relatives within two generations?" Aiden continued.

"Cordell O'Riordan was an only child born to Connor and Ava O'Riordan. Ava had one brother, Liam Sheerin. He and her parents, Dylan and Ciara Sheerin died before Cordell was born. Connor, like his son, was an only child. He was born to Sean and Aileen O'Riordan. Cordell had no children."

"Now what?" I asked.

"Who were Cordell's known associates?"

"Cordell was employed as a biochemist at Payne MedCorp

in Dayton, Ohio. His supervisor was Michael Webster, his coworkers were Brian Williams and Nicholas Isham, and he had two assistants, David Protos and Kaori Maru."

And there she was.

"That's her! That's the Zero! What became of Kaori?" I asked.

"Kaori and David were both last seen on June 19th, 2015, the same day Kaori was a target of an attempted kidnapping. One suspect was captured but he died in custody. No clues were ever found in their disappearance."

"They skipped time. There is no other explanation," said Aiden.

"200 years? That just does not seem plausible."

Aiden turned back to the Archive.

"When was the first Class discovered?"

"Classes were originally known as Anomalytes and the first was an unidentified Glider identified on November 4th, 2013 in Dayton, Ohio."

"Kaori worked in a biomedical lab in the same town where the first Class was discovered," said Aiden, "then she and her coworker disappear and she shows up 200 years later with an intimate knowledge of our powers. That is no coincidence."

"So, why are they here? Do you think they skipped accidentally?"

"No," Aiden replied. "I do not imagine skipping 200 years is an easy feat that happens by chance. I think they came here to do something that they could not do in the past."

The Zero was clearly tied to our history, although I was uncertain just how. I needed more answers.

"How can we tell where she is now?" I asked Aiden.

"Archive, where was Dayton, Ohio in relation to where we are today?" he queried.

The Archive projected a map.

"Dayton, Ohio was located at 39.7594° N and 84.1917° W, sixty-six miles southwest of this location."

I immediately recognized the spot on the Archive's map. It

was near the reported sightings of the Zero. I used my holo to overlay my sightings map onto that of the Archive.

"Archive, indicate where Kaori Maru lived," I ordered.

The Archive showed four locations on the map. None of them were near the sightings.

"Where is the lab where she worked?"

It was also out range. I was out of ideas, but Aiden was not.

"Where did her parents live?"

Also not a match.

"Where did they work?"

"Kaori Maru's mother did not work outside of the home, but her father was an engineer at an automobile factory in Moraine, Ohio for most of his life."

The factory was at the epicenter of the sightings. We had found her hiding place.

"Josiah, I would like your sponsorship for an application as a special Gendarme Agent."

"Consider it done."

Chapter 13
Kaori

After a few months of rest, I was almost back to normal. I could move around without headaches or assistance. With my independence returned, I decided to do some investigating. I found a lab and an electron microscope and used it to examine some of my blood samples.

Why was this in me? Where did it come from?

I had an idea where it came from, but I just didn't want to believe it. But more importantly, I didn't know exactly what it was.

"Kaori, what are you doing..?"

I was so engrossed in what I was doing that I didn't hear Medic come in. She had this look on her face like Truman did when he found out his whole life was a TV show.

"I..."

Over the past few years, lying had come so naturally to me. It didn't matter if it was to save a life or just because it would be easier than telling the truth. But despite my moral waverings, I had no lie to explain what Medic saw. Blood samples, plate reader, thermocycler and me staring into an electron microscope.

Medic slowly made her way over to me while looking at the equipment. She turned off the thermocycler and removed a sample.

"Kaori, are you a doctor?"

"Not, exactly..."

Looking me in the eye, she stepped closer, wanting to have a look at what was under the microscope. I took a step back to oblige her. As Medic leaned over, she kept her eyes on me, like she didn't trust what I might do next. She finally directed her attention to the microscope and after a few seconds, she stood upright.

"Is that your virus?" she asked.

"Yes."

"So, you're a scientist, like your friend from the past?"

"I was..."

I noticed Medic's breathing grew heavier as her lip

quivered.

"You never indicated you had any medical knowledge."

"I never thought it was relevant..."

"You never thought it was relevant? As many times as we have been injured or sick? What are you hiding, Kaori?"

"That's a part of my past. It's not who I am anymore."

Medic looked around at the equipment again.

"Apparently it still is."

I couldn't look at her. I felt if I did, she'd cull the truth from my eyes, and I couldn't risk that.

"What makes one a Class, Kaori?"

"Genetic anomalies usually occurring on the seventh and thirteenth chromosomes," I replied, trying to bury her curiosity in terminology.

"What makes one a Class, Kaori..?"

I dropped my eyes to the floor and shook my head. She wasn't letting it go, and rightfully so. I had betrayed her trust and graduated to insulting her intelligence. Lying, evading, neither would make things better, if that was even possible. I had made so many excuses for keeping the truth hidden that I had started believing them. I pretended I was protecting my friends, but I was really just hiding my own guilt.

"A virus," I replied.

"What kind of Event creates a virus?"

"A planned one."

Medic spent the rest of the day avoiding me. She didn't say anything to the others. I was thankful for that, but I was still anxious as I had to wait for the other shoe to drop. It was only a matter of time before someone realized something was wrong. I was cozying up to Godspeed *(probably as a distraction)*, Gracie was emotionally distant, and Medic wouldn't look me in the eye.

"Pay up, brother," said Deadeye.

Gadget, Godspeed, Gracie, Jinx and I were all gathered in the rec room when Deadeye walked up and held his hand out to Gadget. Gadget rolled his eyes, reached in his pocket and retrieved three pieces of gold for Deadeye.

"You just got lucky, old man," Gadget muttered while glaring at Godspeed and myself.

"Never bet against the backslide, youngster," Deadeye instructed as he gleefully took the gold.

"Wait," said Godspeed, "were you two betting on our relationship?"

"Technically, I was betting against your relationship," Gadget replied.

"Well, some friends you two are!"

"What about you?" Gadget exclaimed. "Your dysfunction is costing me money!"

"Serves you right, Gadget. Betting against us," I said as I held Godspeed tighter.

"Deadeye, double or nothing they break up in twenty four hours!"

"No way am I taking that sucker bet!"

"Hey now!" I replied, but it was feigned indignation.

Our relationship was like a rollercoaster with a weak track.

The ups and downs were fairly predictable, but you never knew when it was going off the rails for good.

"Well, this is making me ill. I'm going to check for chatter on the coms," Gadget said as he left the room.

I watched him pass Gracie and Jinx, and I took notice of their play. I was starting to miss how Gracie never wanted to leave my side, but I knew it was good for her to have someone who at least seemed like her own age. She was smiling and laughing and having a good time.

"Anyone seen Medic?" Deadeye asked.

Not wanting to speak on the matter, I averted my gaze.

"When I last saw her, she was looking for more medical supplies," Godspeed replied.

"She has been keeping to herself lately," said Deadeye.

"I noticed that too," said Godspeed.

I felt the anxiety wrapping itself around me like a python. *What would she tell them? What would I tell them?* I needed to get up before the nervous energy shook me apart. I walked over to

Gracie and Jinx who had started drawing pictures.

"Ay, KK! We're drawing!"

"I see that, Jinx."

I looked over at Gracie's picture and saw what looked like two people fighting.

"What are you drawing, honey?"

"You."

"What am I doing?"

"You're fighting the bad guys. I want you to teach me to fight."

"Why do you want to learn to fight?"

Gracie pointed to one of the figures she had drawn.

"He coulda killed you. If I knew how to fight, I coulda helped."

"You're too young to be fighting."

Without looking up, Gracie replied, "That Gendarme didn't care how young I was when he said he was gonna kill me."

You could almost hear our collective hearts breaking.

"You can't beat those men in a fight, sweetheart."

"I can't outrun them either. So, I'd rather fight."

I knelt down beside her, and I put my arm on her shoulder.

"Okay. I'll teach you to defend yourself."

"No. Teach me to win."

I searched her eyes for the innocence that had brought me back from the edge, hoping it was still there. I needed to know I hadn't crushed one more thing in the grasp of my careless hands. My sins had piled high, and I knew that bill was coming due soon, so, if any part of my life was going to have meaning, I needed to leave at least one other life better than I found it.

"There's still room for you in this world," I said.

Gracie looked like she was about to speak, but Medic arrived. She walked over and sat near Deadeye and Godspeed, never even glancing in my direction.

"Looks like I missed all the fun," she said.

"You missed me taking a young buck's money," Deadeye declared. "I was just getting ready to make dinner though. I hope everyone is in the mood for some questionable rice."

He was looking at Medic when he spoke, and when she gave no response, he looked over at me. It took less time than I thought.

"That sounds wonderful, Deadeye," I replied with far too much enthusiasm for what would surely be a barely palatable meal.

I had hoped everyone would blame it on my renewed affection for Godspeed, but that didn't seem likely. Medic started walking in my direction and the panic began to set in again. My heart pounded against my chest so hard, I thought for sure the others could see it. I couldn't tell if she was walking towards me or just in my general direction. I feigned a smile and tried to ready myself for whatever she might say, but Gadget burst in and I never got to hear it.

"I just received word on Whisper's whereabouts!"

Godspeed and Deadeye leaped to their feet in reaction to Gadget's troubled tone.

"Where is he?" Godspeed asked.

"He's in Darke County due to be auctioned off in two days!"

"I'll get the vehicle, Deadeye, you and Gadget gather the weapons..."

"No," I said.

The others looked shocked at my objection.

"We'll do this without violence."

We lived in a world of unmitigated hostility where the solution to every problem was thought to be found with some form of aggression. But the one thing that everyone needed the most would never be found at the end of a sword.

"Are you planning on politely asking the auction house for Whisper?" Gadget asked.

"In a manner of speaking. We'll buy him back."

Gadget didn't see the wisdom in my plan.

"Whisper might be getting long in the tooth, but he could still fetch a handsome price at auction."

"So..?"

"So, buying him could wipe us out, and it's not like any of us have paying jobs."

"Kaori is right," said Godspeed to everyone's surprise. "The last fight took a heavy toll on us, and you can't put a price on the life of someone you care about."

All the while, he was looking at me... like you used to. It's funny how the very thing that draws a person in could also chase her away.

"Okay," said Gadget, "we'll need someone to do the buying."

"Medic," Deadeye chimed in. "She's less assuming than most of us and hasn't been seen in public."

Deadeye's suggestion caught me off guard. I didn't figure Medic would want anything to do with such a plan and even less to do with me, but I guess I was projecting a little. I wasn't quite ready to talk to her directly, so I assumed *(perhaps even wished)* she felt the same.

"I don't think Medic wants to be out there on the front

line…"

"I'll do it," she said.

"Oh…" I replied. "Well, we don't have a lot of time so we should get moving."

I gave Medic a nervous smile, and she returned one with far less emotion than the one I delivered.

I sent Godspeed out to get a car. We needed something expensive, worthy of a wealthy socialite, as the average Class didn't own slaves. Godspeed acquired the equivalent of a 21st century town car, something roomy, shiny and justifying the need for a hired driver, which of course would be Godspeed.

Gadget inspected Medic's internal jammer to make sure she passed all scans, but that wasn't enough. Since she was going to mingling with the *uppercrust* for an undetermined amount of time, Medic needed to be able to fake a power, and a Shocker was fairly easy to simulate. Gadget found an old defibrillator and managed downsize it into something that fit close to the skin. It wasn't very powerful, but it would get the job done.

We didn't exactly dress to the nines, so Medic needed some really nice clothes. Most of our clothes were salvaged or bought cheaply, but wealthy people in the market for a new slave didn't usually shop in the bargain bin, so I had to dust off my sewing needle and come up with something tailor made. That meant intimate one on one time with Medic, and I wasn't looking forward to that.

I found her later that day in one of the examination rooms that she used as her quarters. I knocked on the open door, and she seemed surprised to see me.

"Kaori..? Uh, come in."

"I need to measure you for your outfit. Is this a good time?"

She looked at me curiously.

"Measure me?"

"Yes. In order to look the part, your clothes need to be custom made. I couldn't find a measuring tape but I did find this string and a yardstick."

The brief silence was a bit awkward, and I considered just

eyeballing her frame.

"I can come back later if that's better for you…"

"No, now is fine. Should I undress?"

"Yes," I nodded.

Medic turned her back to me and started disrobing, and I didn't know where to direct my eyes. Having a conversation with Medic was awkward enough without her being half naked. As she removed her shirt, I was mortified by what I saw. The freckles on her shoulders drifted down her back, leading to unsightly scars. Some were deep, some were raised. I couldn't imagine anyone believing a kind soul like Medic deserved such treatment. She caught sight of my horrified expression in an eyewash station mirror and spoke without turning around.

"My former master was cruel. His wife would tend to my wounds."

"Is that when she started teaching you medicine?"

"Yes," she replied as she turned to face me.

"I never knew."

215

"Had you asked, I would have told you the truth."

That was obviously a dig at me, something I didn't expect from Medic, but I guess my dishonesty had hurt her at least as much as the lashes she once received. I walked over and began taking her measurements.

"Why didn't you tell the others about me?" I asked.

"What would I tell them? I'm not certain of what all you're hiding, and I'm not sure I even want to know. Regardless, I could never do that. When you came into their lives, you gave them hope. You gave them something to believe in, and I will not take that away."

I wished I could have been more like her, selfless and caring. Nothing I ever did was really for anyone else. Even my most seemingly altruistic acts were just attempts to mitigate my own pain. I paraded around as if I was making some big sacrifice when in reality, if I saved all of mankind, I would only be breaking even. I finished taking Medic's measurements and left the room.

Chapter 14
Aiden

"How may I help you sir?"

After a few months, I went back to Gendarmerie headquarters asking for Josiah knowing full well he was out that day. The admin at the front desk informed me of such, but I was determined to get to the lift.

"Agent Griffin has sponsored me for a position here, and I wanted to see how that is progressing."

"Well, Detective Price, you can leave a message, and I will ensure that Agent Griffin receives it."

"I am sure you are well aware that an endorsement from a high ranking official such as Special Agent Josiah Griffin is a guarantee of my employment. I would just like to get a headstart with my registration."

The admin looked at his monitor and pulled up my information.

"Yes, I can see that Special Agent Griffin has started the process and is requesting you enter at a higher rank than normal."

"He finds my eagerness impressive."

The admin tapped his fingers on the desk, looked around, then shook his head as he keyed something into his computer.

"I shouldn't be doing this, but since you might very well be my superior soon, I'll let you in."

He took a badge out of his drawer then placed it on a coder next to his desk. He finished my badge and handed it to me.

"This badge gives you very limited access to the building, but the rights are sufficient to get you everywhere you need to go for now. Scan your badge on the lift, and it will take you to the correct floor. If you need to go anywhere else, you'll need an escort."

"Thank you very much.".

I took the badge and wheeled myself over to the lift. I got inside and placed my badge in my pocket, but just as the doors were closing, another fellow slipped in.

"Room for one more?" the agent joked.

I feigned a smile, frustrated at his presence.

"Where are you headed?" he asked.

"I need to go to registration."

"Oh, well do you have a badge? If you scan it, the lift will take you right there."

"I knew I was forgetting something."

I pulled the badge from my pocket and scanned it. The agent then scanned his palm.

"Were you in the army or are you being sponsored?" he asked.

"Sponsored. I have been working with Special Agent Griffin."

He seemed quite surprised when I told him that. Apparently we were a topic of great interest around the office.

"You were in that battle in Zero Alley? Is that how you wound up in the chair?"

"Yes."

"Wow. From what I heard, that was one crazy fight. Is it true you were bested by Zeros?"

"They were armed terrorists backed by Sympathizers," I said defending a rather humiliating loss.

The doors opened on his floor.

"Well, this is my stop, but I would love to hear more about what happened," he said stepping out of the lift.

"I am sure I will see you around."

"Good luck with registration!"

The doors closed, and I quickly put my hand against the scanner. The lift stopped, and I chose Level A.

I made my way back to the Archive room, trying to prepare myself for what I had seen before. Apparently, we were capable of committing unspeakable acts against anyone, not just those we deemed lesser than ourselves. I was already starting to believe the words of the fugitive, but I had to know for sure. I took a breath and spoke.

"Archive, describe societal attitudes towards

homosexuality."

"In which country?"

"North America," I replied.

"Present day?"

"Fifty years ago," I replied as my heartbeat sped up.

"Societal attitudes towards homosexuals have not changed in the past fifty years. Homosexuality was a cultural norm during that time."

I breathed a sigh of relief, but that was to be expected. After all, I was fifty-three years old. I continued.

"One hundred years ago."

"Societal attitudes towards homosexuals have not changed in the past century. Homosexuality was a cultural norm during that time."

My heart rate slowed down to a relatively normal pace. I decided I had been worrying for nothing. I concluded that Kaori knew nothing of history and her *queer* reference must have been grossly exaggerated for my benefit.

Smiling I asked, "And one hundred fifty years ago?"

"Societal attitudes towards homosexuality were near the rate of acceptance that they are today. Most governments and religions had adopted a more tolerant attitude towards homosexuality than in the decades before, and the majority of the country had legalized same sex marriage."

That time my heart stopped.

Near the rate? Most governments? Legalized? Had my marriage been illegal at one time?

I was terrified to hear the answer, but I pressed ahead.

"200 years ago…"

"200 years ago, North America consisted of three distinct countries, Canada, the United States of America and Mexico. Your current region was part of what used to be the United States of America. During that time, sixteen of the fifty states and one district had legalized same sex marriage. Thirty-three states had a ban. However, approximately 60% of the population believed homosexuality should be accepted by society."

Should be? We were not accepted by all of society?

"Many states still had laws against homosexual acts, although such laws were rarely enforced, unlike in foreign countries during the same time. The three major religions of the time, Christianity, Islam and Judaism traditionally forbade homosexuality, however, within each of these religions, there were sects that had adopted a more favorable stance. Even with a growing acceptance of homosexuality, there was still a strong opposition from people with more traditional values."

"Opposition to my existence was once part of a tradition?"

"In a manner of speaking, yes."

I had learned more than I ever wanted to know, but I suspected there was more, a lot more, so I presented one more task.

"Compare today's societal attitudes towards Zeros to those of homosexuals in the past."

"Societal attitudes towards homosexuals in which decade and which countries?"

"200 years ago and earlier in any country."

This time the Archive projected images.

"Attitudes about today's Zeros and yesteryear's homosexuals are very similar. Prior to the twenty-first century, many countries had laws against sexual relations between members of the same gender with some countries imposing punishments such as fines, imprisonment, whippings and public executions. No country had yet recognized same sex marriages and many stereotypes abounded. Homosexuality was synonymous with sexual deviancy and prior to 1970, it was considered a mental disorder."

I wanted it to stop, but I was too flabbergasted to speak.

"Homosexuals were blamed for outbreaks of diseases such as AIDS, a life threatening syndrome which reached epidemic levels in the late twentieth century. Some religious groups blamed homosexuals for natural disasters and the decline of civilizations. Throughout the world, homosexuals were the targets of violence, and it peaked during the Holocaust where more than 15,000 were killed and many more were imprisoned or institutionalized.

Homosexual slurs included but were not limited to bone smuggler, butt pirate, cock gobbler, dyke, fag, faggot…"

"Stop…"

"Fairy, homo, lesbo, muff muncher, mary, queen, queer…"

"Stop!!!"

I had heard enough. The mere thought of living through any of that made me want to cry. Knowing I had treated others the same way my people had once been treated made me sick to my stomach.

"We were the Zeros of that time…?"

"Throughout history, social minorities have always been subject to differential treatment through oppression and unintentional exclusion."

"So it happens to everyone? It is cyclical?" I asked rhetorically but the Archive answered anyway.

"Based on my records, most demographics have been treated as Zeros at some point in history."

So, Classes were not special. We were not superior. We

were just blessed to be born in a century where society allowed us to sit at the head of the table. I watched the Archive's projections and grew increasingly more disturbed. The Trail of Tears, the Holocaust, Slavery, Zulu Kingdom, the Haiti Massacre, Manifest Destiny and others. History was filled with atrocities of mankind. The irony of it all was that I had seen all of this being done to the Zeros, and never once did it give me pause. For the first time I saw myself as I truly was, a monster, and I had dehumanized others to justify my behavior.

Hours later, I rolled into our condominium drained and dejected. You were sitting on the couch watching the holo when I entered. You asked what was wrong, but at that point, it felt more like curiosity than concern. I just shook my head. Even if I could have found the words, I did not have the strength.

"Aiden, there is clearly something wrong. What is it?"

My heart was too heavy and my spirit too low to reply. Still, you persisted.

"Your eyes are red and sunken, you are disheveled. You are

almost never at home. I don't think you even sleep. Tell me what is going on with you!"

"I's fine!" I yelled.

You were taken aback and, at the time, I was not quite sure why you had such fear in your eyes, and I wish I had known that was the last time I would see them. You backed away then retreated to our room.

I steered my chair into the bathroom and locked the door behind me. Then I pulled the liquid Nitro from my pocket and stood up from my chair. I looked at myself in the mirror, but only briefly. My reflection was more than I could bear. I removed the dropper from the bottle and placed a drop in each eye. I had not yet become accustomed to the burn, and I winced at the pain. Once the burning subsided, my body was overcome with a sense of cold. I felt jittery and my heart started racing. That was followed by euphoria and a feeling of invulnerability. One of the more longer lasting effects was a dry mouth and a rather numb tongue, but that was a small price to pay for the feeling I received. I did not need the Nitro anymore because I had done what I needed to do, but it still beckoned me. And honestly I did not care.

That night I dreamed I was chasing Kaori and her friends through the woods. I was closing in on the driver when he tripped over a tree root and landed face first on the forest floor. When I reached him, I turned him around and saw his face was mine. As I strangled the life out of him, I too struggled to breathe. I was killing myself and could not stop. I awoke in a panic.

My mouth was still dry, so I rolled out of bed to get a drink of water. Something did not seem right, but I was too groggy to worry about it. I ambled into the bathroom and turned on the light. I filled a tumbler with water and quickly finished it. I filled it again, and took another long drink, but then I noticed a note on the mirror.

It simply said, "Goodbye."

The tumbler shattered on the travertine floor, and I rushed back to the bedroom. I turned on the light and sent out a pull, opening all the drawers and closet doors simultaneously. All of your things were gone. I began to gasp for air and my heart raced uncontrollably. My com was in my ear, and I tried to ping you, but I could not get it to work. I had used it everyday, but in my panic I could not trigger the correct signals. I found it harder and harder to breathe as the walls were closing in. I started to collapse, so I grabbed the dresser and as I did, I looked in the mirror and I saw the face of the monster and the victim. I screamed, shattering the mirror into tiny shards and shaking our entire building as everything went black.

I awoke the next day to Josiah rapping me on my forehead with his knuckles. I had not moved from the spot where I had fallen.

"I sponsored you for a position with the Gendarmerie and this is how you thank me? Falling into a Nitro induced stupor?" he asked calmly.

"None of that matters now," I replied, resting my face back down on the carpet.

Josiah looked around at the empty drawers and sighed. He

229

lifted me up onto the bed then left the room. He came back with a glass of water and handed it to me.

"Drink this. You're dehydrated, and it'll lessen the symptoms."

I just wanted to sit there with my face buried in my arms, but my mouth was very dry, so I accepted his offer. I finished the glass and let it drop to the floor. Josiah picked it up and stared at it as he showed a fleeting moment of compassion.

"They are… a casualty of the job. What we do, at this level, it doesn't allow us the comfort of companionship. But what we do is important, and it's worth the sacrifice..."

We were the only two people in the room, but his words seemed as if they were meant for someone else.

"Worth it to whom?" I asked.

Josiah looked up from the glass and turned to me.

"We all have regrets, Aiden, but we can't change the past. All we can do is move forward and try to create a better future. It won't make up for everything, but it does make living with our choices a little easier."

Oddly, he was right. I had lost faith in myself, and I had lost you, and without either, I had nothing left. But Josiah had unwittingly shown me what I really needed to do. I could not make up for all the evil things I had done, but I could try to make a better future.

Josiah stood up and placed his hand on my shoulder.

"Get yourself together and get clean, then help me find her, so this is not all in vain. That's what will make it better."

"Yes," I replied, "finding her will make it better."

Chapter 15
Kaori

Godspeed had installed traps, or hidden compartments, in the car, so I was filing them with weapons when Gracie climbed into the back seat next to me.

"What are you doing, little one?" I asked.

"I'm coming with you."

"I can't allow that, Gracie."

"Why not?"

"Because it isn't a good idea."

"Because it's gonna be dangerous?"

"No, not at all."

"Then why so many weapons?"

I looked down at the gun in my hand then over at a rather self-satisfied Gracie. She had her arms folded waiting for my impossible response.

"These are just for Plan B in case something goes wrong."

"And what if something does go wrong?"

Gracie wasn't backing down. Before, she was afraid, pleading for me not to leave her. Now she had become... demanding.

"I need to be there in case it does go wrong!" she exclaimed.

I didn't mean to laugh, and clearly Gracie didn't appreciate it, but I couldn't help it.

"You need to be there so you can protect me?"

"No, I'm just afraid you're gonna die..."

I dropped the gun and wrapped my arms around her.

"Oh Gracie, I thought you were over your fear of me dying."

"I'm not afraid of you dying. I'm afraid of you dying without me."

Confused, I leaned back to look at her.

"Gracie, what are you say..."

"If you're gonna die, then I'm gonna die with you."

I was overcome with anger and sadness when I grabbed her firmly by her shoulders.

"Don't you ever say that! Your parents gave you to me so you could have a long happy life, not so you could wind up like me!"

"But I am like you, Kori, and I can't be happy if you're gone too."

She wasn't even sad about it. She was just certain and determined. I couldn't bear the thought of that sweet little girl resigned to the same fate as myself. There had to be something better for her than this. Better than me, at least. She didn't deserve me, and I certainly wasn't deserving of her.

"It's better that we don't go out in public together since a lot of people are looking for us now. I can't take you with me, but I promise I won't die without you."

Gracie hugged me and gave me a big smile, and, for the first time, her smile made me sad.

Everyone was ready to go, so I went looking for Medic. I

found her in a restroom looking in the mirror and mumbling something. I assumed from her demeanor that she was practicing.

"The trick is to just believe that you belong. If you believe it, so will they," I advised.

"Thanks," she replied softly.

There was still so much tension between us. I just couldn't stand it.

"Medic, I wish I could tell you everything, but…"

"Kaori, stop. I'm about to go watch people be sold as slaves. I cannot possibly imagine how horrible it's going to be, but right now I'm wearing a dress for the first time in a long time, and I feel good."

I nodded and let it go. I hadn't thought about what was best for her. I was just so worried about the guilt and shame that it didn't occur to me that maybe the distance and silence that was killing me was the very thing she needed. I owed her at least that much.

"We're ready," I said and headed back to the car.

It was another silent car ride until we got closer to the auction house. I decided that it would be a good time to give Medic a refresher course in human auctions. The car had a partition, and I pressed the button to raise it, but Godspeed didn't appreciate that.

"What are you doing?" he asked.

"You're a Zero servant. Your master isn't likely to be chopping it up with you."

My explanation left Godspeed no more appreciative, but I raised the partition anyway.

"Okay, we're almost there, so I need to give you some tips."

We had come up with a backstory for Medic that I quickly went over again. Her name was Virginia King, and her parents were applied science engineers out west whose patents provided her with a trust fund. I gave her two bags of gold, one for the deposit before the auction, and the rest for completion of the sale.

"Now, we obviously want Whisper, but you have to act like a real customer and check out all of the merchandise. Go up to them before the auction and inspect them. Check their eyes, arms, legs, teeth…"

"Their teeth?? Like a horse?"

"Yes, like a horse. They're not human to you. They're just property."

"I don't know if I can treat someone that way..."

"We're trying to save Whisper's life. It's this or we go in there with guns blazing and risk more lives than necessary."

"I know," she said pensively.

Medic took the mantra of *primum non nocere* quite literally. She didn't like hurting people, even if it meant helping someone else. She had suffered and seen so much pain in her life that she couldn't bear to pass it on. Admiral, but such traits made martyrs, not survivors. Then again, that didn't matter to Medic. For her, surviving at all costs was futile since we all die anyway.

She once told me, *"How long you live is far less important than how you live."*

"You don't have to treat anyone badly," I reassured her.

"Just do your best to ignore the situation, and show no emotion."

"I'm not like y…"

"Caught the train before it left the station, eh?" I asked.

"Kaori, I didn't… I don't know your sins, and I have no right to judge. Whatever you've done, I know you're working hard to make it right. I'm sorry I was so cold towards you, but I was hurt, and I didn't know how to deal with it."

"It's okay. I deserved it."

"No, Kaori, you did not. I love you. And it's not contingent upon how much good you do in the world, or because you're smart or beautiful, or for anything you have or haven't done. I love you because I love you, and nothing should change that."

They were words I had never heard before, not like that. Not from my parents, not from you. I grabbed Medic and pulled her close. We weren't back, but we were getting there.

"We're here," said Godspeed through our coms.

"Okay, when it's time to bid, be calm and confident. The auctioneer will raise the bid in increments, but if you have competition, you can jump the bid."

"Jump the bid?" she asked.

"Yeah, that's when you yell out a bid significantly higher than what the auctioneer would've offered. It shows the other bidders that you mean business and that can intimidate them. Although, this can also lead to a bidding war. Our pockets aren't as deep as everyone else, so try not to drive the price up too high."

"Well, how do I outbid all other bidders without risking a high price?"

"Only make eye contact with the auctioneer, show no emotion and speak clearly. Let them know you won't be leaving without Whisper."

I told Godspeed he needed to open Medic's door then wait by the car.

"If you believe you belong here, then they will too," I reminded her.

I lowered the window just enough to watch the events while Godspeed stood next to the door. We watched Medic walk over to register at the outdoor auction.

"What if this doesn't work?" Godspeed asked.

"I stashed Plan B in every trap in this car."

Medic made it through registration and headed over to the stage where the slaves were kept. It was kinda far, so I pulled out some binoculars to get a closer look. Medic casually looked the slaves over, then stopped at Whisper. He stood there with his head hanging low. I never thought I'd see him so broken. After Medic checked out his body, she placed her hand under his chin and raised his head. Even from that distance, I could see the hopelessness on his face. Whisper had never met Medic, so he had no idea of our plan. Medic only knew his face from the auction catalogue. I just wanted to reach out and let him know that he still had friends in the world.

"How's it going?" Godspeed asked.

"She's keeping it together so far. Looks like a few people have shown some interest in Whisper, but I'm not worried just yet."

I looked at the faces of the bidders, happy and excited about the day which was in sharp contrast to the faces on stage. The fish and the fisherman share the same story, but they tell it very differently.

Based on the assigned numbers, I could see that it would be awhile before Whisper was up, so I decided to have a snack. I took some jerky from my pocket and offered a piece to Godspeed through the window.

"Thanks," he said, accepting my offer.

"You're standing too proud," I told him.

Godspeed looked at himself then over at me. His head was high, his shoulders were back, and his arms were folded in defiance.

"I know you're a badass, however, the Enforcers don't need such info."

He gave me a half smile, relaxed his posture and took another bite of jerky. It was nice being normal again, or whatever passed for normal between us. We were both well aware that this was just the eye of the storm and the opposite wall would be upon us soon, but rather than waste precious time worrying, we chose to enjoy the calm skies.

"Aren't you concerned about this Backtracker's interest in you?" Godspeed asked.

It was out of nowhere, but I was a little surprised it took so long.

"Somewhat," I replied.

Actually, I was very concerned. Someone posing as a Backtracker was looking for me and I had no idea why.

"You're certain travelling backwards in time is impossible?"

"Very."

"So why would he pose as a Backtracker?"

"I guess he knows I'm displaced in time and figures the hope of getting back where I belong will lure me to him."

"Do you think he's setting a trap for you?"

"No, I think he needs something from me. I just don't know

242

what."

As I continued peering through the binoculars, I noticed Whisper taking center stage.

"He's up!"

Medic briefly looked in our direction then turned up the mic on her com so I could hear. The auction started off slowly with an opening bid of thirty-three ounces of gold, which was about $50,000 in yesterday's money. Medic raised her electronic card, indicating her bid which sent a signal to the auctioneer. A couple others joined in but dropped out early. The bid got up to forty ounces, which was fine because we came with 150. Just as it looked like we were home free at forty, two men entered the bidding.

"What's going on?" asked Godspeed as he noticed my demeanor had changed.

"We have some late bidders."

Godspeed took the binoculars from me.

"I think they're twins," I said.

"Are you sure?"

"Well, they're either twins or they're lovers and one has a Liberace complex," I said as I took the binoculars back.

The brothers looked to be in their fifties, with matching short, blond hair and finely tailored black suits. I thought the whole *let's dress alike so people know we're twins in case they don't notice our matching faces* thing would've gotten old around twelve. Apparently, these two were riding that one trick pony until the hooves fell off.

The bidding had gotten intense, Medic was reaching our limit, and those doppelgangers didn't want to give up. I was ready to tell Godspeed to strap up when the brothers finally conceded at 140.

Medic walked over to collect her winnings and register her new property. She kept her cool throughout, but the discomfort on her face was obvious. She had this faint, tight-lipped smile haloed by pain-filled eyes. That whole scene was torture for her, so it meant a lot that she came through for us.

Once the transaction was complete, a guard escorted Medic and a shackled Whisper over to our car. I slid to the other side so as not to be seen. The guard thanked Medic for her business and went on his way. Godspeed had his head down, so Whisper didn't notice him when he opened the door. The jig was up when he got in the car and saw me smiling.

"What, what's going on here..?" Whisper asked with an expression somewhere between pleasantly surprised and cautious.

"We're here to rescue you, old man. This is my friend, Medic and that's Godspeed up front driving."

"Godspeed?"

Whisper turned to the front of the car, and Godspeed gave him a wave.

"I appreciate your help, but I had my own escape plan."

"Come on, Whisper. You couldn't escape from a paper bag in the rain!" I chided.

Whisper laughed and we hugged as Godspeed drove off. Whisper then turned to Medic, introducing himself and thanking her for her help.

"You know, I'm kind of disappointed that such a beautiful woman isn't going to be my master…"

Medic responded with a silly grin on her beet red face.

"Okay, Loverboy, leave her alone. I need a favor."

"Ha! I knew this new and improved, selfless, altruistic Kaori was too good to be true!"

"You know, technically, you're still our slave," I teased.

"Not if your friend Medic here is a Zero, which I suspect she is."

"Well, I guess we should turn around and return you to your rightful owner…"

"Okay, okay. What do you need?"

I told Whisper about the guy named Shift who was looking for me, and he said someone actually came around asking about me after our melee. Apparently, the news of the fight was a lot more than a buzz. We were practically folk heroes and that was the reason for the raid on Zero Alley. Zeros didn't have the numbers, resources or unity to pull off any sort of coup, but they were an important part of the labor force, and killing them off was bad for business. So, before there was any attempt to revolt, the feds arrested hundreds of people to break their spirits before they even developed. Whisper said the stranger didn't give a name, but he claimed to be a Backtracker who could be of great assistance to me. Whisper denied knowing who I was but kept the guy's info.

"So you know how to reach him?" I asked.

"Yes, I can arrange a meeting if you want."

"That would be great."

"Are you sure, Kaori? This guy seemed a little shady. He might be trouble."

"Oh I'm certain of it, but I still have to meet him," I replied.

We were on the road for about twenty minutes when I noticed Godspeed repeatedly looking at his rear cam. I turned around and saw a black luxury sedan behind us.

"Is there a problem, Godspeed?"

"Someone is following us. Doesn't look like law enforcement."

"Should we outrun them?"

"This vehicle isn't exactly built for high speed chases, of course, neither is theirs."

"Maybe they're just going the same way?" said Medic.

"Doubtful," said Godspeed. "I've taken a few out of the way turns. You guys might wanna strap up."

Just then, the car behind us accelerated, blowing past us then cut us off. Godspeed had to slam on the brakes to avoid hitting them. He reached for a handgun and hid it in his belt while I grabbed an automatic rifle.

"Godspeed, get out of the car and see what they want. Don't get too close or engage them until we know what we're up against," I instructed.

Godspeed complied and stepped out of the car but stayed behind the door and kept his hand on his firearm. Medic and Whisper were a bit shaken up. They weren't used to altercations, but I assured them it would be okay. I wasn't so sure though when twenty seconds went by without any signs of movement from our visitors. A door finally opened and the driver walked over to the passenger side and let a rather large man out of the car.

Huge, muscular frame, wide jaw, oversized hands. **Hitter.** *Limited range of movement. Disorient and attack from behind.*

Behind him were Tweedle Dee and Tweedle Dum from the auction. Apparently, they hadn't given up after all.

"We wish an audience with your master, Zero," said Tweedle Dee.

Godspeed didn't appreciate the disrespectful demeanor, but he kept his cool and opened the door for Medic. He knew we needed to end this as peacefully as possible. Medic looked at me, and I nodded. She was very nervous and didn't know what to expect, but she trusted me. She exited the vehicle but remained close to Godspeed.

"How might I help you gentlemen?" Medic asked as her voice cracked.

"I am Vindego and this is my brother, Vicente. I believe you recall us from the auction."

"I do," Medic replied.

"Well, we were quite disappointed at losing that fine specimen, so we thought we would make you an offer."

"Whisp… the Zero is not for sale, Mr. Vindego. Have a good day," replied Medic as she started to get back in the car.

"Wait! You have not yet heard our offer. It is very generous…"

"I'm sorry, but…"

"We are offering you seventy ounces," interjected Vicente.

"Seventy?!" cried Godspeed. "We paid 140!"

"Why is this Zero speaking to me directly?" asked Vicente. "And why does he say *we* paid?"

"Your offer is refused. Now, we must be on our way."

Medic tried to speak with forcefulness but she was growing fearful of their intentions.

"You have not heard the best part of our offer," said

Vindego.

"It allows you to live," his brother said, and Godspeed pulled out his gun.

"You arm your slaves? Are you a pathetic Sympathizer who buys Zeros only to release them back into the wild?" asked Vicente.

"I doubt this is going to be the smartest decision you make today," said Godspeed.

"Come now," Vindego mused. "You think your two Zeros and you are any match for my brother, our bodyguard and myself?"

That was my cue to join the conversation, so I got out and brandished my fully automatic pulse rifle. It was good for 1,000 shots without recharging and could rip through steel like it was paper.

"Well, now. What kind of party is this?" asked Vindego, surprised at my presence.

"It's about to be a slumber party if you don't get out of our way," I advised.

"Another Zero, I presume?" asked Vicente. "Well, you were warned."

The twins gave no obvious clues as to their Classes, but that was because they were Swaps. Swaps were siblings, usually twins, that could exchange powers on the fly, which made them difficult to fight. If you suppressed one power, they could easily switch to another. That even held true if you hit them with a neutralizer.

The bodyguard made the first move, leaping into the air and smashing the hood of our car. Godspeed and I both hit him with several rounds midair, but he was wearing an impact suit, and it took the brunt of the blasts. Vindego, a Speeder, ran full speed at Godspeed while dodging his bullets. He clipped Godspeed and knocked him over as he flew by and rounded the car towards me. I sidestepped and tripped him into the bodyguard who was coming at me as well. The impact was enough to knock the wind out of the Hitter, and Vindego, so I took my shot. The Speeder got away, but

I ran up on the guard and shot him in the head.

Vicente, a Shocker, sent out an electrical blast at Godspeed, who dove inside the car. Godspeed shot through the windshield, and Vicente ducked behind his car door. The shot to the guard's head only stunned him. Apparently, the suit provided peripheral protection to exposed body parts. He reached through the windshield for Godspeed, and Whisper shot him in the face from the back seat. Unfortunately, that only angered him. The car was still driveable, so Godspeed floored it and drove straight for Vicente and the other car. The twins swapped and Vicente sped out of the way. The guard flew into the other car.

I tried to nail Vicente, but Vindego hit me with a bolt of electricity. Thankfully, I had come prepared with a suit of my own. It provided impact, fire and electrical resistance, but it still hurt like a mother. The suits came in handy as a backup, but it was never a good idea to take a direct hit if you could avoid it. Vindego was coming at me for another shock when Medic grabbed him around the throat and sent a shock through his brain stem with her makeshift electrical harness. He was disoriented, but the twins quickly swapped again and Vicente sent an electrical blast at Medic while Vindego sped off after Godspeed. Medic had no suit so I leaped into the path of the electricity. Again, it hurt like a mother and did some damage to the suit. I managed to take aim at Vicente who was wide open. He panicked and swapped so he could get away, and I immediately turned to the newly slow Vindego and shot him in the back. Vicente cried out as if he had died too. I had never killed a Swapper before, so I was a bit surprised when Vicente became a Diploid, a Class with two powers. He came at me like a lightning bolt surging with energy. He managed to dodge shots from Godspeed and myself, but luckily Whisper knew what an electromagnetic pulse gun was. He shot Vicente in the side and brought him to a complete stop, and I finished the job with a single shot. The bodyguard came to and grabbed Godspeed from behind, but Godspeed used his free hand to shove his pistol into the bodyguard's mouth. The suit offered no protection there.

The driver had been hiding in the car during our skirmish, so Godspeed knocked on the passenger window with his gun. The driver slowly exited the car with his hands raised.

"Turn your hand around," Godspeed ordered with his pistol aimed at his head.

The driver turned his left hand around and revealed the zero burned into the back of it. Godspeed lowered his gun and motioned for the driver to come around to the other side.

"You're a free man if you want," I told him. "But we'll need your word that you'll never speak of this."

He looked at me then back at Godspeed. I figured he'd be elated and heap gratitude upon us. Instead, he reached for a gun lying on the seat on the ground, so Godspeed made him a free man anyway...

We decided that the twins had the most driveable car, so we took theirs. I found a neutralizer in the trunk along with a ball gag and a sex swing. I pulled my sleeve over my hand and grabbed the neutralizer. We moved our car off into a wooded area and placed the bodies nearby. I saw Godspeed staring at the driver like he was waiting for him to answer a question.

"Does it bother you that he was one of our own?" I asked.

"He wasn't one us. He was nothing more than a pet snake trying to shed his own skin."

We dropped Whisper off near Zero Alley before heading back home. He agreed to get back in touch with us once he heard from Shifty. It was fairly late when we got home, but everyone was still up. Gadget had made some rudimentary laser tag guns and sensors so he, Gracie and Jinx were playing in the lobby. Gracie came running around an overgrown palm tree and almost knocked me over. She saw our battle wounds and tattered clothes, then looked down at her laser gun and handed it to me.

"Welcome home."

Chapter 16
Josiah

"Welcome back, Detective Price."

Aiden had pulled himself together and was no longer abusing drugs. He said he had begun taking nitrocodone because his husband had left him, but I wasn't certain. I was also curious about the dosages he had been taking. At a certain dosage, a Class either dies or becomes extremely dangerous, and Aiden obviously had not died. Nevertheless, I allowed him back on the investigation and made him a Gendarme. He was vital to finding the fugitive, and he seemed to have a renewed interest in the case.

We had raided the automobile factory months ago, but due to his injuries, Aiden wasn't with us, and we never saw any signs of the fugitive or her friends. I decided to return and bring Aiden with me. The factory was barren and well combed, but Aiden still managed to find more evidence. I watched Aiden as he pored over some scraps of metal.

"Old automobile parts?" I asked.

"Some, but other parts are an alloy I have never seen before. I suspect these items were modified to build weapons. It also looks like at least five people might have been living here."

"Any chance it's just a coincidence? Maybe someone else was holed up here? It's common for Zeros to take up residence in abandoned buildings," I said.

"Unlikely. I have found evidence of soldering, metallurgy, surgery. All skills that your average Zero does not possess, and most Classes do not need. However, these are the exact skills that Kaori and her associates would require."

"Any idea how long they've been gone?"

"Maybe a month before you started observing, but that is just a guess. They did a very good job hiding their tracks."

"Not good enough, apparently."

I was extremely frustrated that they had slipped away before we got to them, but Aiden assured me that all was not lost. Since some of the materials they had used were not easy to come by, narrowing down their suppliers was our key to picking up their trail again.

"Did anything come from the raid in Zero Alley?" Aiden asked.

"Not really. Most of the big players escaped our net. Including D'Arco."

"Do you think D'Arco is connected to her?"

"What is D'Arco not connected to?" I asked.

It didn't matter that D'Arco and his crew escaped. Even if he knew the girl, he would never betray her, even though she was a Zero. It wasn't that he was so honorable or noble or even a Sympathizer. In fact, he was an absolute cad, but his hatred of authority outweighed his lack of love for anyone else. D"Arco would rather have died than give us the hour of day.

"I ran a query for local suppliers," said Aiden, "and found one nearby."

"Come on then."

Once Aiden and I reached the outside of the factory, we

saw some Zeros standing around.

"They look us in the eye now," I said.

I looked over at Aiden, but he seemed distracted, not the focused detective I had come to know.

"Aiden?"

"I am sorry. I was elsewhere," he said.

"Do you see them?"

Aiden looked up and saw the Zeros openly watching us. Usually, they ran and hid in the presence of any Class, let alone law enforcement. Gendarmerie should've had them scattering like rats.

"They're starting to question our might," I said.

I had come to expect violent outbursts from Aiden when it came to Zeros, but there was nothing. He barely even acknowledged what I had said.

"Let them stare. They cannot harm us," he replied.

"Not too long ago, we would've said the same thing about the fugitive."

The electronics supplier was in a rundown area of an old city, thirty minutes from the factory. It was a four story warehouse with peeling paint and filthy windows. We entered the building and saw the owner beating one of his Zeros with a rod while others looked on as if they had no fear of retribution. The tearing of flesh echoed throughout the warehouse. The errant Zero, however, took the caning in silence. I noticed Aiden had a clenched jaw and narrowed eyes, seemingly troubled by what we were seeing. I was confused as he had mercilessly tortured Zeros and even leveled a building trying to catch our fugitive, yet he was somehow disturbed by what lay before us. The punishment ended when the rod shattered on the Zero's back, causing the splintering wood to slice open the owner's hand. He cried out in pain. As he assessed his wound, he caught sight of us near the entrance.

"Uh, hello…"

The owner greeted us with caution and anxiety as he wrapped his bleeding hand in a rag.

"I am Special Agent Griffin and this Agent Price. We are

with the Gendarmerie. Can I assume that you are Bardon Louse, the owner?"

"Yes, yes I am," replied Bardon. "I'm sorry you had to witness that. Zeros get out of line from time to time. Sometimes you need the rod to put them back in their place. You know how it is," he said while looking at Aiden.

"I do not," Aiden replied.

I began to wonder how much of his behavior was attributed to Carson leaving.

"Mr. Bardon, have you seen this woman before?" I asked showing him a holo of the fugitive.

He looked at the image but failed to recognize her.

"I would remember if I had. I don't get very many women as customers."

I was fearful that a promising lead was just another dead end, but Aiden had not quite given up.

"Do you have any customers who frequent your establishment, looking for items such as these?"

Aiden pulled out some circuitry and some metal parts from his coat pocket. Bardon looked them over.

"These circuits might have come from anywhere, but this alloy, this is my own special recipe."

"Do you keep records of all of your customer purchases?" I asked.

"Just the electronic ones." He replied.

"We are looking for someone who always makes purchases with gold, a frequent customer who possibly lives close by," said Aiden.

"Oh, you are looking for Tinker…"

"Tinker?" I asked.

"I don't know his true name. I call him that because he buys a lot of this stuff to make things."

"Is he a Zero?" asked Aiden."

"No! Never!" Bardon anxiously replied. "I would never sell such things to a Zero. They're not even allowed in my shop without their masters present!"

"Relax, Mr, Louse. You're not in trouble, but we will need you to have a mind reading," I said.

"Certainly," agreed Bardon.

I called headquarters and ordered a Reader to meet us at the warehouse, while Bardon waited nervously in his office. Once Aiden and I were away from other ears, I questioned the earlier performance.

"Since when do you care what happens to a Zero?"

Aiden wasn't shocked by my question, and his response was rather matter of fact.

"I do not," he replied without looking at me.

"So, that rod shattered on its own?"

Still, without looking, Aiden replied, "If you push long enough and hard enough, something is going to break."

Clearly, Aiden was still pursuing the fugitive, but I couldn't help believing he had other motives. Nevertheless, he was still my best option. I just needed to keep an eye on him at all times.

After Bardon had his reading, we returned to headquarters

to go over the evidence with the lab technicians. The Reader had culled an image of a black male, possibly in his early thirties, six feet in height with an athletic build. He didn't match any of the suspects we had on file, so we used facial recognition on the Zero database. We soon found a match for a RWitt08. He belonged to a man named Renore Witt who worked as an applied and mechanical engineer. Witt ran a very successful business designing weapons and security systems for government entities until Sympathizers launched an attack on him. His slaves were freed and everything he had was destroyed. It appeared RWitt08 had the rare drive to learn from his master and built on that knowledge. Knowledge which made him a very dangerous man.

"I guess this explains how she can appear to be a Class at will," I said with frustration.

I could only imagine what other surprises lay in store.

"Clearly, she is supported by some very knowledgeable people," Aiden responded, almost with a tone of admiration.

"She might only be the tip of the iceberg. There could be a

whole network of Zeros and Sympathizers involved," I replied.

"Kaori is the only one we need. Once we find her, this all ends."

I didn't understand why Aiden said that. She obviously had powerful people helping her that could undoubtedly continue to wreak havoc in her absence, and we had yet to discern their intentions, but Aiden had already determined what it took to end all of this.

"What makes you so certain?" I asked.

"It all began with her."

I was not satisfied with his answer, but it was clear that Aiden had no intention of revealing all that lay in his mind. I decided to wait it out. Sooner or later he would play his hand.

I left the lab and headed towards my office so I could prepare for a meeting with Governor Mathias. He had ramped up the the anti-Zero rhetoric, and Congress was in talks to vote on bringing back martial law. I needed to talk the governor out of moving forward with it.

On my way back to my office, I was stopped by a service tech.

"Special Agent Griffin, I'm still working on the ventilation issues on Level A, but I had to order some parts. Hopefully I can have it fixed soon."

I was quite perplexed as to why he felt the need to tell me that, and he must have seen the confusion on my face.

"Since you've been accessing that floor a lot lately, I thought you might like to know."

"Oh. Yes, I appreciate that very much."

Somehow someone had cloned my biometric signature in order to access the Archive. I knew not of any powers that could do that, but I did know who might be determined enough to find a way.

I returned to my office and pulled up the log of my activities in the building. There were several entries showing I had visited the Archive over the past few weeks even though I hadn't. I pulled up the accompanying holographs and each one was out of focus. So much so that I couldn't tell if the impersonator was a male or female. I didn't know what power could clone biometrics, but I did know that a level 10 Mover on nitrocodone could easily bend light.

I knew the Governor would hold me responsible if my trainee was any type of traitor, so I decided to keep my suspicions to myself. As I pondered the situation, Mathias contacted me through my com.

"Good afternoon, Josiah."

"Hello, Mathias. Is our meeting still as scheduled?"

"Somewhat. Meet me on the roof."

"The roof.." When, sir?"

"Now."

It was an exceptionally windy day, probably more so being on the roof. Mathias was waiting for me at the rear of the building standing uncomfortably close to the edge. I walked over to him, but didn't venture as close to the edge as he.

"Nice day isn't it, Josiah?"

"It's a bit windy, especially so close to the edge."

Mathias turned and pulled me closer.

"Josiah, surely you are not afraid of death?"

"No, sir, I'm not afraid of death, but I'm in no rush to meet it either."

"Of course not," he said, looking out over the cityscape, "Not with so much beauty lying before us. The city looks so peaceful, but somewhere out there in a back room or a hidden attic is someone who wants to destroy that peace and upset our perfect balance. Zeros have the opportunity to live a good life as long as they follow our laws and know their place, but these upstarts are giving them ideas, causing them to question our way of life."

"Sir, are you campaigning…?"

"Actually, I'm working on a speech to rally support for the return of Martial Law. You know, two very close friends of mine were murdered by those fugitives."

"I'm sorry to hear that."

"Don't be. While I mourn their loss, it still works in my

favor. Tomorrow I'm holding a press conference."

"A press conference, sir?"

"Yes, Josiah. Not every war is fought on the battlefield. The public needs to know that we will protect them. I want you and Agent Price with me."

"I don't know if that's a good idea."

"Why? I'm not asking you to speak."

Aiden was too unstable to stand beside the Governor during a national broadcast. He was too unpredictable, but I couldn't tell the Governor that.

"I don't project well."

"I did not envision you as a vain man, Josiah."

"I'm not. I just don't enjoy the public eye, and I don't imagine Agent Price does either."

"Nonsense. The Zeros have their face of this conflict. It is time we showed the nation ours."

Later that day, I informed Aiden that we were to be the face of law enforcement for the nation to counter the cult of personality that the fugitive was creating. I stressed that he needed to be at his best during the broadcast.

"Are you saying that I do not know how to behave myself in public?"

"You just haven't been yourself lately, Aiden, and I'm concerned."

"You need not concern yourself with me, Josiah. I have everything under control."

His words brought me no comfort at all. In fact, they concerned me more.

The next day, a huge crowd gathered outside of Gendarmerie headquarters to hear the Governor speak. Several streets were blocked off for security. Ordinarily, the Governor didn't take such precautions, but he wanted to reinforce the threat that Zeros could pose if they got out of control.

Aiden and I stood near center stage waiting for the Governor to arrive. I looked over the crowd and noticed some strategically placed Zeros. They had much bigger smiles than I was used to seeing and showed great enthusiasm for the Governor, but that is the nature of politics. Nevertheless, those Zeros were no concern of mine. I was keeping my eyes open for the fugitives. I looked over at Aiden who appeared to be in another world. His eyes seemed to meander through the crowd with no sense of purpose.

"Any sign of them?" I asked.

"She will not be here. The Governor is not her target."

"What makes you so sure?"

"None of this begins or ends with him."

"And you believe that's her goal? To end our way of life?"

"Or maybe just to end hers."

"Are you getting soft, Aiden? Life has winners and losers, so for them to win, we must lose, and it's our job to ensure that we do not lose," I said adamantly.

"A Zero-sum game?" Aiden mused at his pun. "No need for a philosophical lecture. I was merely offering a possible explanation."

Aiden's reply was so evenly keeled. Not in the way of contentment, but more like there was something missing. Either Carson, the nitrocodone, or encounters with the fugitive had taken something from him. Or maybe something was missing all along and he had just realized it.

Governor Mathias soon arrived and took the stage. He began his speech and a hush fell over the crowd.

"Greetings my fellow North Americans. I come to you today with a heavy heart, laden with grief. I am certain the majority of you have heard of the attacks on law enforcement officials by Sympathizers and Zeros in Zero Alley. Some have tried to glamorize these people as heroes, but they are not. They are outlaws. They are terrorists. Three weeks ago, they slaughtered two brothers, family men, in cold blood and left their bodies on the side of the road to rot. These criminals' very existence threatens the peace and harmony that we have all come to enjoy. If these terrorists continue their assault on our way of life, then I will have no choice but to impose curfews and authorize more raids.

273

Martial Law must return! Anyone aiding these felons will be charged as co-conspirators and held equally responsible for all crimes committed. However, anyone aiding in their capture will be rewarded with 30,000 ounces. In addition, if the informant is a Zero, he or she will be granted full emancipation."

The feigned enthusiasm became quite real when the reward was mentioned. Anyone so easily bought did not deserve freedom.

"Here beside me is Special Agent Josiah Griffin and Agent Aiden Price. They are the leads on this manhunt. Combined, they have many decades of experience, and I assure you they will catch these terrorists, but your assistance would still be beneficial."

The Governor continued his speech to the thunderous applause of the audience as Aiden looked right through them.

Chapter 17
Kaori

"Please tell me you're watching a holo."

"I am, Gadget," I replied back into my com.

I was in the middle of training Gracie when I saw Governor Mathias holding an extremely rare press conference. He had connected us to the twins and was offering 30,000 ounces of gold for our heads, as if my life wasn't complicated enough.

"They're showing images of you, Gracie, Jinx, and… me! How did they get my image?! I've never been seen with you!"

"They are Gendarmerie. They have their ways."

They didn't show Deadeye, Godspeed or Medic, so I assumed Gadget's trips for supplies are what put him on their radar. I figured it was only a matter of time before we were all named.

"Now Gadget is in trouble," said Gracie. "If you hadn't met me that day, no one would know who you were."

I didn't want such a young child trying to bear the burden of guilt.

"If I hadn't met you, then my life wouldn't even matter," I said, touching her face.

"We still need to address the matter of my face being projected all over the country!" said Gadget.

"Relax, Gadget. It might get you some groupies."

"Groupies? What's a groupie?"

It had been a few weeks since the auction, and I'd spent most of that time training Gracie in self defense. I was so proud of her progress, but it pained me just the same. A little girl should have the opportunity to be a little girl. I guess there were no little girls left, though. Just survivors. Things were still tense in Zero Alley, so Jinx remained with us. She was a great help with Gracie, and provided some much needed levity to our group.

"Hey! Just heard from Whisper!" said Godspeed as he flung open the door to my room.

Whisper had us meet him in a city called Circleville. It was about thirty minutes from where we were living, but we took back roads for safety reasons and stretched it out to an hour. We had no clue who this Shifty was, so I took Jinx, Deadeye and Godspeed with me. We met Whisper in the parking lot of some greasy spoon. I was tempted to try their home fries, but we were on a schedule. We started to get out, but Whisper squeezed into the front seat with Godspeed and I instead.

"We need to talk," Whisper said with urgency.

"Where is he?" Godspeed asked.

"I'll take you to him, but first we need to talk about the fiasco after the auction."

"Why? What's going on, Whisper?" I asked.

"Drive down this road for about five miles. Those twins you rescued me from...."

"Yeah, we saw that they connected us to their deaths," I replied.

"How they know was you?" asked Jinx.

"We used guns, which means the culprits were most likely

Zeros, and we're the most likely Zeros. After all, we've made quite a name for ourselves when it comes to killing Classes," I replied.

"You don't understand," Whisper continued, "these men were personal friends of the Governor. That speech he gave was a ruse. He is coming down hard on all Zeros regardless and blaming you guys for everything."

"How can he blame us for his raids?" I asked.

"They're making false claims about you hiding in neighborhoods and taking refuge with citizens. They're labeling people as Sympathizers then killing them. He's trying to make everyone afraid to be within 100 yards of you. His ultimate goal is to legalize Martial Law and have absolute power."

"We won't be safe anywhere if that happens," I said.

"Not everyone hates you. There are still people, Zeros and Sympathizers alike, who stand behind you. They see through what the Governor is doing," said Whisper.

"And what about this Shift character we're meeting?" Godspeed asked. "How do we know he's not someone who wants our heads?"

"Trust me, he doesn't. Turn here."

We turned down some old dirt road that lead to what appeared to be an abandoned farm. I saw a barn in the distance that looked as if it could be razed by a good sneeze. There were no other buildings, and the fields were nothing but overgrown grass.

"What do you see, Gadget?" I asked.

"I only have one heat signature, and it's coming from that barn."

Everything looked okay, but I had a bad feeling. If were in a movie, that would've been the part where the audience yells, *"Don't go in there!"*

Godspeed stopped a safe distance from the barn, and we all cautiously stepped out of the car and looked around. Well, except for Whisper who trotted right up to the barn door.

"Come on," he beckoned.

"Whisper, I swear if this is a trap, you're gonna be pouring drinks with your feet!" said Godspeed.

Whisper just shook his head and went inside. One by one we entered. I took up the rear making sure no one came up behind us. Once I entered, I turned to see everyone staring at a shadowy figure.

"Hello, Kaori," he said in a voice that triggered my anxiety.

I couldn't understand why I felt so uneasy until he stepped forward and showed his face, and then all I saw was red. After that, I just remembered Deadeye and Godspeed pulling me off of him. His blood covered his face, my shirt and my hands.

"Kaori!" Deadeye yelled, "What are you doing!? Who is this guy?"

I managed to flip Godspeed onto his back, shove Deadeye away and leap back on the bastard.

"Kaori," he pleaded, "you don't understand..!"

"I understand you're a lousy piece of shit, and I'll fucking kill you!"

This time all three guys came for me, but after a few low blows, they quickly regretted that decision. Jinx stepped in and blinded me with a flash of light.

"KK, stop. He cannot hurt you."

I looked up at her, and even with my vision impaired I made out the fear on her face. I looked down at the frail pathetic waste of skin, and Jinx was right. He couldn't hurt me, not anymore than he already had. I stood up and walked over to a post and released my fury on it with a single punch. It felt like the rickety structure would collapse on our heads, and that was just fine with me. *Shift* struggled to his feet with Jinx's help and wiped the blood from his face with his tattered jacket.

"Not quite the welcome I was hoping for," he said with blood-stained teeth.

I made a move for him again, but stopped when Deadeye stood in my way.

"It's not in your best interests to test her," said Godspeed.

"Trust me, Godspeed, I know her far better than you do."

"How do you know my name?"

"I know all of you."

"I saw you die," I said as the words crawled through my grinding teeth.

"I survived. Unfortunately, I won't for much longer without your help."

"You want my help??!!"

"I offer mine as well."

"What could you possibly offer me?!"

"The cure," he replied, then coughed up blood and collapsed.

"Who is he?" asked Deadeye.

"David Protos. The fucking traitor who stole my life from me."

At first we thought I had seriously injured him, but it was soon apparent that something else going on. The others convinced me that we needed to get him back to Medic. They figured if there was a chance he could help, then it was worth hearing what he had to say. Personally, I just wanted him dead.

We made it back home, and Protos was coming back

around. I managed to allay my anger long enough to really look at him. He was much paler than I remembered and his face was sunken. He was having trouble breathing and could barely walk without assistance. Something was really wrong.

"Is this the Backtracker?" Medic asked when we got inside.

"It was all a lie, Medic," Godspeed replied. "This fellow is Kaori's Skipper."

Medic looked on with shock.

"He doesn't look well," she said.

"That's because I'm dying, my dear."

"Then die already," I ordered.

"He needs medical attention," Medic insisted as she looked him over.

"There is nothing you can do, doctor," Protos replied.

"What do you want?" I asked. "Why are you here?"

"Well, our dear friend, Cordell, infected me with a virus, a deadly one…"

My mouth fell at his words and my eyes met Medic's.

"I got sick soon after we skipped, and after a little investigation, I realized my Class was killing me."

My mouth trembled and my heart raced. I didn't want to hear those things.

"Why... why would Cordell do such a thing..?"

"Insurance," Protos replied before coughing up more blood.

"I need to check you out," Medic insisted.

With Deadeye's help, she took him to an examination room.

Gracie and Jinx went off to play while the rest of us waited in the Rec room for hours. I sat in a corner by myself trying to make sense of what Protos had said.

Why would you infect us with a virus. Was I going to die too?

For so long I had seen Protos as my mortal enemy. Suddenly I didn't know what to believe.

Medic entered the room, and I jumped to my feet. The others mistook my anxiety for concern.

"Well?" Godspeed asked.

"He's infected with a virus…" Medic answered as her eyes found mine, "…but it's unlike anything I've seen before."

My body and soul exhaled with relief.

Medic continued, "I've managed to get the infection under control, but his condition is still terminal. He said he needs the same cure that we are seeking."

"If he knows where the cure is, then we don't need to go back to D'Arco," said Godspeed.

"He could be lying," I replied. "We should just give him over to D'Arco and be done with it."

"Don't let your feelings cloud your judgment, Kaori," said Godspeed.

"My feelings?" I practically screamed. "He dragged me 200 years into the future, robbing me of everything I have ever known, and you think we can trust him!? If he knows where the cure is, why doesn't he have it?"

"Because I need your help getting it."

285

Protos was out of bed and standing at the door. He looked better, but still similar to something a cat coughed up.

"I'm obviously dying, so there's no reason for me to lie."

"I'd rather take my chances by giving you to D'Arco," I said.

"I'm not surprised," Godspeed quipped.

"That's why you sought me out? Because D'Arco wants me? What's he offering you?"

"He can help us get the cure," Deadeye answered.

A weak laugh escaped Protos' mouth.

"How would D'Arco know where the cure is? You don't need him. Only I can get the cure."

"Honestly, Kaori, checking out Protos' story seems a lot easier than rummaging through the Archive," said Deadeye.

"The Archive?" Protos asked.

"D'Arco will give us access to the Archive in exchange for you," I replied. "I figure the Archive can tell us what happened the day we skipped, and perhaps lead us to where the cure might be hidden.

Protos slumped into a chair and covered his face.

"Great..."

"What?" asked Godspeed.

"I had hoped you already had access to the Archive," he said.

"What does that matter?" Deadeye asked.

"I know where the cure is supposed to be, but I need the Archive to find the exact location."

"You're worthless! Let's just deliver him to D'Arco! He doesn't know any more than we do!" I said.

"Cordell told me he would hide the cure for us to find in the future in case things didn't go as planned," said Protos.

I was taken aback. His words made no sense.

"What are you talking about? If he told you he would hide it for us to find in the future, that means he knew that mob was coming and how far we'd skip. There's no way he'd send me away knowing that. And he certainly wouldn't do it without telling me."

"Just like he wouldn't give me a deadly virus?"

For all of his shadiness, I couldn't think of a reason why Protos would be lying. He was indeed dying, and like us, he needed the Archive. Tying his life to our mission certainly would ensure that the job was done, but you would never do that. Infect him... me... without telling us. *Would you?* My head was spinning as I questioned everything I thought I knew.

"So basically," Godspeed began, "If we take you to D'Arco, we get the Archive, but we won't know what to query. But if we don't turn you over, we'll know where the cure is, but have no way to find it."

"Essentially," Protos replied.

"You could tell us what to query," I mumbled.

"Seriously? Why would I do that? Out of the kindness of my heart?"

"Silly me," I replied. "For that, you'd need kindness and a heart!"

"We could get the cure and come back for you," Deadeye

suggested to which Protos let out a sickly laugh.

"Even if I trusted you, I would be long dead by the time you returned. You think D'Arco wants to have a gentlemanly talk to clear the air?"

"We could pay D'Arco off," said Gadget. "We have sixteen ounces."

"Sixteen ounces?"

Protos was confused.

"You think D'Arco will accept, what, $25,000 for me?"

He let out another laugh which sounded more like Whooping Cough.

"Why wouldn't he?" Deadeye asked. "That's what you owe him."

"Is that what he told you? That I owe him sixteen ounces of gold? This isn't about money. This is about you," Protos said, looking at me. "I left D'Arco's camp shortly before any of you joined. I wound up getting myself in some legal trouble, so I offered law enforcement a tip…"

289

"That was you?!" said Godspeed. "You were responsible for that raid? We could've been killed! Or worse!"

"I know. I was desperate. Apparently, D'Arco and Kaori were having troubles, and you were turning her head."

Godspeed and I looked shamefully at each other.

"The raid went down, and everyone scattered. By the time the dust settled and everyone got reunited, you two were all hot and heavy."

"You fool! D'Arco is after you for ratting him out. Not because of me!" I argued.

"Then why did he lie about the money?"

It was a valid question, another of which I had no answers for.

"The raid is part of it, but it was really more about him losing you. You were gone for months. He blames me for depriving him of the chance to fix what was wrong. All the money in the world won't satisfy him."

"So we're done. There is nothing we can do," said

Godspeed.

He expressed a sentiment that we all shared. We could threaten Protos for the information, but he was dying, so he really had nothing to lose, and it was unlikely that D'Arco would settle for anything less than Protos' hide. All seemed lost.

"There is one way we could pull this off."

We all looked at Protos, waiting for whatever unscrupulous suggestion might spill forth from his mouth. He did not disappoint.

"We could doublecross D'Arco."

I was so appalled I wanted to throttle him.

"Are you insane?" I asked.

"I'm willing to hear a more plausible plan if there are any available," Protos replied.

As dangerous as it was, it seemed like our best bet, but still, I didn't want to even consider such a thing.

"Maybe, Shift is right," said Godspeed.

"His name is Protos!" I shouted. "And he is not right! We can't do that to D'Arco."

"Why not?" Godspeed asked.

"Because I cannot bear to hurt him anymore than I already have."

Protos had robbed me of love, and I had paid it forward to D'Arco. I lived with that pain cutting through me like a dull knife everyday. Betraying D'Arco again would destroy him, along with any self-worth I had left.

"Your feelings for him mean more than saving millions of lives?" Godspeed asked.

"Don't go there, Godspeed. This isn't about us. D'Arco is our friend..."

"No, he is your friend! He can barely stand me," Godspeed retorted.

"Maybe we should consider this," Deadeye spoke.

"Et tu, Deadeye? What is wrong with everyone?" I cried.

"Honey, I get that you don't wanna betray D'Arco," Deadeye replied. "I don't either. But if I have to choose between indulging his grievances and ending this war..."

"You don't understand…"

"I understand that D'Arco's pain matters more to you than that of everyone else," Godspeed replied.

I didn't really feel that way, but I guess, essentially, that's what my words were saying. I had to choose between his pain and theirs, and, ironically, I had caused them both.

"Jinx would never go along with this," I muttered.

"She's right. Jinx won't betray D'Arco," said Deadeye.

"Then what?" Gadget asked. "We just don't tell her?"

"I think she'll catch on when bullets start flying," Godspeed replied.

"If it comes down to an altercation, we'll explain it to her, then let her decide," I said.

Tears streamed down my face. I couldn't believe what I had agreed to do. I was preparing to turn on people I had known and loved for years. No matter what the outcome, I knew there could be no real winners, only more pain left in the wake of the storm known as my life.

We decided it was best not to tell D'Arco that we were coming. The less prepared he was the better. We, on the other hand, needed to be prepared as possible. Gadget brought the twins' neutralizer with us. He said it was just in case we encountered the law again, but we all knew it was for Jinx. I gave it to Deadeye because there was no way I could have used it on her.

Once again, we were leaving Medic and Gracie behind, and Gracie was none too happy about that. She thought the few lessons I had given her made her qualified to run missions with us.

"You're not ready, little one," I told her.

She rolled her eyes and folded her arms as she watched me gather my weapons.

"I went with you to Zero Alley last time."

"First of all, that was a mistake. And secondly, we're not going to Zero Alley. D'Arco has a new hideout."

"Why can't I go?"

"I told you. You aren't ready."

"But, Kori, you need someone to watch your back."

"You needn't worry about that, Gracie. Everything is gonna be fine."

Jinx came in the room to let me know everyone was ready. While she was there, Jinx said goodbye to Gracie.

"I not know when I be back, Gray. Dee prolly miss me lots."

"I'll miss you lots, Jinx…"

Jinx reached down and gave Gracie a big hug.

"No worry, Gray. I see you again."

"Promise?" Gracie asked.

"Promise."

Jinx hugged Gracie again and they kissed each other on the cheek.

"Don't be strange," Gracie told Jinx.

"Stranger," I replied. "Don't be a stranger."

"Oh yeah, don't be a stranger."

"Jinx never be a stranger to you, Gray."

As Jinx stood to walk away, Gracie smiled and held onto

her finger. Jinx turned around and continued walking until Gracie was holding on by just the tip. Jinx paused, smiled, then took another step as Gracie released her grip, but their hands lingered in the air for several seconds as if still connected.

"They sent me to get you two," said Medic as she entered the room.

"We're leaving," I replied.

"Why all the guns?" Jinx asked.

"In case shit gets real," I replied.

"Is the shit not real?" Jinx asked.

I looked down at Gracie and saw her head nestled in Medic's side.

"Everything's gonna be fine," I said.

"You should stop saying that," Gracie replied. "You're always wrong."

I held onto the door jamb briefly before following Jinx out the door and starting our long drive.

Zero Alley was still hot, so D'Arco took up residence in

one of our old hideouts fifty odd miles away. It was an old McMansion, reminiscent of 90's decadence. It was in rather surprisingly good shape for a 220 year old house built using shoddy materials and subpar construction. Nevertheless, it was Jinx's favorite hideout, because it was the only one that felt like a real home. Real bedrooms, bathrooms not restrooms, a kitchen, even a fenced in yard. Truth be told, it was my favorite too.

When we got close enough, I commed D'Arco. We wanted to arrive unannounced, but not too unannounced. A strange car pulling into a cul- de-sac would put them on their guard, and that was the last thing we wanted.

"D'Arco, we're close, and we have your package."

"Kaori? How close? I thought you would've called first," D'Arco replied.

"I'm calling right now. We're five minutes away. What's the matter? You're not decent?"

"I am. We're just about to have dinner. I'll just have Cleves set a few more places at the table."

"Make it five more. Six if you plan on giving your prisoner his last meal."

Protos didn't appreciate my last remark, but I had to sell it.

The house sat at the end of the longest cul-de-sac I had ever seen, which made an easy getaway somewhat problematic. We took notice of the guards looking out of the windows of the two houses at the cul-de-sac entrance.

"One way in. One way out," said Deadeye.

"One way is all I need," Godspeed replied.

Jinx was too preoccupied with excitement to catch what they were saying. She was just happy to see her family again. Bully was at the end of the driveway when we pulled up. He came out armed, but that wasn't unusual. He motioned with his automatic rifle for us to park our car in a neighboring garage. He stood there stone faced as we approached until Jinx ran and teleported into his arms.

"Bully! Missed you much!"

"Hey, Jinx, girl! Missed you too! Been gone long time!"

Bully looked over Jinx's shoulder and saw me escorting Protos in shackles. We were all armed, but Bully must have assumed it was for Protos and didn't bother to ask us for our weapons. He put Jinx down and walked over to Protos.

"Been gone long time for you too, Shift."

"What's the matter, Bully? You miss me?"

Bully hit him in the jaw with the butt of his rifle, knocking him from my hands.

"Hey! Watch it! He's still mine until I hand him over to D'Arco, and I'd like to hand him over intact!"

I picked Protos up and shoved him up the driveway.

"He won't be intact for long," Bully said.

Most of us knew the way, but Bully still escorted us to the dining room. One side of the huge dining table had been reserved for us and the food was plentiful. Apparently, there was some sort of celebration we were crashing.

"Come in! Come in!" said D'Arco.

Jinx ran over and gave him a hug and told him how much

she missed him.

"What's the occasion?" I asked.

D'Arco smirked.

"I'm hurt," he replied. "I thought you chose this special day on purpose."

It was his birthday… I was always bad with dates, but was especially so after the world went to hell. If forgetting his birthday was hurtful, pulling a gun out on him during cake and ice cream was gonna kill him.

"Happy Birthday! Here's your present!" I said, offering up Protos.

"Hello, Shift. You're a difficult man to find," said D'Arco.

"Hey, D'Arco, I called. I left messages. I even sent you letters, but you didn't leave a forwarding address."

"Still every bit of a smart ass, eh? Nevermind that for now. Today is a celebration."

D'Arco motioned for his goons to bring Protos to him then sat back down in his chair.

"Let's all eat!"

"There's still the matter of our payment," I reminded him.

D'Arco looked up to see us all still standing. He knew then that something wasn't right.

"Sit," D'Arco insisted.

He nodded to a guy on the other side of the room who nodded back and then left.

"I didn't forget your payment, but let's have pleasure before business. Cleves, come serve my guests."

I nodded to my group, and we all took our seats. Cleves entered from the kitchen and prepared our plates. As he served each of us, D'Arco and I did not break eye contact. All of D'Arco's crew had begun eating by the time the one fellow returned with a box which he handed to me.

D'Arco wiped his mouth and pointed to the box.

"There are gloves and contact lenses in there that will get you past the biometric scanners. They will cycle through several hundred possible bio codes to ensure your entry. There is also information on where you can find the Archive. The closest one is in Gendarmerie headquarters. These things will get you inside, but I cannot guarantee that you will survive. I hope whatever it is you wish to find in there is worth it. Now, let's enjoy this fine meal."

I took a deep breath and exhaled whatever normalcy was left in my life. D'Arco took a pause from his merriment and noticed none of us were eating.

"Is the food not to your liking?" he asked which gave his crew pause as well.

I reached into my pocket and placed the bag of gold on the table.

"We wish to renegotiate the terms of our agreement," I replied.

A cacophony of forks clanging against dinner plates followed. We immediately felt a thick cloud of tension move into the room, and everyone's hands disappeared below the table.

"Renegotiate?" D'Arco asked. "You delivered my package, and I gave you access to the Archive. There is no negotiating after the fact."

"There are sixteen ounces of gold in that bag, the amount you said Protos… Shift owes you. We'd like to buy his freedom."

I tried to speak casually as if what I was proposing was perfectly reasonable, hoping that somehow my Jedi mind trick would convince D'Arco of such, but that was a fool's hope. D'Arco picked up the bag and examined its contents.

"Have you two suddenly become the best of friends? Or is this the latest stud you've allowed in your stable?"

Godspeed tensed and started to raise his gun, but I quickly grabbed his arm.

"Shift is the Skipper who brought me here."

D'Arco looked at Protos then back at me as if he was trying to make sense of it all.

"So, you're wanting to enact your own revenge?"

"No, D'Arco. I'm not looking for revenge. A pound of flesh is the most expensive cut of meat you'll ever buy, right?"

D'Arco smiled.

"Well, I've been saving up, so I can afford it," he answered.

"We need him to finish our mission," I said.

I was almost pleading, but D'Arco was unmoved. In fact, he was becoming more and more agitated.

"That is not my concern."

He threw the bag of gold back across the table.

"There will be no further negotiations."

D'Arco picked up his fork and began eating angrily while the rest of us watched with caution. I took a deep breath and raised the stakes.

"We cannot leave without him," I said firmly.

D'Arco placed his fork gingerly on the table and then wiped his mouth again.

"You mean you will not leave without him?"

I guess at that point we had both made up our minds about how it was all going down. We just needed a catalyst.

"Fine," I said, "We will not leave without him."

With that, D'Arco pulled out a handgun, leaped to his feet and put it to Protos' head.

"You want him? You can have him! But just his corpse!"

Then it hit the fan. Everyone leapt to their feet and drew their guns. I took aim at D'Arco. Bully pointed his gun at me, and Deadeye had Bully in his sights. Everyone else had picked a target as well, except for Jinx. She stood there with her mouth agape, unable to comprehend the sudden turn of events.

"Seriously, Kaori?! You would choose the life of this pedazo de mierda over me?!" cried D'Arco.

"Drop your weapons now!" Bully yelled.

"You first, Baldilocks!" replied Deadeye.

"Dee, what happens here?" Jinx asked with the fear of a child in her voice.

"What happens, Jinx, is that Kaori has come to kill me. She has come to kill us all!"

"KK..?"

"No, Jinx. I am not here to kill anyone."

We were in one big powder keg, and it wasn't going to take much of a spark for it to explode.

"She wants us dead, Jinx! We welcomed her into our home, and she pulled guns on us!"

"D'Arco, you know that's not true!" I cried.

"I know that this is a man you hate even more than your own pathetic life and yet you choose his side over mine!"

"That's not it, D'Arco! I need him."

"Oh, so you no longer need me? Is that it? Now, I'm just another discarded heart in your long line of expendable assets?!"

"No, D'Arco..."

Tears filled my eyes as we prepared to cross the Rubicon.

"Yes. You see, Jinx? Kaori has no friends. Only stepping stones. You have to stop her."

"KK, I not your friend..?"

"Jinx, sweetie, listen to me. I'm sorry that it's come to this. I never wanted you in the middle. I just need you to know that it doesn't matter what you decide to do. It doesn't matter what happens because I love you, and nothing can ever change that."

Jinx cried silently as we all stayed focused on our targets, waiting for the spark to ignite. It came when Cleves returned from the kitchen with a cake. As he entered, we were all momentarily distracted, except for Bully who let his hammer fly. I immediately shot the gun from D'Arco's hand, and Deadeye put one between Bully's eyes, but it was too late. As all hell broke loose, the impact hit my chest like a sledgehammer, knocking me to the ground. I figured the bullet tore through my vest when I felt the warmth of my blood spilling over my neck and down my sides. With eyes closed, I lay there listening to the hail of bullets flying and my only thought was *finally*. But then I opened my eyes, and I realized it wasn't my blood. Jinx was lying on top of me with her big brown eyes staring at me and blood spilling from her mouth. She had teleported in front of me and took the shot in her back. I rolled her over and checked her wound as Deadeye covered me. It was bad. The shot had torn through her back, out her stomach and stopped at my vest.

"K... K..?"

"Don't try to speak, baby. Just stay with me."

I tried to stop the blood, but there was so much. I had her apply pressure to her stomach while Deadeye and Godspeed used suppressive fire to help me get her out of the room. Protos managed to get over to Gadget who helped him get out of the room as well.

Guards appeared at the front door so we were trapped. We gave Godspeed cover while he darted up the stairs. The houses were somewhat close together so Godspeed was able to dive out of the window and through one in the adjacent house. We were outmanned and outgunned, but Godspeed came barrelling through the house with our van. The sudden explosion of debris and dust gave us a chance to dive into the van and speed off. D'Arco's gang jumped in their cars and took off after us while Deadeye picked them off one by one. All the while, I worked feverishly on Jinx.

"Just stay with me, okay Sweetheart? Give me the first aid kit! Gadget, you have a torch, soldering gun or a laser or something on you?!"

"Uh y-yeah," he stammered.

None of them knew I had any medical training up until that point, so they were all confused. I reached into my pocket and gave Jinx several nitrocodone. Gadget handed me the kit and a laser cutter.

"Can you adjust the power on this thing?"

"Yeah, yeah," Gadget replied.

He showed me how to adjust the laser, then I cleaned it and my hands with alcohol from the kit.

"Jinx, grab Gadget's hand and squeeze tight okay?"

She nodded, and I proceeded to wash out her wound with a saline solution. She winced in pain but did her best not to scream. I reached in and started cauterizing her wound, but it was hard to see through all the blood. I turned her on her side and worked on the wound from her back, but the blood kept coming. I went back to her stomach, washing away the blood with saline to see where she was hemorrhaging.

"Do you know what you're doing?" Gadget asked.

"I have to stop the bleeding!"

She was still losing blood, but I couldn't give up. I wouldn't. Then Jinx released Gadget's hand, reached for mine and pulled it away from her wound.

"No matter what happens, I love you, KK, and nothing change that…"

I stopped what I was doing and pulled Jinx into my arms and sobbed as I held her close.

We arrived home and pulled into the parking garage as Medic and Gracie walked out to greet us. Gadget slid the side door open and stepped out while Godspeed walked around from the driver's side. Over Gadget's shoulder I could see a hopeful smile on Gracie's face as she strained to see me. Gadget stepped aside, and Gracie saw Jinx's lifeless body in my arms. Her cries of agony echoed throughout the garage and my very soul.

Medic wasn't trained in mortuary science, but she did the best she could. She stood over in a corner of the examination room while I looked over Jinx's body. The white sheet draped over her blended seamlessly into her pale skin. I ran the back of my hand over her cheek, my thumb across her lips then gingerly held chin between my thumb and forefinger. I had forgotten how cold a body gets or maybe it just never mattered to me before. After all, I had been around many dead bodies in my life, just never one of someone I loved. I felt... everything. Joy that I had known her, sadness that I had lost her, anger that he took her, and guilt for letting it happen. I agonized over everything I thought I had done wrong and what I could've done differently. I knew it wasn't healthy, but I couldn't help it. I could've told her to stay back, or I could've shot first or just let D'Arco have Protos. Anything would have been better than watching her die. I leaned over and pressed my lips against her forehead and then matched Gracie's gentle sobbing that I heard coming from the hallway.

I walked out and saw Deadeye trying to comfort Gracie. Gadget and Godspeed stood helplessly off to the side. I purposefully avoided looking at Protos and went to Gracie. I squatted down and turned her from Deadeye. When Gracie saw me, she collapsed into my arms, throwing her arms around my neck. She squeezed so tight it hurt, but I didn't care. I could feel her warm tears running down my back. I just kept telling her it was going to be okay, but okay was the most it could ever be. One day we would cry less. We would learn to hold our heads high enough to see the horizon again, but our hearts would remain scarred, reminding us there would always be a piece missing.

Gracie pulled away and held up a handcrafted necklace made of leather and beads and sobbed as she spoke.

"I-I m-made this for Jinx. Gadget h-helped me make the b-beads. I was gonna give it to J-Jinx when she came back to visit us…"

Her little face was so red and the blue of her eyes was obscured by tears. Seeing her in pain made mine all the worse.

"Jinx knew you loved her, baby. You were always by her side, always together. She knew."

I pulled her back to me and held tight until Medic came out

of the room. She placed her hand on Gracie's head and asked if she wanted to see Jinx. Gracie looked at me, and I nodded, then she took Medic's hand and went inside the room.

Godspeed handed me a towel, and I used it to clean my face. Protos took that opportunity for an ill-timed apology.

"Hey, Kaori, I'm really sorry about Jinx. I knew her too and.."

I just turned around and swung with everything I had, sending him across the tiled floor.

"I swear to you, if you don't get us to that cure I will kill you in the most painful way imaginable!"

"Hey, I'm sorry this happened, but it's not my fault..." Protos said with a mouthful of blood.

"200 years, Protos! 200 fucking years!! We were never supposed to go that far! If it wasn't for your stupidity or selfishness, or whatever it was, this would all be over by now, and I'd be home. Everything that has happened since we left is your fault!"

"Are you really so blind as to think a control freak like Cordell would leave anything up to chance?"

I didn't like where he was headed.

If Cordell didn't want me to skip 200 years, he wouldn't have given me the power to do it."

Medic came out to see what was happening.

"What do you mean, gave you the power?" asked Deadeye. "I thought Classes were the result of an accident.."

"Everything that happened was by design," said Protos.

"Don't try to turn this around..." I replied to his insinuations.

He smiled and shook his head.

"You're so quick to point out my sins. What about yours? Do your friends know about your contribution to all of this?"

"What's he talking about, Kaori?" Godspeed asked.

I lowered my head and decided it was time I told the truth. The whole truth. I told them that we intentionally created superhumans using a virus for a government contract, and it eventually spread out of control. The Classes grew mad with power and we had to stop them, so you came up with a cure that would render Classes powerless. Everything fell apart when that mob attacked the lab, and I lost the cure just before Protos skipped us into future.

"You did this?" Godspeed asked.

"It wasn't meant to be this way," I replied. "None of this was supposed to happen."

Protos finally picked himself up off the floor and laughed smugly to himself.

"You still think he was this great man who loved you dearly, don't you? He didn't love you."

"He... loved me," I said holding back the tears.

"He used you."

"Cordell would never use me or anyone for that matter!" I insisted.

Then why am I dying?"

I was angry but couldn't say at who.

"Why 200 years?" I asked, afraid to hear the answer.

"To teach the world a lesson. You give a mouse god-like powers, he'll want to be a god..."

"Then at the height of his power, take it all away..." I said completing his words.

"Now, you're catching on."

"This was all a game to you people," said Godspeed.

"I didn't know what Cordell was planning..," I said.

"But you knew how this all started, and you let us believe a lie," said Godspeed.

"I was afraid you'd blame me for all of this."

"I do blame you. And as far as I'm concerned, every scar on our backs bears your name."

Godspeed left, then Deadeye and Gadget followed. At a loss for words, Medic went back in the room to check on Gracie, leaving me alone with Protos.

"He sent me away, knowing he would never see me again, and he never even said goodbye."

"Jesus, Kaori. He was also responsible for the deaths of millions, but you go ahead and focus on that heartache thing."

"Fuck you, Protos. You're just as responsible as any of us!"

"Yeah, but I don't play the victim."

Chapter 18
Aiden

Even though I was getting closer, Kaori still managed to evade me. Before I would've been confused and angry at such events, but I began to admire her ingenuity. She had survived everything thrown at her and was still going strong. For so long we had believed the Zeros were these inferior weaklings deserving our scorn, but she had proved us wrong. She was demanding our attention and respect, and that was frightening to most Classes. She had earned reverence while we wanted honor simply for being born. Kaori was not proving to be equal. She was proving to be superior.

Josiah was still watching me closely. He needed my help, but he still did not fully trust me. I was able to somewhat allay his concerns by using the drug Cloak to hide the side effects of the Nitro, which I was still using daily. I had initially taken it to get to the Archive, but there was a far greater task ahead of me, and I needed every advantage possible. In order to remain on the case, I had to make progress in finding Kaori, but the closer I got to her, the closer Josiah did as well. So, really, there was only one way this could end.

"I hope you have some better news for me than last time."

Governor Mathias was micromanaging our case, which made it even more difficult for me to get close to Kaori undetected. The Governor respected my skills, but he confused my calm demeanor with a lack of urgency. I wanted Kaori just as much as he, but for entirely different reasons.

The Governor had accompanied Josiah to my office for our briefing and wanted some answers.

"I want to know why those Zero bastards attacked my friends," he asked.

"They were not attacked," I replied.

The Governor did not appreciate my flip and concise response.

"Then perhaps you can tell me why they were found dead

in the woods."

With a decided lack of enthusiasm, I looked up from my work and explained that Vicente and Vindego Vitali had been at a flesh auction just hours before their deaths. The Vitali's were bidding on a Zero named Whisper who was one of the people picked up during the sweep in Zero Alley. Witnesses said the brothers were quite miffed when they were outbid by a woman named Virginia King, whose identity was later proven to be false. I suspected the auction was simply a rescue mission for Whisper. The car found at the scene had been used by Miss King, not the Vitali's.

"Are you saying the Vitali's attacked the Zeros?" the Governor asked.

"Had Kaori and her people drawn first blood, it would have been in the form of an ambush. It is clear from the heavy damage sustained to the Zeros' vehicle, this was not the case," I replied. "Besides, they won the auction. They would have had no reason to pursue the brothers."

"And what reason would the Vitali's have to pursue this woman?" the Governor asked with incredulity.

"Well, the Vitali's were hotheads who were accustomed to shrewd business practices. I believe they tried to take Whisper by force after the auction. It was a decision that cost them their lives."

The Governor was clearly annoyed by my accusatory tone, so Josiah stepped in to keep the focus on finding Kaori.

"The Vitali's car was equipped with a tracer. The tracer was located fifty miles west of the murder scene, but the car was nowhere to be found," said Josiah.

"Then look in every direction except that one," I replied.

Josiah was confused.

"Why?"

"Anyone smart enough to remove a tracer from a stolen vehicle is smart enough to remove it before heading home. They probably attached it externally to another vehicle and it fell off at some point," I explained.

"So are you telling me we have another dead end?" asked

the Governor.

"No. The key is Zero Alley. There is someone there that can help us find her. Someone there knows what she is after," I replied.

"We tried that, remember?" the Governor snidely responded.

Clearly, he was not very fond of me.

"I read the arrest reports. No one who was arrested received a reading," I replied.

"It was meant as a scare tactic, not reconnaissance," the Governor replied.

"Well, I believe a vital opportunity was missed."

"So what should we have done, Agent Price? Over 300 Zeros were arrested. We do not have the resources to read them all!"

His patience with me was well worn, but I was not concerned.

"Out of those 300 people arrested during the raid, Kaori

and her friends only rescued one. I propose we find the one called Whisper and bring in a Reader," I replied.

The Governor was satisfied with my answer, and perhaps I should have left it at that, but, as you know, I have always been quite vocal with my opinions.

"I also propose you remove the bounty from her head."

Concern for my safety washed over Josiah's face as the Governor's finger turned red while he pressed it into my chest. The Governor was born a Diploid. He was a Burner and a Hitter, a deadly combination, but it was nothing that I could not handle.

"If I didn't know better, I would say you were a Sympathizer," he accused.

I discreetly removed just enough oxygen from his personal space to prevent adequate gas exchange, effectively snuffing out the budding flame on his finger.

"Clearly you do not know better. I am no Sympathizer. I know want to spread hysteria through propaganda, but placing an unusually large bounty on her head makes you seem scared. And people aren't as likely to follow a coward."

I could see the Governor was feeling lightheaded but it was clear he did not know why. Josiah, however, was a lot more observant as he cut his eyes at me.

"I realize that you have been vital to this man hunt, but I suggest you tread lightly," the Governor warned while bringing his hand to his head.

"I meant no disrespect, Governor Mathias, but on this matter, I am certain even Special Agent Griffin agrees."

Josiah did not appreciate me dragging him into the maelstrom I was creating, but it had to be done. The Governor was becoming a problem and I needed a distraction. He turned towards Josiah and gave him a questioning look.

"The large bounty could backfire and be perceived as weakness, sir," Josiah grudgingly admitted.

The Governor glared at us both as his breathing returned to normal.

"The bounty stands," he declared as he left the room.

"The Zeros are not to be underestimated," I called after him.

The Governor returned just long enough to deliver a warning.

"I am not to be underestimated, Agent."

I smugly watched the Governor walk away as Josiah shook his head.

"Do you wanna die, Aiden?"

"Desire is irrelevant, Josiah, as death is inevitable."

"That's no reason to expedite your demise with the foolishness you pulled on Mathias! If he even suspected you had used your powers on him..."

"Are you truly concerned for my life or just your career?" I asked.

"I have other interests at stake which include my career, and I will protect those interests to the best of my ability. But your life is an interest as well."

"Just not as high on the list as capturing Kaori."

Josiah seemed exasperated by my response and let out an audible sigh.

"Perhaps our heart to heart a while ago caused some confusion. I don't care who you are or how valuable you are. If you ever do anything like that again..."

"Josiah," I interrupted, "I suffer no delusions of grandeur. I am well aware that I am seen as an expendable asset within this organization. Nonetheless, I will fulfill my duties and find your fugitive."

I had really pushed my luck with Josiah that time, but I knew how much rope I could afford to take. I was getting close to the end anyway. Kaori had presumably flown under the radar for quite some time, then suddenly she was showing up everywhere. She no longer cared, or she was at a stage where discretion was no longer an option. Either way, I was certain it was all coming to a head.

I did not know what I would do when I met her again. I assumed she would probably attempt to kill me for the third time.

Of course, it would be well deserved. And maybe that was it. Perhaps I wanted her to take my life, and that would be the penance I needed. I suppose Josiah was right. I had been courting death lately. For life to be worthwhile, one needs love and a purpose and I had neither. Without a reason to go on, I thought that my death could provide the meaning that my life could not. And perhaps news of my sacrifice would make its way across the miles and that one final act of altruism would make you love me again.

People are creatures of habit. They find comfort in the familiar. Be it prison or a bad relationship, people often come back to that which they know, and that is how I knew Whisper would return to Zero Alley. A few days after being chastised by the Governor, my team of Enforcers in Zero Alley had caught Whisper. I was cautious about which info I made Josiah privy to, but I knew that if I was caught hiding something important, everything would be for naught. I decided to inform him, but keep him at a distance.

"Josiah, I have Whisper."

Josiah was out of the office that day so I told him via com as I made my way down to Zero Alley.

"You have him with you now?" he asked.

"No, there are Enforcers holding him for me in the Alley. I am on my way there now."

"That is good news. Do you have a Reader with you?"

I did not want to risk harming another person, and Readers were notoriously careless with Zeros' minds. They did not care if they burned their brains as long as they got the information they needed.

"I believe I can get the information on my own," I replied.

"Aiden, I know you are on some philosophical, bleeding heart journey right now, but this is far too important to just hope this Zero betrays his friends due to a sense of civic duty! I'll get a Reader and meet you there!"

Josiah was determined to make this difficult for me, so my only hope was getting to the Alley well before him and attempt to cull the information from Whisper myself. Not only would I be able to save his life, I could choose which information to share.

I made it to Zero Alley in record time which gave me about thirty minutes to get what I needed from Whisper. I reached the old warehouse where the Enforcers were holding him. He was tied to an overturned chair being mercilessly tortured. I immediately stopped his tormentors and sent them outside. Once they were gone, I levitated the chair upright and and took a seat across from him. He looked at me through his swollen eyes with caution.

"It is Whisper, correct?"

His only response was labored breathing.

"Whisper, I am here to help you, but I need you to help me first. I need to know the whereabouts of your friend, Kaori Maru and what she is seeking."

"I don't know a Kaori…"

"Whisper, I know that you were picked up in the sweep and auctioned off to a friend of Kaori's and you all subsequently found yourself in a battle with two brothers."

"I swear to you, I do not..!"

I knelt in front of him and grabbed his shoulders and he immediately tensed up as if preparing to be struck.

"I am not going to hurt you, but the man coming after me surely will. He is bringing a Reader who will not hesitate to lobotomize you in an effort to get information. I know you do not trust me as you have no reason to, but you must know how the Gendarmerie work. We do not have much time."

Whisper knew my words to be true, but I suppose he thought voluntarily giving up his friend was a far greater transgression than having it forced out of him.

"I cannot…"

"I am certain Kaori did not save your life so you could needlessly throw it away in a futile attempt to protect her. A Reader will get whatever he needs from you, so you must know I am only trying to help you. "

My words were sinking in. He knew I was speaking the truth.

"I don't know where she is…"

"Why is she here, in the present?"

He was shocked that I was aware of Kaori's time traveling origins.

"She's here to fix everything.".

"Fix everything how? Explain!"

We heard a vehicle pull up outside. It had to be Josiah with a Reader and the urgency of the situation must have shown on my face.

"You cannot let them see what is inside my head…"

"You did not get started without us did you, Detective Aiden?" Josiah asked accusingly.

"What is she doing here?" I asked with derision.

Riser smiled.

"Good ta see you too, Pussycat."

"I told you I was bringing a Reader."

I walked over to Josiah and pulled him aside.

"We do not need a Reader that powerful, or unstable for that matter! She could kill him!"

331

"Why do you care?"

"I care because that maniac almost killed me!"

"Don't be so dramatic, Aiden."

"You do not even like the woman."

"That's true, but I brought Riser here because I expect resistance, lots of it."

Josiah gave me this stern looked as he walked away, and I caught Riser with a smile looking a little too pleased with herself. It was then that I realized why Riser was really there.

"Hello, Whisper. My name is Special Agent Griffin, and this is Riser Kilroy. She is a Class 10+ Reader. I am sure you know what that means, but at the risk of insulting your intelligence, I'll tell you that you can resist her if you like, but I guarantee you won't survive it."

"Oh, Tomcat, what make you think the Zero will survive either way?" Riser said smugly.

"Please, I don't know anything more than what I told him," Whisper begged while motioning towards me.

Josiah looked over at me.

"I guess we'll know for sure soon enough."

Riser smiled as she walked over to Whisper. He looked at me with pleading eyes, but I was not sure what to do.

Riser grabbed him by his face and her veins lit up even brighter than I remembered, then Whisper shook violently. He tried to scream, but Riser's hand was over his mouth. She jackhammered her way into the recesses of his brain, all the while, looking at me. I felt electrical charges in the air and surmised that Riser used them to pull information from Whisper, so I began changing the charge to disrupt the communication. It must have worked, because then I felt it. This tingling sensation started radiating throughout my head. Riser was trying to burn her way into my brain as well!

"How's it going, Riser?" Josiah asked.

"A lil troublesome. He a little tougher than ah thought." Riser replied, still staring a hole through me.

"I'm sure you can handle it."

Riser increased her assault on my brain as I continued to push back. She was not even touching me and was still managing to get inside of my head. I had no idea she was so powerful. Defense alone was not going to work. I tried increasing the pressure around her head but I could not. I assumed she was blocking my powers and that must have weakened her because I felt less tingling in my head. We were both trying to assault one another and fend each other off at the same time. We were well aware of what was happening, but we pretended just the same. What was Josiah trying to prove? That he was in control? Showing me what would happen if I crossed a line again? Our battle was escalating when I noticed blood coming from Whisper's ears.

"I doubt you will get much more," I squeaked while pointing at the blood.

"Enough," Josiah ordered. "We should have all we need."

Riser sent one last jolt into me, and I almost vomited.

"The Zero seen betta days, but it look like you have too, Pussycat."

"I'm fine," I replied.

"What did you get, Riser?" Josiah asked.

"Not much. The lady Zero is far from home and looking for a cure."

"A cure for what?".

Riser walked over to Josiah and touched his face.

"A cure for us," she said.

Josiah looked at me briefly.

"What does that mean?" he asked.

"That, I dunno, Tomcat. His head was a mess"

I must have limited Riser's access to Whisper when I was trying to protect myself. She had to have known what I was doing, yet she said nothing. As I pondered my next move, one of the Enforcers came back inside and called to Josiah.

"Special Agent Griffin, there is someone outside who wishes to speak to you."

"Who is it?"

"I don't know, but he says he has vital information for

you."

"I'll return shortly," said Josiah to us as he followed the Enforcer outside.

Riser looked over at me.

"Looks like you might have more Tom in ya than ah thought, Pussycat."

"Don't call me that."

"Aaw, Risa mean no harm. Ah like the new Aiden. You go from Enforcer to Gendarme to… Reaper…"

"I am no Reaper."

"True. A Reaper wouldn't try to stop the swelling in a poor Zero's brain…"

She knew I was trying to save Whisper, and I thought for a moment that it was going to get very unpleasant.

"Not worry ya pretty lil head. Ah wanna see how this play out," Riser said with a most nefarious smile.

Then Josiah burst back inside the warehouse with excitement.

"I know how to find her!"

Later that night I went home and began writing. Of course, I am using *home* rather loosely. I knew when you left I would never know home again, and I suppose that is what made my decision so easy. As I said, life requires love and purpose, and without either, we are just moving to the beat without ever really hearing the music, and I so desperately wanted to hear music again. I needed to feel the melody of your touch passing over my body, causing me to sway back and forth to the rhythm. I needed to believe that, in spite of everything I had done, my presence or absence in this world meant something to someone. Instead I am left with the low hum of white noise and a painful numbing in my heart.

I know that as a husband and a man I deserve no more than this life that lay before me, but acceptance is not an anesthetic, so the pain remains. I love you, Carson. I am sorry it took me so long to say that again, and I am sorry that it comes too late. I only hope my sacrifice leads you to forgive me for the undeserved anger and callousness I cast before you. I hope it shows I still had a heart filled with compassion and a willingness to change. Let my final act in this life be my penance, and the world I leave behind be my gift of love to you.

Love always, Aiden.

Chapter 19
Kaori

I sat on the rooftop with my back to the world, sick with longing and regret. Everything I thought I knew was wrong, and I was still losing everything that I loved. I had always told myself that no matter what I lost, the sacrifice would be worth it in the end. That is what gave me the will to carry on, but I was no longer certain. My life just seemed like one great act of futility as everything I did only seemed to make things worse.

I could still hear the gunshot. I could feel the force throwing me to the floor. I could still see Jinx's chest rise and fall slowly until she slipped away.

Out of the corner of my eye, a figure approached that could only be Medic. She walked across the roof towards me, but I kept my head low so that all I could see were her legs.

"I brought you some clean clothes."

I looked down and saw that I was still wearing the same

blood stained shirt from the altercation. I guess I felt if I took it off and washed it, I'd be losing the last little piece of her that I had, and I was so tired of losing.

I took the clothes from Medic and lay them beside me. She squatted down and placed her hand on my knee.

"It's been four days. We miss you."

"Really?" I asked. "Is that why only you and Gracie have spoken to me since…"

I was determined to walk alone in my grief, but when I looked at her eyes, they were as red as mine.

"I've had time to process this. The others haven't."

"They'll never trust me again," I said as I lowered my head to my knees.

"No one blames you for Jinx's death, Kaori."

"I blame me."

"From what the others have told me, Jinx knew what she was doing. I believe she gave her life for you, because she loved you, and she knew you weren't finished here."

340

I had never really heard Medic support the mission before. She was always more concerned with staying true to who we were than anything.

"Since when did you care about such things?" I asked.

"Since that young lady died for you. She didn't die so you could waste away on this rooftop wallowing, Kaori. I believe there is a life after this that matters more, but I also believe that we weren't meant to live like this. You have the power to make it right."

"I'm not sure it's worth it anymore."

Medic reached for my chin and forced me to look her in the eyes.

"How could it not be? We've come too far and lost too much to give up."

"That's just it. We've lost too much. Every battle is at best another Pyrrhic victory, and I just keep hurting and losing the people I love. What if I do finish this? What if we save the world and the world left behind isn't even worth saving?"

341

"As long as there is love in the world, it's worth saving."

I sat there staring at the fresh clothes while Medic's words settled in my mind and couldn't help but to wonder, *What if there's no love left in this world for me?* The number of people I loved was getting smaller all the time, and the number of people who loved me was almost nonexistent. Once I was alone, would my guilt be enough to get me through the mission?

"I don't wanna lose anyone else, Medic. It hurts too much."

"I know it hurts, but it is really a blessing."

"A blessing..?"

"If we live long enough and love hard enough we will eventually lose someone, and if that loss hurts us deeply, it is only because we have loved deeply as well, and that is never something to regret."

Her words wrapped me in bittersweet nostalgia, like a much needed hug that was a bit too tight.

"Tell me, would you trade one minute, even one second of your life with her just to mitigate this pain?"

I closed my eyes as they welled with tears and shook my head.

"No."

I followed Medic back inside so I could shower and change. We agreed that getting cleaned up and eating something would make me feel better. I walked into the unisex shower room and found Protos shaving.

"It lives," he quipped.

I offered my middle finger without looking in his direction.

"Can you get out?" I asked.

"I'm not done."

I sighed and then, much to Medic's surprise, I started undressing.

"What are you doing?"

"I don't have the energy to fight with this jackass. I don't even have the energy to care."

My eye caught Protos as I spoke, and a smirk flashed across his face. At our best, we were indifferent towards each other, but our feelings had grown into restrained contempt. If we ever reached a point where one no longer needed the other, something bad was going down.

"I'm going to check on Gracie," said Medic as she excused herself.

Protos stayed and continued shaving. I could tell he was taking his time, and not just to annoy me. I turned on the shower to let it heat up.

"They haven't killed you, so that's a good sign, for you anyways," I said with a towel wrapped around me.

"That's only because Cordell never developed a *if looks could kill power,*" he joked as I stepped into the shower.

I hated hearing him speak your name. Whenever he did, it reminded me of my doubts and fears. It was as if your name still fell from my lips with with love and reverence, but it slithered from his, sending a chill throughout my body despite the heat rising from the shower.

"Do they hate me too?"

"Not yet," Protos replied.

"Yet?"

Protos looked around cautiously, making sure Medic was gone before continuing.

"We should leave, Kaori. We can finish this ourselves."

"You expect me to just take off and leave my friends who I love and trust for *you* of all people?'

"Not for me. For the mission. Besides, I'm not so sure how much love and trust they have left for you."

"You're the one who pushed the issue. They didn't have to know!"

"They would've discovered the truth eventually. Sooner or later, everyone will."

"I'm not leaving, Protos. I won't just abandon them. They're the closest thing to family I've had since... since we left."

"This is why Cordell didn't trust with the whole plan. He knew you weren't strong enough to make the hard choices. He knew your weaknesses."

"If you're so trustworthy, then why is he trying to kill you?"

"Because he knew my weakness too."

I used to look for signs or notes or messages from you, but there was nothing. You knew you'd never see me again, and you didn't care. You just let me leave. After awhile I knew you weren't truthful with me. It was just easier to believe that Protos took you from me. I wasn't ready for the truth, because I couldn't lose what you meant to me too, even if it meant I was in love with a lie.

"Why did you do it? You knew you'd lose everything too."

"I never really had anything to lose, Kaori."

"So, he sent you on a mission, then gave you something to lose so you would complete it."

"That's pretty much it."

Protos looked away when he spoke. Every part of me knew he was hiding something, and my mouth took it upon itself to ask what my ears were afraid to hear.

"What else, Protos? What else don't I know?"

I held my breath and stared at the shower floor as I waited for his response. He hesitated much too long.

"Nothing."

I knew he was lying, but I was too afraid to push. I just didn't know if he was protecting me from the truth or himself. It was probably the latter, but I wasn't ready.

"I chose you over my friends once before, and I will regret that until my dying day. Ask me to do that again and I will leave you for dead."

"So be it. I just thought I'd save you the pain of having to see the looks on their faces when they find out the whole truth," Protos replied.

Protos left the room, and I dressed in silence, wondering what to believe. For so long I thought my life had fallen apart in the last three years, but I was starting to realize I was a mess long before that. It was just easier to blame Protos or this world than it was to admit that I made some poor choices and put my faith in the wrong people. I hated that it was taking someone like Protos to help me see that.

I went looking for the others later and found Deadeye, Gadget and Godspeed sitting at a table in a conference room. Gadget kept opening and closing the box from D'Arco, Deadeye was cleaning a gun, and Godspeed was twirling a pen in his fingers. They all looked like reluctant guests waiting for a chance to leave.

"You didn't have to wait for me to start the party," I said in jest.

Deadeye and Gadget looked up at me, but Godspeed, whose back was to the door, didn't bother to turn around.

"Hey, Kaori," said Gadget, "We were starting to worry."

"I couldn't tell," I unintentionally said aloud.

I knew they were hurt, but so was I, no matter how much I deserved it.

"What did you expect?" Godspeed asked as he turned around.

"For you to remember that I'm still me."

348

"Well, we don't know who that *me* is," he replied. "You lied to us, Kaori, and now you expect us to continue on like nothing has changed."

"I'm sorry, but I didn't think you'd trust me if you knew the truth."

"Well, now we don't trust you anyway."

"Take it easy, Godspeed," Deadeye said as he stood from his chair. "We were all taken aback by what Kaori said, but we still have a job to do."

"And what job is that?" Godspeed asked. "I still don't think we know the truth."

"I told you the truth, Godspeed," I replied defensively.

I knew I had no right, but defending myself was a force of habit.

"The whole truth?" he asked.

"You know as much as I do."

"Why do I have the feeling that's not much?"

"A lot of blood has been shed on this journey, so if there is

349

some good to come from this, we should see it to the end," said Deadeye.

Even though I could hear the apprehension in his voice, I knew he was on my side. Still, I had a long way to go in order to gain his trust again.

"I'm glad you feel that way, Deadeye," Protos said as he entered the room, "because we have a lot of work to do."

My friends had granted me some benefit of the doubt, but the same courtesy was not extended to Protos. His overconfidence was not well received.

"Let's be clear, Skipper," said Godspeed, "if we have doubts about Kaori, you can be certain that you are close to the top of our shit list."

"Fair enough."

"So, where do we go from here?" Deadeye asked.

Gadget pulled a mini hard drive from the box and loaded it into his holo, and a wireframe layout of Gendarmerie headquarters appeared.

"We have the schematics for the building and biometric cloners for access, but there are facial recognition scanners all over the city," Gadget began. "The scanners are connected to the Gendarmerie criminal database. Kaori and I are definitely in the system, and there is a chance the rest of you are too."

"Is there a way to block the scanners?" Deadeye asked.

"I could disrupt the scanners with a virus, but the firewall they have in place is impenetrable. I would have to do it from inside the building, and we wouldn't get within a quarter mile of the place without setting off alarms."

"And we're back to where we started," said Godspeed.

"I could get your virus inside," Protos offered.

"Are you a computer hacker now too?" Godspeed asked.

"He wouldn't need to be," said Gadget. "I could build a device that delivers the virus wirelessly, but he still couldn't just walk inside, even as a Class."

"I could if I brought them something they wanted."

The others looked at Protos, then at me.

"No one is going to believe you subdued Kaori," said Godspeed, dismissing the suggestion.

"Not Kaori," Protos replied.

My eyes turned red, and I swept Protos' legs from behind, dropping him to the floor, then I grabbed Deadeye's gun from the table. I jumped on top of the Skipper and put the gun to his head.

"You go anywhere near that child and you won't have to worry about that virus killing you!"

"I wouldn't actually turn her in! It's just to get us in the door!" said Protos.

"Well, you have a history when it comes to turning people over to the authorities," said Gadget.

"Gadget is right," Godspeed chimed in. "How do we know you wouldn't try to make another deal?"

"I need the Archive, and the Gendarmerie would never make a deal for that," Protos replied.

I had made my point so I got off of his chest and tossed the gun back on the table. It slid across the table into Deadeye's hand.

"Regardless of your intentions, you're not endangering Gracie. If something went wrong, she could be killed or spend the rest of her life as a slave," I said.

"I'm a Skipper, remember? I can get her out of there if necessary."

"The building is one big neutralizer," said Gadget. "You would be powerless in there."

"I'm an Outlier. I can handle it."

"The Reapers are Outliers. There's no way you're that powerful," said Godspeed.

"I skipped 200 years into the future. How would you rate me?"

"Why is this still being discussed? We're not using Gracie!" I shouted.

"Then someone needs to come up with a better idea, because unless we get to the Archive, Gracie is gonna wind up living in slavery anyway, and the rest of us will probably be dead," said Protos.

He was definitely right about coming up with another idea. The Governor wanted us badly, and we had become far too infamous for him to ever give up. We needed to get to that Archive somehow.

"I'll come up with an idea that doesn't endanger the life of a child," I told them.

"Unlike the one you had 200 years ago?" Godspeed chided.

That hurt. A lot.

"That was unnecessary," I replied, eliciting a faint amount of regret from Godspeed. "For now, let's assume we know how we're getting the virus inside the building and work from there. Gadget, work on your device to administer the virus. Deadeye, gather up the lightest, most powerful weapons we have. Work with Gadget and Medic on some modifications. Godspeed, I want the fastest van or SUV you can find."

"And what should I be doing, your majesty?" Protos asked snidely.

"You can work a lot harder on not saying things that might

354

get you shot in the face."

I left the conference room and headed back to my quarters, all the while thinking about what I was going to do. I had no idea how to get into Gendarmerie headquarters, but I knew Gracie was not an option. I tried so hard to protect her from harm, and it seemed all I had done since we met was put her life at risk. I began to wonder if she would be better off without me. Actually, I guess just about anyone would. I thought about Protos' offer to leave. We probably wouldn't have had a chance, but the others could have. Without me, they might have had a chance at something close to a normal life. I tried to tell myself that they'd soon forget me, but I knew that wasn't true. They had the misfortune of loving me, the poster child for self-loathing. I had spent a lifetime seeking love from everyone but myself and never feeling I deserved any of it. It seemed as if love was a prize I had cheated to win, and it constantly reminded me of my ill-gotten gain. So every chance I had, I was throwing away the one thing I wanted more than anything, then desperately searching for it again.

I made it back to my room and collapsed like dead weight onto my bed. I was Sisyphus watching my boulder roll back down the hill, and I didn't know if I had the strength to roll it back up again. I needed my bottle, but I didn't see it anywhere around my bed. I looked around the room to no avail, then I remembered I had last seen it on the roof.

I could hear a storm calling in the distance as I neared the roof. I opened the door and the sweet smell announced the coming rain. I was given fair warning, all the time I needed to seek shelter from the storm or embrace its wrath. All too often I picked the latter.

I was surprised to find Gracie there just listlessly swaying in the wind. The coming storm and her proximity to the ledge had me more than a little concerned, so I walked quickly, but not so fast as to startle her.

"Gracie, you shouldn't be here. It isn't safe."

She rubbed her arm and I noticed the long scar she received from our car chase in the Alley.

"It hurts when it rains," she said.

"I'm sorry."

She just looked at me briefly and made a partial attempt at smiling.

"Why are you up here, Gracie?"

"I wanted to see how bad the storm is."

I looked out at her view of a clear sky. The approaching storm was behind us.

"The storm is back there," I told her.

"They don't like it when you look at them. It makes them angry."

"The storms?" I asked.

"Yes."

"Why?"

"Because that means you're not afraid."

I squatted next to her and placed my hand on her shoulder.

"Are you afraid of storms, sweetheart?"

"A little," she replied.

"It won't always be like this, Gracie."

"Did you think of a way to get inside the building?" she asked.

"Were you listening to us?"

Gracie looked down and nodded her head.

"How much did you hear?"

She shrugged her shoulders.

"A lot, I guess. I didn't wanna interrupt."

I pulled her close to my side and ran my fingers through her golden locks.

"Don't worry about such things, baby. I'll figure it out."

She pulled back and looked me in the eye.

"I wanna go with Shift, so he can get inside the building."

Panic seized my body, and I squeezed her arms tighter than I should have.

"No, Gracie! There's no way I'm letting you do that!"

"Why not?"

"Because you could get hurt or you could die!"

"I've been hurt, and I'm not afraid to die."

"You don't know what you're saying,. Dying is ugly and final. You just don't know what that's like."

"Is it anything like losing someone you love?"

I stiffened my lip and nodded.

"Probably," I muttered.

"Then I've already died three times."

Her words tore through my heart like shards of glass.

"Gracie, there is a life out there much better than this, and you don't need to die to find it."

Gracie held out her hand and gave me my pill bottle, and my shredded heart sank to my feet.

"Neither do you," she replied.

I couldn't look her in the eye, so I stared at the bottle.

"Gracie, I keep that for…"

"I know why, Kori. It's the same reason I go out in storms."

When I met her, she was this sweet, innocent little girl who wore dresses and played with dolls. Her parents said they couldn't protect her, but they had managed to shield her from all of the ugliness in the world. I had tried to give her the tools she needed to survive, but in the process, I had taken something else much more precious from her.

"Gracie, you're not like me. You're better than me, and there is something good in this world worth having. I don't want you to give up before you find it."

"I'm not giving up, Kori. I wanna help so I can live again, like before in a house with a family. I wanna play in a yard and sleep in a real bed. I wanna be a normal kid again."

I pulled Gracie close to me, and she rested her head in the curve of my neck.

"If I take you with us, I might lose you, and I cannot bear that," I told her.

"If you leave me behind, I might lose you, and you promised you wouldn't die without me."

I was so worried about losing her that I didn't really think about what it would be like if she lost me. One more person for her to mourn and one less for her to love. She'd be alone at the mercy of an evil world, and my last moments of life would certainly be spent agonizing over hers. Of course, I hadn't been that successful keeping her safe as it was, and sooner or later, our luck was going to run out. Everything I did or didn't do was a risk at that point, so I needed to just make a decision.

"No matter what, I won't let the bad guys get you, Gracie."

"Are we going to run away?"

"No, baby. We're gonna face the storm."

The next morning I went to the maintenance office that served as our machining room. Gadget had brought in a lot of fabricating tools and such for his inventions. Deadeye and Godspeed used them too for their guns and vehicles respectively. Gadget was fitting some type of device on Protos' hand. My team was quite resourceful... and resilient. Despite all we had lost, all the pain we had suffered, despite all the awful things we had gone through, we were still here. We were tired, it felt like we had more scars than skin, and we certainly weren't any stronger, but we weren't dead yet either, and that was all the reason we needed to go on.

The guys all stopped what they were doing and looked at me.

"How's it going?" I asked.

"About as well as it can without knowing the plan," Godspeed replied.

I walked over and removed the device from Protos' hand and gave it to Gadget. Then I stood Protos up and looked him squarely in the eye.

"You don't let them touch her. They'll try to separate you and take her into an interrogation room with a Reader, but you stall as long as you can. Give us time to get to the Archive. If you can't stall them or this goes sideways, you quickstep her out of there. You got it?"

Protos smiled and nodded. There was still the concern of the scanners detecting Gracie's face too early, but it was the best plan we had.

Medic wasn't keen on the idea of using Gracie on this mission, but she understood. Gadget designed the viral delivery system in two parts. One for Protos and the other for Gracie. Separate, they were completely innocuous, but combined, it would wirelessly infect the Gendarmerie security system, allowing us to get inside without facial recognition scanners detecting us. I was too recognizable, so I planned to sneak in from below with Gadget while Deadeye and Godspeed entered through the employee entrance disguised as agents. I would wirelessly transfer the Archive to a nearby hard drive that Gadget installed in the getaway vehicle. If anything went wrong, Godspeed and Gadget would be close by to make sure Gracie made it out.

After a couple months of planning, Gadget and I went into the city do some recon. We found a tall building just outside of the range of the Gendarmerie's scanners. We set up on the roof. As Gadget unpacked our surveillance equipment, I took notice of a wounded sparrow fluttering about on the roof. I could tell by the markings that it was female. I walked over to her and held out my hand, but she was wary of my intentions. I had crackers for snacking in my satchel, so I offered them to the timid bird. I crumbled the crackers in my hands and tossed the crumbs her way. She tilted her head at first, then cautiously accepted my gift. She inched closer, pecking her way towards the final crumbs that lay in my extended hand. The sparrow paused just before reaching my hand and looked at me. I smiled and she looked back into my hand, but with blinding speed, a hawk swooped down and took the little bird. I instinctively drew my gun and took aim, but Gadget reached out and grabbed my wrist.

"You can't save her," he said, motioning to the great distance the bird would fall to the ground below.

I watched them soar ever farther away until Gadget beckoned me.

"Come look at this."

I walked over to Gadget, and he handed me the tracking-goggles.

"Anchor one," he said, and the goggles guided my eyes to the front door of Gendarmerie headquarters.

"That's where Protos and Gracie will enter. Anchor two."

The goggles steered me to the street near our vantage point.

"We'll be waiting by that sewer drain. As soon as we get the signal that all perimeter sensors are down, you and I will head into the sewer and make our way to the target."

"I'm not loving this sewer entrance."

"We can't use the front door."

"Can't we use the roof or a window?"

"I'll handle any rats we run into. Anchor three."

I was shown a side entrance.

"Deadeye and Godspeed will go through the restricted entrance."

"Did anyone ever reach Whisper?" I asked.

"No, but I found someone else to leak the information."

We had been trying to reach Whisper for weeks to no avail. We needed him to spread the word that we had been spotted. That would lead to a dispatch of Gendarmes, thus leaving fewer of them for us to contend with at headquarters. Gadget's guy did his thing, and the Gendarmerie took the bait and set up a sting for the following week.

"We don't have time to find Whisper, but make sure our eyes and ears are still looking for him," I said.

Gadget got quiet and just stared at the hawk picking away at the sparrow on rooftop one building away.

"Do you really think he can get her out of there?" he asked.

"Can Protos get Gracie out? Yeah, he can quickstep her out."

"What's a quickstep? Is he a Speedster too?"

"No..."

Quickstepping was a little something I theorized and shared with Protos before we skipped. He undoubtedly perfected the technique and used it to trick people into thinking he could backtrack. Skipping only allowed one to open a portal and travel through time but not space, so no matter how far in the future you went, you'd be in the exact same spot when you reappeared. A really patient attacker could just wait for your return. With quickstepping, you could open successive portals and begin running simultaneously, thus allowing you to cross time and space. As impressed as Gadget was by my explanation, he still had his doubts.

"But with the neutralizers, will he be strong enough to do it?" he asked.

"He's an Outlier"

"So, if he's strong enough to escape the Gendarmerie, how did he get caught by local law enforcement and made to rat you guys out?"

Good question. Maybe he was weak from his illness at the time, maybe they caught him surprise, or maybe he was betraying me again. Whatever the case, I knew we needed to watch Protos closely, and I informed Gadget of such.

"The device that you're using to deliver the virus, can you make it an implant?" I asked.

"Sure," Gadget replied.

"Can you give the one for Protos a secondary function?"

"'I guess. What else do you want it to be?"

"A bomb."

I started keeping a closer eye on Protos. I had never fully trusted him, but I figured it best to start sleeping with both eyes open at that point. I had always wondered why you kept him around. After all, he was nothing like us. But perhaps I was the one who was different than the two of you.

I was so apprehensive the night before the big mission. Godspeed had secured a van, and I was loading up our equipment when Medic walked into the garage.

"Do you have everything you need?" she asked.

"Just about."

I feigned a smile then sat in the doorway of the van. Medic walked over and sat beside me.

"Worried about tomorrow?" she asked.

Yeah. I know you think I'm stupid for doing this."

"No. I don't like that Gracie is involved, but I understand that she has been in harm's way since birth, and this might be her only hope."

"Well, I think I'm stupid. I mean, my whole plan hinges on David Protos! I need him to take out the security, protect Gracie, and help us find the cure, and I'm not sure I can trust him to do any of it. What was I thinking? I was a fool to think I could…"

My words dissipated into the air, and I fell silent.

"But you have never really trusted Protos, so this isn't about him, is it?"

She was right. Protos was useful, but he was far from altruistic, so anytime he was involved, there was always a contingency plan.

"No, it's not about him. I trusted Cordell with my life because I believed in what he was trying to do, but I'm not even sure what that is now. For all I know, we've been risking our lives for nothing."

"Do you really believe that?" Medic asked.

"I don't know. I don't know what to believe or who to trust anymore, especially myself."

"Part of loving someone is trusting them, and I don't think you should give up on either."

"So, I should continue to risk being a fool?"

"Kaori, I would risk playing the fool a hundred times over."

"Why?"

"Because I came into this world to live and to love, and I will not allow fear to deny me of either."

"Do you trust me?" I asked, uncertain if I even wanted to know the answer.

"I do."

"Even after all my mistakes and my lies?"

"You have a good heart, Kaori. I know you love Gracie and all of us and truly want what is best for everyone, so yes I trust you, and whatever you decide, I'll support you."

"Sadly, that makes me feel worse," I said with my head in my hands.

"Why?"

"Because, Medic, I don't deserve your trust or support. You're holding me to a standard I cannot live up to. I carry on everyday, not because I believe in myself, but because I don't know what else to do. I'm so confused and lost."

"You feel doubt and confusion because you gave a man something that was not his to own, your worth. That belongs to you, Kaori, because if you give away your worth to a man, he won't return it when it leaves."

I had let you define me. I wanted your approval so badly that I gave up everything to get it, and in the end, I lost you and myself. I wanted to hate you, but I couldn't. I willingly gave my all to you and left nothing for myself. You said you would give me the world, but you never said I'd have to carry it on my shoulders.

Despite my doubts, I chose to finish the mission. No matter what secrets you had kept from me, I chose to believe that you would not allow humanity to suffer indefinitely.

I hugged Medic and thanked her for helping me once again,

then she left to finish packing. There was a good chance we'd have to take the quickest route out of town after crashing Gendarmerie headquarters, so returning was not an option. I finished loading the van and went back inside.

When I got to Gracie's room, she was fast asleep. I stood over her bed wondering how she could be sleep so peacefully knowing what tomorrow was going to bring. Maybe she knew it was all going to be over one way or another and she was relieved. It made me sad that such a little girl would have to be so grown up, but it was better than living in fear. I climbed into bed with her and placed my hand on her shoulder. She stirred a bit then pulled my arm down across her chest and let out a soft sigh.

I probably slept a total of thirty-five minutes that night, and then only in seven minute increments. I was beyond apprehensive. The lives of everyone I loved were in my hands, so I was wrought with guilt and fear. It was quite a burden to bear. I looked over and saw that Gracie was awake. She looked at me and smiled. I smiled back and stroked her golden locks.

"Did you sleep well?" I asked.

Gracie nodded then nuzzled her head against my chest.

"Are you scared?"

She nodded again and buried herself deeper. I held her against me and told her that she didn't have to go through with the plan.

"Yes, I do."

Deep down I was kinda hoping she would change her mind so I wouldn't have to put her through it. She was going straight into the lion's den, and I was going to be half a mile away at the time. Only 2,640 feet, but it might as well have been a light year away. If things went badly before I reached the building, it would be up to Protos to save her, and that thought was not very comforting.

After a bit, we all got dressed and made our way to a conference room. Everyone was muted, like when you're getting ready for a funeral. People talk, but they use short sentences and even shorter words to make polite conversation. It's usually unrelated to the deceased and nothing more than an attempt to stave off the inevitable for as long as possible, all the while preparing for that very thing.

The clock was ticking, and we could no longer afford to play with time, so we went over the plan once more. Godspeed and Deadeye would be in a fed's car just outside of the perimeter, while Medic would be close by in the van which housed the wireless hard drive. Gadget and I would be in a sewer which led to a renovated section of the Gendarmerie headquarters. Protos would take Gracie through front door and ask to see an agent about collecting the reward. Once inside, Protos would take Gracie's right hand in his left and their implants would activate, disrupting the security system and signaling the rest of us to move in. Gadget and I would make our way through the sewer to the spot where an older building used to be and break through the foundation into a sealed room. From there, we would make our way into the main building and to the elevator leading to the Archive floor. Deadeye and Godspeed would enter from a private entrance using stolen security codes. Medic would wait for us at the rendezvous point in the van. All the while, Protos needed to stall the agents so he wouldn't get separated from Gracie. Once Gadget and I started the download from the Archive, we would make our way out while Deadeye and Godspeed provided an exit for Protos and Gracie. If we got separated, then we were to meet up at this old salvage yard outside of town.

"Is everyone clear on what they need to do?" I asked.

Everyone just nodded giving barely audible acknowledgements. We had been on many dangerous missions, but none more so than the one that lay ahead. We all knew there was a good chance that we wouldn't survive, but no one was willing to say goodbye… except me.

"Godspeed…" I called as he opened the car door.

"What?" he snapped.

Clearly time had done nothing to temper his anger with me, but still I pressed him.

"Godspeed, I just want to say…"

"We need to leave. Can't this wait?"

"Yeah, I guess."

He was hurt. I was hurt. We knew our roles all too well, but I was tired of playing mine. I walked away and joined Protos, Gadget, Gracie and Medic in the van.

Deadeye waved to me from the passenger seat of the car. I returned a faint wave and even less of a smile. Godspeed knew that could be the last time we saw each other, and he was perfectly willing to risk ending things with such toxicity.

Gadget was our driver, so our trip was somewhat less aggressive. Gracie squeezed my hand and took deep breaths. She was trying so hard to be brave, but Protos let her off the hook.

"It's okay to be scared, little one. In fact, it's best. They'd get suspicious if you weren't."

Gracie smiled at Protos and then looked at me.

"Are you scared, Kori?"

"I'm terrified. You guys are the last good things in my life, and I don't want anything to happen to any of you."

"Something's gonna happen to us," Gracie replied. "I just hope it's good."

I put my arm around her and kissed her on top of her head.

"Me too, sweetheart."

I looked over at Medic and saw her eyes were closed and her head was bowed. She was praying. I remembered praying once or twice as a child, but I didn't have a religious upbringing. Becoming a scientist gave me even less of a reason to indulge in any kind of spirituality. It all seemed so pointless and illogical, but when Medic opened her eyes and looked at me, I saw she had something I never did, peace. She had this calmness about her that was so foreign to me. It was like, no matter what happened, she was going to be okay. I realized that regardless of whose belief was right, we were both destined to leave this world behind, but she was the one who could do it with an unburdened heart. I looked out the window towards the sky and struggled to find words of contrition, words that could lend compassion to an unworthy soul, but it was to no avail. My only hope was that if He did exist,

He would understand why I couldn't believe, and perhaps show mercy despite my doubt. And if He could not, at least allow me the chance right my wrongs.

I considered saying *"Amen,"* but I wasn't sure I had prayed at all. As I pondered whether my thoughts had even risen beyond the roof of our vehicle, Medic reached out and touched my arm.

"He knows your heart."

It took us a couple of hours to reach the city, so my anxiety had plenty of time to escalate into full blown neurosis. Still, I did my best to keep it from showing as Gracie didn't need to see it. I could tell she was nervous and trying very hard not to let it show. She kept giving me these strained smiles and rubbing the scar on her arm. Gadget was uncharacteristically tense and quiet, but I guess levity was in short supply for everyone. Protos was rather stoic about it all. He was on borrowed time and the odds weren't in his favor, so I guess he figured *que sera, sera.* And of course Medic was still calm as a placid lake.

Gadget pulled the van into an alley for our first stop and

checked in with Deadeye and Godspeed.

"Dispatch, this is vehicle Thirty-Two. We have arrived at our destination and the package is ready to be delivered."

"I expected you earlier," Godspeed replied through his com.

"I didn't want the delivery delayed by traffic stops, dispatch. Some drivers respect the laws of the road."

I opened the side door and helped Gracie out of the van. The others got out as well. I gave Gracie a long hug and just breathed her in. Gadget came over to check her implant, but I didn't want to let her go. I couldn't. Gadget decided to check Protos' first instead.

"It looks good. Just remember, your left hand has to touch Gracie's right for five seconds for the device to activate."

"I got it," Protos replied.

Gadget came back to me, and I was still holding Gracie. He looked at Medic, and she came over and touched my shoulder. I knew it was time, but I still wasn't ready. I realized at that moment

379

that you didn't hug me like you weren't going to see me for a long time. In fact, you let me walk out of your life without telling me how you felt. Actually, I guess you did...

I released Gracie and looked her in the eye.

"We'll get out. I promise."

"I know, Kori. Everything's gonna be fine."

Gadget checked Gracie's implant and gave her a few last assurances.

"Okay, Gracie, your implant is good. As soon as you guys get inside, Protos will take your hand and activate the device. Your com implant will allow us to hear everything going on and provide an echo-visual of your surroundings until you're inside, and then we'll have access to their cameras. We'll be there in forty-five seconds at the most, okay?"

An echo-visual was a 3D, monochromatic image created by soundwaves, another one of gadgets inventions.

Gracie nodded and gave Gadget a hug, then Medic.

"Be careful, little one," Medic instructed.

"You too, Medic."

Gracie looked over at me with a longing in her eyes for one more embrace, but we both knew we would never let go, so instead, she pointed to her eye, her heart and then to me. I did the same and held up two fingers at the end. Protos and Gracie walked out of the alley and out of my sight.

"Dispatch, the package is en route. Readying delivery of second package. Stand by for delivery of third."

"Acknowledged, Thirty-Two. Dispatch standing by," Godspeed replied.

Gadget climbed into the van with Medic and turned on the monitors.

"Okay, Medic, the echo-visuals will be on this screen. You'll be the eyes for the rest of us until I get inside since Protos and Gracie won't be in a position to talk to us."

Gadget went to the back of the van and unloaded a motorcycle. It was no Tomahawk, but it had to do. He rolled it in front of the van as Medic got in the driver's seat. I sprayed a perimeter around the bike with an accelerant called Burnout as Gadget collected our weapons. I loaded up then got on the bike. Gadget climbed on back then hit the Burnout with an electrical charge. The ellipse burned bright blue before cutting through the asphalt and sending us into the sewer below. Medic quickly moved the van over the hole.

"This is disgusting," I told Gadget as I looked around at the murky water and the stained sewer walls.

"It's just a storm sewer. Human waste doesn't lead here."

"Well, it smells like it does."

I sat there in the darkness, silent and still, barely breathing, listening intently for any sign of trouble, but my heart was beating so hard I thought it would drown out any cries for help. Gadget must have sensed my anxiety, or maybe he just heard my thundering heartbeat, because he called in.

"Spotter, what does it look like out there?"

"The package is still en route," Medic replied. "It's about halfway to its destination."

"We're fine, Gadget," Protos chimed in. "We'll be there shortly."

"Stick to nomenclature, delivery man," Gadget replied.

I turned off the mic on my com and leaned backward.

"How do I pull up the EPS on here?" I asked.

EPS stood for Epicenter Positioning System. It used Earth's inner core to track movement on the surface. It was found to be far more reliable than GPS as it wasn't dependent on vulnerable satellites.

"It's a straight shot," Gadget replied.

"Yeah, but I want us there as fast as possible, and I need to know precisely when to decelerate."

Gadget turned on the EPS and programmed the bike for the maximum amount of speed while allowing us to stop without crashing. I started the bike and gave the controls a once over. The motorcycle was a lot lighter than what I was used to, but it was necessary for the terrain.

After a few minutes, I heard the faint sounds of sirens.

"Did you hear that?" I asked..

"What?"

I turned my mic back on.

"Did any of you hear that?" I asked.

"Nothing over here," Deadeye replied.

"Me neither," said Medic. "And no visuals."

"I hear it," said Protos. "I think it's... oh, shit..."

"Protos, what is it?!" I cried out anxiously, but the only response I heard were pounding footsteps and heavy breathing amongst sirens.

"Protos?!!" I cried out again. "Medic, what do you see?!"

At that point, all codes names were out the window.

"It looks like they have agents coming at them from all sides!"

"Dammit, the scanners must have recognized Gracie's face!" said Gadget.

"We gotta get them out of there! Protos, can you skip out?" I asked.

"Yeah, but are you sure you want me to?"

"No!" yelled Gadget. "The plan was always to get them inside, and this works just as well!"

"Are you crazy, Gadget?! She could get killed out there!"

"She will definitely be killed if we try to shoot it out with them in the open while their defenses are still up!"

"Come on, Kaori!" Protos insisted. "Make the call!"

I knew we couldn't take them on like that, and if Protos skipped out of there, we might not get another chance at the Archive, but still I didn't wanna do what I knew had to be done.

"What are we doing?" Godspeed asked.

My hands grew numb and my stomach turned.

"Let them take you…"

We sat quietly, helplessly as we listened to the Agents bark their orders.

"Release the girl and get on the ground!"

"He's a Skipper!"

"I've come to collect my reward!" said Protos.

"Release her now!"

"I'll only surrender her to Special Agent Josiah Griffin!"

"I won't tell you again!"

"I'll be well into the future before you can pull that trigger..," said Protos.

The coms went silent, and I was all set to track their location when I heard a familiar voice.

"Stand down, Agents. This man is our guest."

"It's Griffin!" said Medic.

The immediate crisis had been averted, but that wasn't the plan. It felt like we were in freefall, and nobody knew who was gonna pull the cord. I disconnected my com from Gracie's feed and spoke to Medic.

"Medic, how is Gracie doing?"

"Her heart rate is elevated and her breathing is labored."

"Is she in physical danger?" I asked.

"No, no one is harming her or showing any aggression, but I fear she is having a panic attack."

I re-engaged my com with Gracie's and spoke softly.

"Gracie, baby, we're still here. You don't have to face the storm alone."

"We're all still here," said Deadeye.

"I can see you, Gracie," said Medic.

"We'll get you out of there soon, buddy," Gadget added. "Just hang in there."

"It's going to be okay, kid" said Godspeed.

"Her heart rate is going down!" said Medic. "She's relaxing."

In turn, my stress levels dropped as well. We weren't out of the woods yet, but at least I was breathing again.

"How close are they, Medic?" I asked.

"They just walked up to the front doors."

Gadget took a look at a monitor on his wrist.

"Okay, gang, stand by. We go in on my signal."

I started the motorcycle and put on my goggles while Medic continued her updates.

"They're being escorted through the front entrance. The signal is being interrupted. They're inside, but I can't see what's happening..."

"Something is scrambling the signal," said Gadget.

"Are we going in?" Godspeed asked.

"No," Gadget answered. "I haven't received confirmation that security is down."

"Are you sure it's still working?" I asked.

"Pretty sure."

"Pretty sure..??"

"I'm locked into the scanners!" said Medic.

Gadget looked at his monitor.

"Security is down! Go!"

I accelerated so quickly that Gadget almost fell off the back of the bike. It was a good thing he held tight, because I'm not sure I would've gone back for him. I tried to ignore my disgust as my bike tore through the murky sludge, but it was hard when it began hitting my face. Just as I feared, we came on a group of rats, but I deftly avoided them by riding up the curved walls.

"You can slow down," said Gadget.

"I can. But I won't."

The EPS signalled we were getting close, and it tried to slow us down, but I overrode it and continued at full speed.

"Kaori, getting there quickly doesn't matter if we're not alive when we arrive!" said Gadget.

Our destination was a dead end, and we were dangerously close, so I hit the brakes and skidded to a halt. Gadget almost crushed my ribs from holding on so tight.

"You can let go. We're alive."

Gadget stumbled off the bike and gathered our equipment.

"Godspeed, where are you?" Gadget asked.

"Deadeye and I are entering through the side. Starting com silence now."

"The package has been escorted to interrogation room six on the third floor. They're still together," Gadget reported while looking at his monitor on his wrist.

Griffin hadn't separated Protos and Gracie yet, but it was only a matter of time. Protos told them he spotted Gracie fifty miles south of the city and recognized her from the news. He said she was with a woman, and he grabbed her outside of a restroom. Protos refused to turn Gracie over until they delivered the reward. He insisted that they pay him in gold to buy us more time as the Gendarmerie didn't keep it on hand. I figured Griffin was obliging, because he was happy to have Gracie which could eventually lead to me.

Gadget crawled into a smaller tunnel and applied burnout to a sewer grate on the ceiling. He crawled out then blew grate open. I followed him back through sludge covered tunnel that was just barely large enough for me squat in. As I was waiting for Gadget to crawl through the hole, I fully expected to meet my demise at the hands of a rat king. I gave Gadget a little nudge to hurry him along, which he didn't appreciate. Nevertheless, he was a gentleman and gave me a hand as I crawled through the hole.

I turned on my flashlight and looked around the forgotten

boiler room with its cobwebs and rusted machinery.

"There," I whispered as I spotted the former doorway.

On the other side of the wall was a secret prison where the Gendarmerie kept people they weren't quite finished with. The prisoners had more than likely given up whatever they knew, but they were kept around just in case. Basically, they were left to die. The guards only tended to them once a day, and based on our intel, they had already visited hours earlier.

Gadget used a smaller helping of burnout around the area where a door used to be and ignited the compound. He gave the wall slight shoves from edge to edge, slowly sliding the chunk of masonry out of the wall. Suddenly, we realized why the guards only visited once a day. The stench from the room was worse than that in the sewer. As we hurried down the hall between cells, I peeked in a few. There was no running water and the closest thing to a toilet was a hole in the floor. I was pretty sure I saw a dead body too.

We reached the other end of the hall where we found an

elevator. Unfortunately, it wouldn't take us directly to the Archive. We would have to get off on the ground floor and take a different elevator up from there. Gadget and I reached into our packs and pulled out the biometric gloves so we could access the necessary floors. As I was putting on my gloves, I caught a glimpse of a prisoner through a nearby cell window. My eyes met his and my heart split in half...

"Gadget, open this door!"

"Lower your voice..! And no way! We're not here on a rescue mission, Kaori."

"Open the damn door!"

Gadget just stood there so I took his canister of burnout and sprayed the lock.

One shot from my firearm and the door to the cell swung open.

"What's going on down there?" Deadeye asked. "That sounded like a gunshot!"

I ran over to the prisoner huddled in the corner and pulled

him close.

"Kaori, what are you doing?" Gadget asked.

"Talk to us!" Godspeed demanded.

"It's Whisper..."

Shock washed over Gadget's face, and I heard faint gasps over our coms.

"Whisper, how did you get here?" I asked.

"I... I'm sorry... Kaori..." Whisper said weakly.

"Sorry for what?" I asked.

"It... wasn't... me..."

"What wasn't you?" I asked. "Whisper, what are you... they know! Protos, get Gracie out of there now... aaaahhh!"

A shrill piercing cut through our coms and then they went dead.

"They're onto us, Gadget! I need you to get Whisper out of here!"

"Where are you going?"

"I have to make sure Gracie escaped."

"No, Kaori! We have contingency plans in case things go wrong!"

"I don't know if the others even heard me! I have to get up there!"

"Give me a chance to try to reconnect the coms first."

"You're not gonna win this. I'm going after Gracie!"

I handed Whisper over to Gadget and checked my weapons.

"You can't go up there alone, Kaori."

"I don't have a choice. You need to help Whisper."

"Leave... me...," Whisper moaned.

"No, no! We're not leaving you!" I insisted.

"Save Gracie..."

His words slowed me down and made me think. If I was going to save Gracie, I needed all the help I could get. I hugged Whisper quickly and carefully laid him back on the floor.

"We'll come back for you, I swear!"

I placed my gloved hand on the biometric scanner to open

the elevator door. Gadget followed me inside, and I took a deep breath then pressed the button. As the elevator climbed up to the ground floor, Gadget worked feverishly to further compromise the Gendarmerie's security.

"They're trying to regain control of their security systems!"

"Can you stop them?"

"I think so, but I need some time, and we have a welcome wagon."

Gadget's monitor showed several armed agents waiting for us outside of the elevator. Most agents couldn't use their powers inside of the building, and most of them weren't trained with weapons other than neutralizers either. That gave us slightly better odds than if we were duking it out on the street. Still, extending our one floor elevator ride was a tall order. Just as the doors opened, I threw the can of burnout into the air above the agents and shot it. Fire rained down upon them, burning straight through their suits and flesh.

"Is that enough time?" I asked.

"Just enough. Got it."

Gadget regained control and locked them out of the cameras, but he hadn't managed to restore our coms. We ran down the hall to the main elevators.

"Are they still on the third floor?" I asked as we got inside.

"I don't know! They're not in the same room!"

More agents came running towards us pointing their weapons and ordering us out of the elevator.

"Well, find them, Gadget!"

"They're on the fifth floor!"

I hit the fifth floor button and shut the elevator doors. Gadget spotted Gracie being taken down a hallway, and that's where we were headed. She had been separated from Protos who was nowhere to be found. On top of that, security wasn't giving up and was still trying to wrestle control back from Gadget.

"We need to split up so I can take these guys out directly," he said.

"Are you sure?"

"Yes, if they keep getting back online, they'll know our every move and we really need our coms back. I've yet to locate Protos, Deadeye and Godspeed, and Medic is probably panicking."

We reached the fifth floor and I stepped out while holding the doors open.

"Turn right, go all the way down the hall, then turn left. I think she's being taken to a holding cell," said Gadget.

"Thanks, Gadget," I said as I let the doors go. "Be safe."

I was surprised to see an empty hallway, but I didn't have time to ponder the situation. I took off down the hall and rounded the corner to see another empty path. Alarms were going off and the whole building was on alert but this floor was like a ghost town. My spidey sense was tingling, but I saw the door just down the hall. I sprinted to the door and kicked it open. There was Gracie tied, gagged and being held by two agents. I made quick work of them with my rifle and rushed over to Gracie. She shook her head in fear as I pulled off her gag and untied her.

"Don't let the door close!" she cried.

397

I turned to see the door slam shut followed by a clanking sound that could only have been magnetic locks engaging. I was set up.

I figured if they went to the trouble of luring me into the room, they chose one that was virtually inescapable, but I had to try. Bad idea. The blast ricocheted around the room before dissipating.

"That was a rather disappointing effort. I expected more out of you than that."

We looked across the room and saw a holograph of Agent Griffin with Agent Price in the background.

"There's no way out, so save your energy for the futile struggle you'll undoubtedly put up when we come down there. Oh, and we'll have your friends shortly."

The holograph was gone, and I quickly searched every inch of the room for a potential exit.

"Do you know where they were projecting from?" I asked.

"I heard them say something about being right upstairs,"

Gracie replied. "I guess they're on the sixth floor."

"That gives us sixty, maybe ninety seconds to get ready."

"Get ready for what?"

"To face the storm."

We didn't have much of a chance, but I figured we were gonna take at least one of those bastards with us. I handed one of my pistols to Gracie. I flipped over a table, and Gracie got behind it with me. I looked over at her and saw her chest rise and fall quickly, but she smiled all the while. I touched her face and returned a smile, then I prepared myself. I always thought my life would flash before me towards the end, but it didn't. It felt more like I was getting ready to sleep. Getting ready for that one last final rest for which I had long waited. But I was going to have to wait a little longer.

"Kaori!" Gadget yelled over my com.

"Gadget? You got me back online?"

"All of us!" Godspeed replied.

Despite my earlier resignation, I was ecstatic to hear

Godspeed's voice and know everyone was still alive.

"Kaori, I'm opening the door now! Griffin and the others are coming! I'll get you out, just follow my directions!"

"Lead the way, boy genius!"

The doors opened, and I quickly looked down both ends of the hall. I couldn't see the agents, but I heard them coming. Gadget directed us down the opposite hallway and into a stairwell. As we ran down the stairs, we were almost knocked over by a door swinging open. We quickly raised our weapons, only to see it was Deadeye and Godspeed. We were all demonstratively excited except for Godspeed. He tried to feign indifference to my presence, but I could see a hint of relief on his face. Gadget ordered us all further downstairs, but I wasn't quite ready to leave.

"Gadget, where are you sending us?"

"Back out through the sewer," he replied.

"I need you to find Protos and get me to an elevator that leads to the Archive!"

"Kaori, this place is filled with agents that would like

nothing more than your pretty little head on a platter!" Gadget replied. "The mission is over!"

"He's right," said Deadeye. "We need to leave while we can."

"We only need one person to start the Archive transfer," I said.

"You don't have that much time. By the time you got to the Archive, this whole building will be on lockdown. I wouldn't be able to get you out."

"Tell me something Gadget, after you get us to safety, what's your exit strategy?" I asked.

Silence fell over everyone as the others were suddenly aware of what I had suspected.

"There's no need to sacrifice both of us," said Gadget.

"There is if it means we get the cure," I replied.

"Kori, no!" Gracie pleaded.

"Gracie, you know this is why we came here. It's why I came to this world. It's why I've lost... it's why we've all lost so much. I can't let those sacrifices be in vain."

She wrapped her arms tightly around me and squeezed the sadness from my eyes.

"Be well, Kaori," said Medic through her com.

"I will, Medic. Finally, I will."

"I'm sorry, but everyone who is leaving needs to go now!" Gadget ordered.

I reluctantly released Gracie and lightly brushed the others on the shoulder, saying all I could with a single touch.

"Find Protos and get him out, Gadget," I said.

Godspeed wouldn't look at me in my drowning eyes. Maybe because I meant so little, or maybe because I meant so much. Either way, it pained me to think that think we had lost so much time. It pained me even more to know we had thrown so much more of it away.

Gadget guided them further downstairs while sending me one flight up. I tried to stay focused as I heard gunshots from their coms. Gracie settled me after each exchange of fire.

"We're okay, Kori!" she repeatedly yelled.

Gadget sent me to a floor least likely to get me killed. Unfortunately, it still included three agents. One was a smug Speeder who dropped his weapon against the advice of his coworkers and came running for me. I knew I would probably miss him, so I shot up the floor, and he predictably ran up the wall to his right. In his path was a large window, and I fired right as he reached it. He fell through the window, but the momentum carried him forward and the broken glass tore him to shreds.

Gadget killed the lights on that floor, and I put on my night vision goggles. One agent was a Burner, so he lit up the hallway with a ball of fire, and the last thing he saw was my rifle three inches from his face.

I don't know what the last agent was because he turned and ran away. Gadget gave me back the lights and guided me towards the elevator I needed.

"Okay, Kaori, go around the corner and you will find the lift 300 feet ahead on your right... Wait! You have to turn back!"

"What? Why? I'm so close!"

"They're coming from that way!"

"Can I beat them to the elevator?" I asked.

"No!"

"Then find me another way, Gadget!"

The com went dead.

"Gadget? Gadget!?"

I took the chance and rounded the corner to see a dozen agents heading my way. I took a deep breath and took off at full speed towards them while spraying suppressive fire. I made it to the elevator button maybe five seconds before the closest agents, and I thought it was enough time, but the doors opened and there stood Griffin. I turned and tried to shoot, but he hit me with a fireball that sent me through a doorway across the hall. I struggled to my feet and stood prepared to shoot anyone coming through that door, but several more agents came crashing through the windows behind me. I tried to fight but Griffin's blast took so much out of me, and there were just too many of them. I heard Deadeye say they had made it to the sewer, and he asked if we were okay. I turned off my com and dropped to the floor.

Griffin walked over and squatted beside me. I saw Price standing in the doorway.

"Most of your friends got away, but we'll find them. Besides, you're the big fish that we wanted all along."

"Congratulations, Captain Ahab. You got your prize," I replied.

As usual, my archaic reference wasn't understood, so Griffin heated up the air around me and got closer.

"Were you really planning to *cure* us? Do you think we have some kind of disease?"

"You are the disease."

Griffin smiled and stood back.

"Well, I'll save the interrogation for the Reader we have coming to pick your brain, but before your mind is liquified, there's an old friend who wants to see you."

I figured they were bringing in Gadget, and I was happy

that I'd get to say goodbye face to face, but I was wrong. The agents stepped aside, and D'Arco emerged from the parting crowd. I felt like a dull dagger had been shoved repeatedly into my heart.

"You..?" I asked, barely managing to force sound from my mouth.

D'Arco tried to maintain a look of righteous indignation, but I could tell he was ashamed of what he had done.

"You betrayed me..." he said.

I used what little strength I had left to leap towards him and swung for his face like Casey at bat. Luckily for him, Griffin caught me by the waist and my fist just barely missed contact with D'Arco's nose. He didn't even try to move.

"You felt betrayed so you respond by trying to get all of us killed!!?? You've destroyed lives, ruined all hope of saving humanity..!"

"I never cared about humanity, Kaori! I only cared about you! I loved you..,"

"You don't know what love is! You don't have a clue!

Love is giving everything you have, even when you risk getting nothing in return!"

He couldn't look at me, and I no longer wanted to look at him.

"I hate to interrupt this lovers' quarrel, but we have a Reader waiting," said Griffin as he placed my hands in front of me and put restraints on my wrists.

"I can take her if you like, Special Agent Griffin," offered Price.

"No, I take care of her. Assist the other agents in finding her friends and have someone bring the one from IT down to me."

Price nodded and left the room, then Griffin grabbed me by my fettered wrists and proceeded to walk me out as well. I spoke to D'Arco as I passed him.

"They left Whisper for dead."

D'Arco hung his head lower at my words.

"That pound of flesh isn't such a great deal now is it?"

Griffin took me back out to the hallway and into the

elevator. He placed his palm on the biometric scanner then chose a floor. I noticed the code for the Archive floor and then I remembered I was still wearing the gloves. Griffin stood behind me, reeking of hydrogen sulfide.

"That's not love," he said matter of factly.

"What?"

"Giving everything you have and getting nothing in return is foolish."

"For a Burner, I bet your bed is awfully cold at night".

Griffin leaned forward and spoke into my ear.

"Let's see how easily those quips roll off your tongue when your mind gets turned into confetti."

I slammed my head backwards into his face then elbowed him in the throat. Griffin dropped to his knees, gasping and bleeding while I hit the scanner with my palm and chose the Archive floor. I had next to nothing left in the tank, but I was going to ride those fumes as long as I could.

I didn't have the building specs or Gadget to guide me, so I had to find my way by memory. I reached the end of the hallway, and was trying to remember which way to go when a fireball nearly hit me from behind. I chose to go left.

Griffin stayed in hot pursuit as I randomly darted through the labyrinth before me. I rounded a corner and saw several agents coming my way. I looked back and saw Griffin catching up, so I went down another hallway and into an open common area and ran right into Price.

He levitated me into the air by my shackled wrists. I looked over and saw Griffin and the other agents coming. I was done.

As the others approached, Price just kept looking at me with these fractured eyes. He was not the man I remembered from Zero Alley.

"Why do you want the Archive?" he asked.

I refused to answer and looked at the floor as the footsteps drew nearer. He forced my head up, and I looked him in the eye.

"Can you fix this?" Price asked.

Confusion colored my face as I hung there suspended by

my wrists.

"Can you?" he asked again.

Still, I gave no response. I was unclear as to why he was asking me such things, and figured it best to say nothing at all. My attention was diverted when the other agents caught up.

Griffin looked rather sheepish as he reached for my arm.

"Thank you," he said to Price. "I'll take her from here."

But Price didn't release me. He just kept looking at me as if staring into my eyes might give him a peek into the freak show I called my mind.

"Aiden, release her," Griffin insisted.

Price looked at Griffin, then back at me.

"Can you fix this..?"

"Aiden, what are you talking about?"

A wave of calm came over me, and something inside told me to trust him. I slowly nodded my head to which Price responded with a blast of concussive force that sent Griffin and the other agents through a wall. I hung there in total disbelief as he shattered my handcuffs and lowered me to the ground.

"What are you doing?" I asked as I rubbed my wrists.

"I know a shortcut to the Archive."

He turned and blew holes through three different walls and beckoned me to follow. I thought this could be some kind of ploy at first, but it would have made more sense to just get a Reader to cull whatever they needed it from me. It would have been faster and required a lot less rebuilding.

I followed Price through the holes until we reached a circular, glass walled room. The glass was frosted so I was uncertain what was inside, but I did manage to make out what appeared to be a figure of a woman. Price reached out for the scanner, and I thought he was going to scan his palm but, instead, he blew apart the entire door. He stepped inside, and I reluctantly followed. When I got inside, I saw a floating woman hooked up to what looked like two oxygen tanks.

"Where is it?" I asked. "Where's the Archive?"

Price pointed at the woman.

"Her."

Price quickly explained the Archive was not a group of servers full of data, but a person. Scientists had learned that the human brain was capable of hosting and indexing more data than any computer in the world and found a way to make it possible. They created Archives from Tricksters whose cerebrospinal fluid had been replaced with liquid nitrocodone. With the right dosage, nitrocodone could heighten the cognitive prowess of the brain while numbing emotional impulses. This resulted in a human database and search engine lacking desire and free will. Of course only .01% of people survived the procedure and half of them became vegetables. The successful candidates had the entire known history of the world uploaded into their brains. Tricksters were chosen because of their ability to project images to display query results. At that time, there were only five Archives in the entire world.

The woman before us was pale with steel blue eyes and platinum hair that went down to her waist. Two thin tubes ran from

412

nearby tanks into her nostrils. Her white gown hung just past her knees, exposing equally pale legs and slender feet which hovered just above the floor.

I took notice of the vacant look in the Archive's eyes, the listless sway of her body as if a slight tremor ebbed through the room. Even as I pitied her plight, I acknowledged that I was a hypocrite as I was about to exploit her as well.

I turned to speak to Price and noticed someone lying on the floor. It was Protos.

"Protos! What are you doing here?" I asked, running over to him.

He was barely able to stand as I lifted him.

"My hand left Gracie's for less than a second, and Griffin separated us with a fireball, then they placed this on me."

Protos turned and showed me the neuro-disruptor attached to the base of his skull. They were the only way to suppress an Outlier.

"How did they know they would need that on you?"

"They scanned me when we got here. I was off the charts, so they were on high alert the whole time. Then they took me up here and did something really weird with 'Carrie' over there. I don't remember much."

"Protos, if you're lying…"

"He is not lying," said Price. "The Governor called and had your friend taken to the Archive."

"Why?" I asked.

"I do not know. Perhaps because she is also a Reader. Now, you are running out of time! You need to take what you need and go!"

"I came here to download the Archive's contents. How am I supposed to download a person?" I asked.

"You will have to take her with you," Price replied.

"I can't get out of here with a drugged up zombie!"

"I will help you," he said. "But I need you to do something for me as well."

I knew it was only a matter of time before the Gendarmerie

regrouped, so I thought it best to comply with whatever it was he needed. Price reached into his jacket pocket and pulled out a leather bound book.

"I need you to deliver this," he said as he handed the book to me.

I took the book and opened it to the first page and saw the name Carson Price. I thumbed through a few more pages and realized it was a long love letter written like a journal...

"There is an address in the back. Deliver it personally, please."

"I will," I said, placing the book inside of my jacket. "I had a friend on the IT floor..."

"He will be in the lower level where you entered. Now you must hurry!"

Price removed the tubes from the Archive and placed the lethargic Diploid in my arms while Protos struggled to his feet.

"Now, go!" Price ordered.

We exited the room and saw the agents had returned in full

force with a very angry Griffin leading the charge. I wasn't going to be able to outrun them with the Archive hanging on me like a bag of laundry, and running seemed moot once Griffin unleashed a wall of fire that liquefied everything that it touched. Fortunately, Price stepped in front of us and forced the fire and heat back. He levitated the Archive, Protos and myself, then tore holes through the floors all the way down to the lower level. He lowered us slowly through the floor as he fought off Griffin and the other agents, and that was the last I ever saw of him. His powers continued to guide us down through the floors while the noise of the battle raged on above us. I wondered how long he could maintain his concentration on both tasks, and I soon got my answer. We had four floors to go when we heard a loud explosion and started free falling. I tried to grab onto a floor as we fell, but it was well out of reach. I figured death had been toying with me all day and she had finally grown bored with the game, but, as usual, I was wrong. We stopped in mid air at the first floor. I thought it was Price until I looked over at some unknown agent gesturing our suspension. I wondered why she bothered to save us until she spoke.

"Special Agent Griffin! Are you alright, sir?!"

Despite seeming listless, the Archive was quite aware of her surroundings. She sensed a Mover close by and disguised all of us as high level agents, so she'd save our lives.

"We're fine, agent," I replied.

Much to my surprise, the Archive had perfectly disguised my voice as well.

"Could you lower us down into the basement, Agent?" I asked.

"Uh, yes, sir…" she replied.

The Mover lowered us into the basement where I found Gadget sitting with his back against a wall. He was clearly in pain, but that didn't stop him from pointing an impact gun at us. The Archive quickly removed our disguises, and Gadget lowered his weapon and smiled with relief.

"You made it," he rejoiced. "Who is she? Did you

417

download the Archive?"

"You could say that. Gadget, meet the Archive."

Gadget was quite confused, but before I could explain, we were knocked to the ground by a fireball. I figured Griffin had caught up to us, but when I turned I saw the Governor.

"Take her and run!" I yelled as I reached for Gadget's gun and blew a hole in the ceiling. The falling debri separated him and the Archive from myself and the Governor.

I tried to fire another shot at the Governor, but he quickly snatched the gun from hands and crushed it. I flopped on my back from exhaustion.

"It's nice to finally meet you, Governor," I said as I lay there completely spent.

"I assure you, the pleasure is all mine, Miss Maru."

"Can we just get this over with?"

My arm lay over my eyes as I heard him chuckle, so I leaned up on my elbows.

"If you think I'm going to be someone's slave or sex toy,

you're insane. I will leave this world like a zeppelin with a smoking section taking as many of you assholes with me as I can."

The Governor knelt beside me, pulled a handkerchief from his pocket and handed it to me.

"What makes you think I want you dead?"

"I don't know. Maybe because we are a plague on this world, and we threaten your way of life?" I said as I ignored his offering. That time, he gave a much more audible laugh.

"You really think I see you as a threat?"

"Your speeches, your crackdowns…"

"There was a rise in Sympathizers, and my popularity had been waning, and do you know what brings people together better than anything else? Hatred. Nothing creates unity quite like a common enemy, and you gave me that."

"It's not enough that Zeros are at the bottom of the food chain, you had to make us out to be the boogey man too?"

"I know it might seem counterintuitive to tell the spider that his greatest threat is the fly, but it really makes perfect sense and is relatively easy to do. Convince a man that his enemy lies beneath his feet, and he'll never notice the strings that you've tied to his hands."

I wanted to be angry, but it was nothing I hadn't seen before. The privileged blaming the pauper was a tactic played over and over throughout history, and if it ain't broke...

"What are you going to do with me?"

"I'm going to set you free."

"Why..?"

"Because you aren't done."

Then the Governor burned a hole in the pile of debris blocking the tunnel, and motioned for me to leave. I knew there was something up his sleeve, but I had to get back, even if I was playing right into his hands. I cautiously stood and walked past him. My pace quickened the further away I got until it was a full on sprint. I made my way out of the sewer, and ran through the streets, easily evading law enforcement, although I was certain the Governor had helped with that.

Gadget had returned without me, so for all anyone knew, I was dead. Luckily, Gracie was more optimistic than most and demanded they wait for me in that old salvage yard. Godspeed was sitting on the hood of a rusty Chrysler, while Deadeye threw rocks at the headlights of random cars. Medic sat shotgun in a Mustang while Gracie pretended to drive them around town. When I walked into view, Gracie jumped out of the car and sprinted for me. I took a few steps and just dropped to my knees and opened my arms wide. Gracie leaped into my arms with such force that she sent me to the ground.

"I knew you were alive!" she said. "I told them you'd meet us here, and I was right!"

"Yes, you were, baby," I replied as I soaked up her love. The others gathered around showing their relief at my return as well. After a few seconds, Gracie sat up and looked at me solemnly.

"I'm sorry about your friend, Kori," she said.

I sat up on my elbows and gave her a quizzical look.

"My friend..?"

I looked at the others and realized someone was missing.

"Whisper..?"

Everyone avoided eye contact, except for Medic who shook her head.

"He was in really bad shape," she said. "Travelling only made it worse."

I sat up and grasped the gravel at my sides and squeezed until my hands began to bleed. Gracie stood up, looked at my hands then touched my shoulder. I smiled at her and wiped my hands on my pants.

"Take me to him."

We went inside an old trailer office, and I saw a figure lying on the couch under a rust stained tarp. The shape was smaller than I remembered Whisper being, so it seemed impossible that he could occupy such a small space. I walked over to the couch and ran my hand along the contour of his body, then I knelt down beside him. I took a deep breath and pulled the tarp back from the face of my friend. Whisper was barely recognizable, like a poor rendering by an untrained artist. His eyes were sunken and his cheeks too shallow. I fixed his hair with my fingers and caressed his face. Then I covered him with the tarp and returned him to his sleep.

Godspeed pulled me aside as I stepped out of the trailer.

"How did you escape the Governor?"

"He just let me go," I replied casually.

Godspeed made an uncharacteristic grab for my arm as I tried to walk away.

"What do you mean he let you go?"

"Just that," I said, jerking my arm away. "What's wrong with you?"

"The man has a bounty on our heads! He's not going to just let you walk away!"

"You don't trust me now, Godspeed?"

He gave me this look like maybe he never did. I knew it didn't make sense that the Governor would just set me free, but that was no reason to doubt me, no matter what we had been through.

"Causing trouble is apparently good for politics. I know there's more up hs sleeve, but I chose to run for me life instead of pressing the matter."

"We need to get going if we're going to get to our next base by nightfall," said Gadget.

I pulled Price's book from my jacket and scraped away bits of blood from the cover with my fingernail.

"Okay, but we need to make a stop first," I said as I pressed the cover of the book with my thumbs.

Chapter 20

Josiah

"Now, this looks all too familiar."

Governor Mathias was none too happy as he stood inside what was left of our headquarters. Nearly a third of the upper floors had been charred beyond recognition, and whatever was left unburned had sustained severe structural damage. I didn't think we should have even been in there at all, but Mathias insisted.

"What do they call that, Josiah, deja vu?" he asked. "It has to be deja vu, because there is no way that a Zero destroyed another law enforcement building."

"She didn't exactly destroy it, sir…"

"No, no, I heard you helped," the Governor replied. "You burned dicyanoacetylene inside of a building? Those are 9,000 degree flames. It's a miracle you didn't burn down the whole city!"

"Sir, Agent Aiden Price was a high level Mover who could block heat, even light. I had no choice."

"Using psychokinesis to block light requires nitrocodone. Who authorized Agent Price's use of the drug?"

"No one, sir," I replied.

"Aiden was using nitro illegally and unsupervised? And you knew about it?"

"I thought he had given it up. He started acting normal again."

"That is called leveling out, Josiah. You should know that. So, Aiden was in a drug induced state and just decided to start attacking his fellow agents?"

"He was helping Kaori escape, sir."

"Along with the Archive"

I had the feeling that Mathias had all the answers he needed and had already made his mind up about what was to come..

"He helped her escape with the Archive, sir."

"So, tell me, Special Agent Josiah Griffin, what makes a highly respected veteran law enforcement officer turn into a traitor and cause the deaths of hundreds of his fellow officers?"

I didn't know what made Agent Aiden Price turn. Perhaps it was his divorce, or the nitrocodone addiction or maybe just the pressure of the job. Unfortunately, the truth was buried with him as my only option was lethal action. The fugitive, Kaori Maru, had been captured with the aid of an informant named D'Arco. I was in the process of taking Kaori to Riser Kilroy for a reading when Kaori attacked me on the elevator and used stolen biometrics to access the Archive floor. Myself and other agents gave chase, but Agent Price intervened and aided Kaori. For reasons unknown, Agent Price freed the Archive then engaged us in battle while she and Kaori escaped along with the other fugitives. Damage to Gendarmerie headquarters was extensive as it required my full might to take Agent Price down. Many agents lost their lives when I maximized my flame. Many more died as the upper floors collapsed. I knew it did not bode well for me.

"I don't know why Agent Price would do that, sir," I replied.

"I wasn't talking about Agent Ptice. Bring me the

427

informant!" Mathias ordered.

One of the agents sorting through the rubble left the room while Mathias and I stood there in silence. It felt like eons had passed while we waited for the agent to return with D'Arco. He was badly beaten with his wrists and ankles shackled. Apparently, someone took their frustration out on him.

"Look at this," Mathias began. "This man is a guest, and this is not how we treat our guests. Remove the restraints."

The agent removed the restraints from D'Arco, and Mathias placed his hands on his shoulders.

"D'Arco, correct?"

He nodded as he wiped the blood from his nose.

"The girl, Kaori, why did she want the Archive?" Mathias asked.

D'Arco looked at me then back at Mathias.

"She needs to find something that she lost."

"Something that she lost? She would only need the Archive if she wanted to find something she lost over 100 years ago,"

Mathias smirked.

"She lost it over 200 years ago," D'Arco replied.

Mathias folded his arms and shook his head.

"Yes, I heard that there was a theory that she was from the past and may have witnessed the Event."

"Governor, I will find her and the Archive…"

"No need, Josiah," he interrupted. "As of this moment, you are officially relieved of your duties."

"But Governor…"

"Your replacements will show you out."

"My replacements..?"

Because of the second attack, Congress held an emergency meeting to legalize Martial Law, and the Governor immediately imposed it, and the dusted hadn't even settled yet.

I turned and saw the last people anyone would ever want to see gathered in one room, Riser and three other Reapers.

Sereno: an Asian Mover in his thirties, calm, quiet, but extremely powerful. It was rumored that the city of Prince George was destroyed when he used his powers to split an atom.

Random: a tall, twenty-something Anglo Polyploid with a penchant for the ladies. He was called Random because he had every power, but he could only use one at a time.

Xiomara: an Hispanic Hitter in her late twenties. Soo, as they called her, could rip steel like tissue paper.

"Guess ah shoulda been here sooner," said Riser stepping over rubble. "Mighta saved you some trouble."

"Mathias..."

The Governor walked over to me and placed his hand on my cheek.

"Enjoy your retirement, Josiah. Riser, escort Mr. Griffin off the premises."

"What about the lil girl?" Riser asked.

"Not yet."

Riser nodded, and Mathias walked out of the building without looking back. The four Reapers and two agents armed with neutralizers escorted me out the back of the building. Everyone we

430

passed looked down or away. Once we were outside, I saw a transport van waiting for us. Riser directed me inside.

"So, Riser, where's the rest of your little gang?" I asked as I stepped into the van.

"This is a limited invite, Tomcat."

Riser sat on one side of me and Random on the other. Sereno and Xiomara sat in the back, then the driver had us on our way.

"Why would we need other Reapers for, Chico?" Xiomara asked. "I can do you myself."

"Now I'm jealous, Soo," said Random. "You promised that if you ever turned to men that I'd be your first!"

"No, I said if all women and men were dead, and I no longer had hands then I *might* give you a chance. You still one nuclear disaster away from poking my panties, Random."

Random turned to Sereno in the seat behind him.

"Think you could help me out and split a couple atoms?"

"Why do we have to drive so far to do this?" asked

431

Xiomara.

Riser looked over at me.

"I've been a Gendarme for a long time. I know how this ends," I said.

Riser smiled at me for a moment then looked back at the road.

"The Govna want it done quiet, Soo," said Riser.

"To hell with quiet, Chica. I wanna hear the pendejo scream!"

"Show respect, Soo," Riser insisted. "Tomcat here can burn cyan."

"Whoa, Chico! You burn cyan?! I don't think even Layo can do that! You coulda been a Reaper!"

Random eased away from me and leaned against the door.

"If this guy can burn cyan, should he be sitting here all unfettered and shit?"

"S'ok, Random. Griff blew his wad earlier today," said Riser.

She was correct. A Burner's greatest expenditure comes from producing flammable gases, and generating dicyanoacetylene left a Burner spent for at least twelve hours. I had no fuel for burning, but Random did. I just needed time for him to cycle to Burner mode.

"Why does the Governor want the girl?" I asked.

Everyone remained quiet. Riser just smiled and looked away.

"I'll be dead soon. You could at least satisfy my curiosity."

Riser looked over at me and ran her fingers through my hair.

"Of everything', that's your last request? Kinda sad, baby."

"I was going to go with set me free, but that seemed unlikely," I replied.

Riser smiled again.

"Archive is a diploid. She a more powerful Reader than me. You take a Reader like that and a Skipper just as strong, and you can read the future."

"They saw something about the girl?"

"That's my guess, but whatever it is, Govna' is keeping it under his hat."

I couldn't imagine what the Archive saw that would make the little girl so important, but I didn't have time to ponder as we were nearing our destination. I considered jumping out of the moving van until I smelled hydrogen sulfide.

I leaned forward then quickly elbowed Random in the solar plexus causing his diaphragm to spasm and triggering his lungs to release excess gas. Then I grabbed Random by the back of the neck and placed my mouth on his. Riser spun me around by my shoulder, and I spit fire in her face. A second later, the whole van was engulfed in flames. I kicked the door open and jumped out then ran down the busy highway as the van exploded. I looked back and saw the Reapers stumbling out of the burning van. I assumed Sereno shielded everyone from the flames and the explosion just in time, but he must have cut it close because they all looked dazed.

Xiomara leaped in my direction but overshot me by 400 feet. She had the greatest resistance to the blast, but I could tell she was concussed. She grabbed a passing car and threw it at me. I had to use my borrowed fuel sparingly, so I dove out of the way, just barely avoiding the car. As Xiomara ran towards me, she grabbed another car and raised it over her head. Behind me was another driver speeding in my direction. I shot a fireball at the driver, and when he swerved to avoid me, he slammed right into Xiomara, knocking her to the pavement.

I got up and continued running, but I felt a tingle inside my head. Riser was trying to get in, but the explosion had really taken a lot out of her. Cars began crashing all around me, but I miraculously avoided them. Enforcer vehicles crossed over from the other side of the highway and halted traffic so I hid under a car.

The Enforcers exited their cars as the Reapers approached.

"Get on the pavement!" yelled one of the Enforcers.

I watched their feet disappear from my worm's eye view and a pool of blood took their place.

"Do you see him?" asked Sereno.

"Nah," said Riser. "Ah can barely think straight. You?"

"Body scans require a lot of focus, and my head is rather fuzzy too."

"The Governor is gonna be raised if we don't find him," said Random.

"Then maybe you shoulda kept your mouth shut, pendejo!" said Xiomara.

"Don't blame me! Riser is the one who wanted to take him on a road trip first!"

"Husha face, you two! Sereno, clear the road!"

I wondered what she meant, and found out a second later. Sereno lifted every vehicle on the road high into the air then slammed them all down with incredible force. I was hanging onto the underside of a car, and just before hitting the pavement, I burned a good sized hole in the road. It was just big enough to keep me from getting squashed into the ground.

I heard them talking as blood leaked through floorboards

onto my face.

"He has to be close," said Random.

"Yeah, but we don't have time for this," said Riser.

"What are we going to tell the Governor?" Sereno asked.

"We gonna tell him you crushed 'im," Riser replied.

"So you want us to lie?" Sereno asked.

"No," I heard Riser say. "Ah want you to crush him."

As they walked away, the ground began to tremble. It was a Richter 9 by the time I lost consciousness from the collapsing earth.

Chapter 21

Kaori

As we drifted down the empty highway, I pored over Aiden's letters, hoping to make sense of the last few hours. Just months before, Aiden had tried to end my life, and he nearly succeeded, but my would-be executioner became my savior, and I was at a loss as to why. Slowly, his words washed away the image I had of him in my mind. I had only seen a madman, a monster, but inside the monster was a man, and inside the man was a martyr. I had left no room for the possibility that there was more to him than my prejudice and his hatred, and perhaps he had done the same with me. But, at some point, Aiden opened his heart and mind and saw something else in me, something worth saving, and I wished I had done the same for him.

I realized Aiden's story was a lot like mine, a reckless heart desperately searching for something we were ill-equipped to find. In the absence of knowledge, our only guides were ignorance and blind luck, neither of which had served me very well. Aiden never recovered the missing pieces of his heart, but he was able to find meaning in his death that was so elusive in life. I wondered if that was my only hope as well.

As I rode shotgun, I occasionally watched Medic tending to the Archive in the rearview mirror. Earlier, she had started going through withdrawal, so Medic was giving her doses of nitro and tapering it down throughout the day. Gracie curiously watched the Diploid, fascinated by her unique appearance. The Archive noticed Gracie and projected a flower above her hand. Gracie smiled and reached for the flower, but it quickly vanished. The Archive seemed as surprised as Gracie, and I wondered if the reduction in nitrocodone was affecting her powers. The Archive focused and projected an entire bouquet of flowers and butterflies, to which Gracie giggled with delight.

"Are we waiting for a special occasion to ask our guest the question?" asked Godspeed.

I understood his impatience. We had the Archive for hours,

and we'd yet to pose our query. The truth was, I wanted answers, but I didn't want any more surprises. Nevertheless, I took a deep breath and turned to the Archive.

"Archive, what events took place at Payne MedCorp on June 19th, 2015?"

"On June 19th, 2015, intruders broke into Payne MedCorp. One intruder, Felipe Cabrera, was apprehended by law enforcement. He confessed to the attempted kidnapping of Kaori Maru and was charged. Later that evening, Felipe Cabrera was killed during a riot at the jail."

"No, that's a mistake. They weren't there to kidnap me. They wanted the cure, so we couldn't use it."

"Records indicate, that after your disappearance, the intruders abandoned their mission."

"No, I dropped the cure right before we skipped. They must've found it and left."

"The vehicle used by the intruders was found. It contained evidence of materials used for a kidnapping. Nothing that would be considered a cure was found."

I thought that maybe Felipe lied to cover their true intentions, but when I looked at Protos, his face didn't share the same look of confusion as mine. He wouldn't look at me at all in fact.

"Archive, where is Cordell O'Riordan buried?" he asked, staring out the window.

"Cordell O'Riordan was buried in Otterbein Cemetery in Westerville, Ohio on August 20th, 2036. Coordinates 40.1216° N, 82.9341° W."

I knew in my head you had to be dead, but hearing for certain hit me harder than expected.

"Those coordinates match the Dregs," said Godspeed. "You still wanna make that first stop?"

"Yes."

We still had a long way to go, so we made a pit stop at some roadside dump that was small enough to be off the fed's radar but big enough to have indoor plumbing. It was the kind of place that people who didn't want to be found could soak their heels without looking over their shoulders. I opted to stay in the van and keep an eye on the Archive. Protos was the last one to exit, so I leaned over the seat and grabbed him by the arm as he did.

"What's inside of me, Protos?"

Protos looked at my hand firmly grasping his arm and sighed.

"Whatever is inside of me, is inside of Gracie as well!"

Protos looked confused, then a sense of revelation washed over his face. He turned to watch Gracie walking with Medic to the restroom.

"She was injured and needed blood, and mine was the only type her body could use."

I could see the wheels turning in his head as he continued to stare in Gracie's direction.

"She'll live," he finally said. "As will you."

He had the strangest look on his face. I noticed later that he was always watching her, so I made sure she was never left alone with him.

After watching Protos head into the men's room, I looked back at the Archive in the rearview mirror. I wondered what kind of life lay before her. Because of her nitro dosage and the length of time she was taking it, withdrawal could kill her. Medic didn't think she would ever be able to stop completely. Her body had learned to metabolize nitro as a sole source of nutrition, so she would more than likely die without it.

"Are you okay?" I asked.

The Archive looked at me as if struggling to understand my question. I turned around in my seat.

"How are you feeling?"

"I am not accustomed to receiving personal queries," she replied.

"Are you unable to answer?"

"I am able. I was momentarily taken aback. I am tired, and my

head is aching. Do you have a historical query?"

443

"You don't have to be my Magic 8-ball."

She paused momentarily, presumably to understand the
reference,

before replying.

"It is why I was created. It is why you took me."

That made me feel ashamed. She had spent her entire
lifetime   being

used and I was treating her no differently, but I wasn't sure if she
could

survive being on her own. Would she have been better off back at

Gendarmerie

headquarters? Choosing between the lesser of two evils was

becoming   the   story

of my life.

"I'm sorry, Archive… what is your real name?"

"I was taken as a child. The Archive is the only name I

have   ever

known. This is my destiny."

"Don't let someone else define you."

"Answering queries is all I know."

"How about you ask me a question?"

The Archive furrowed her brow and seemed more confused than ever.

"I would not know what to ask."

"Ask me whatever you want."

She paused for a moment.

"Have you defined yourself?" she asked.

I didn't expect that question, but I was more surprised that I didn't know the answer.

"I don't know…"

I had been used like Archive, I had believed a lie like Aiden,   and I had lost everything like Gracie. We struggle so hard to set ourselves apart from one another that we fail to see how much we are alike. Was there anyone who had not known pain or laughed until   they   cried?   Who   has   never   broken   a heart or had theirs broken? Yet we repeatedly diminish another's struggle.   No one gets the dictate another's right to feel.

The others returned, and we set back out on the road for another hour or so. It was awkward riding next to Godspeed. He hadn't spoken directly to me for hours, and it had been even longer since he had looked in my direction. I wanted to say something, anything, but I decided I should wait, at least until I had something worth saying.

"We're here," said Godspeed.

I looked around at the open field of prairie grasses and wildflowers that swayed in the evening breeze. I lowered my window and allowed the country air to waft through our vehicle. The Sweet Alyssum scented breeze was welcomed but seemed out of place for a day wrought with such despair. Then again, those are times when such stark contrast is needed the most.

The modest dwelling was a one-story brick ranch with a gravel drive and window boxes full of more flowers. I saw the curtains move, undoubtedly the homeowner was curious about his visitors. I didn't imagine he received much company this far out in the country.

I removed all my weapons and my jacket and stepped out of the van with the journal. I walked slowly up the driveway hoping to allay any fears my potential host might have had. I knocked on the door and heard shuffling about inside. Thirty seconds or so went by before the door finally opened, and a middle aged, blond man with a slight build stood before me.

"May I help you?" he asked, curiously looking over my shoulder at the van.

"Carson Price?"

"I am he. What can I do for you?"

"Aiden asked me to give you this."

I handed Carson the journal which he took with trepidation. He seemed more relaxed after opening it, presumably because he recognized the handwriting.

"Was Aiden too busy to bother delivering it himself?" he

asked as he quickly thumbed through the pages.

"No," I replied, shaking my head.

Carson took notice of my quivering lip and my averted gaze.

"Is he..?"

I nodded, and Carson crossed his arms and brought his hand to his mouth

and then to his eyes. I didn't know him, but I knew his pain, and I so badly wanted to take it all away. I reached out and touched the hand covering his eyes and expected him to pull away. Instead, he opened his hand and squeezed my fingers, keeping them pressed against his face. When the trembling stopped, he released my hand and wiped his tears.

"So how did he... How did he die...?"

I knew how hard it was to hear those words, and how much harder it was to say them.

"I'm a Zero, and he died saving my life."

Carson looked down at my hands then shook his head in

disbelief.

"Why would he do that? Aiden hates… he hated Zeros."

"Well, he hated me at one time."

A look of recognition came over Carson's face.

"You're the fugitive he had been chasing…"

I nodded.

"Why would he give his life for yours?"

"I guess he saw something in me that was worth fighting for, worth dying for. So he fought off the Gendarmerie while my friends and I escaped."

"Aiden always wanted to be a Gendarme, and he wanted your hide more than anything. You must be truly special to have changed his mind."

"I'm not special, but what I'm fighting for is."

"And what is that?"

"Love. It's all in there," I said, pointing to the journal.

Carson held the journal against his chest and breathed deeply.

"Are you okay?" I asked.

"I will be. Thank you..." he paused, waiting for my name.

"I'm Kaori."

"Thank you, Kaori. If you ever need anything..."

I smiled and nodded my gratitude.

I left Carson to pore over Aiden's final words and returned to the van. As we turned around to leave, I saw him standing at the window. He raised his hand and placed it against the pane, and I did the same. Deadeye had taken over driving for the next leg of our trip. I lowered my window and let wind dry my tears as they formed. Reaching into my journal, I pulled out our photo and saw the faces of two people I no longer recognized. I wanted say I had changed, but people rarely change. Time and chance just allows you to see more of who you really are. As I was lost in the facade of who I thought we were, the wind caught the photo and snatched it out of the window. I turned quickly and watched it leave.

"Did you need that?" Deadeye asked.

"No," I said and watched in the rearview as you slipped

further into my past.

THE END

Made in the USA
Middletown, DE
20 January 2020

83468025R00269